ESCAPE

Other Books by Jeff Povey

Shift
Delete

JEFF POVEY

ESCAPE

SIMON & SCHUSTER

First published in Great Britain in 2017 by Simon & Schuster UK Ltd
A CBS COMPANY

Copyright © 2017 Jeff Povey

1 3 5 7 9 10 8 6 4 2

Simon & Schuster UK Ltd
1st Floor, 222 Gray's Inn Road
London
WC1X 8HB

www.simonandschuster.co.uk
www.simonandschuster.com.au
www.simonandschuster.co.in

Simon & Schuster Australia, Sydney
Simon & Schuster India, New Delhi

A CIP catalogue record for this book
is available from the British Library.

PB ISBN: 978-1-4711-1872-2
eBook ISBN: 978-1-4711-1873-9

Typeset in the UK by M Rules
Printed and bound by CPI Group (UK) Ltd, Croydon, CR0 4YY

MIX
Paper from
responsible sources
FSC® C020471

Simon & Schuster UK Ltd are committed to sourcing paper
that is made from wood grown in sustainable forests and support the Forest
Stewardship Council, the leading international forest certification organisation.
Our books displaying the FSC logo are printed on FSC certified paper.

This is dedicated to my illustrious in-laws:
Owen Stewart, Jayne Povey,
Alastair Evitt and Helen Allen.

It's also for everyone who read the first two
novels in the series.

Thank you.

THE TRUTH IS NOT OUT THERE

There's a liar staring at me. He's sitting on a sofa in a small flat and a homemade 'Welcome Home' banner is hanging limply from the off-white ceiling above his head. Crumbs from a celebratory cake (caterpillar-shaped because apparently I had an unnatural desire to actually be a caterpillar when I was four) have been trodden into the ancient rug that slumps, exhausted, between the worn sofa and the small telly.

I'm trying to ignore everything. From the sound of laughter in the room to the thoughts that are lighting a hundred small fires in my brain. How could it all have gone so spectacularly wrong?

'What's so funny?' I ask the liar, but he doesn't reply. He's too busy laughing and smiling with the woman who sits next to him.

It feels like they've been laughing ever since I arrived here thirteen days ago. They laugh and smile while I lurch from bedroom to lounge to kitchen and back again, restless and lost. They say that I should really start thinking about going back to school. I've had enough time off as it is. I think that's supposed to be a joke, but then again they say everything as a joke because all they ever do is look at one another and start laughing all over again.

How did this happen? *I think.* How did I let things turn out so badly?

WORLDS OF HURT

I am standing on a sinking pleasure boat in the middle of a perfect copy of the Thames and I have less than five seconds to reply to a question that I can't possibly answer.

'It's your choice, Rev.' My now-very-ex best friend Billie tells me. 'You can try and save Johnson or the Ape. But you can't save both. So make your wish.'

I'm so stunned my mind goes completely blank before retreating instantly to somewhere safe and warm. For some reason it's an image of me as a little kid making a Christmas Wish List. There I am writing on a piece of paper and slipping it under a tree decked with baubles, chocolates in foil and fairy lights.

Dear Santa,

I would like to not be here on this sinking boat. I would like instead to be back in my own world, on my own earth with all of my friends. I would like everyone to be alive again. Not scattered

*or lost or drowning or dead. I want Billie to be
my best friend again and not be super-powered
and superhumanly vindictive with it. I want
my precious Ape not to be bleeding to death
because a savage, snarling evil version of our
friend, Moth, gutted him. I would like to go on a
date with Johnson rather than having to make a
decision that means I will never see him again.
I would also like Other-Johnson and his band of
merry doppelgangers to stop causing us so much
trouble and go home, back to their own vicious
copy of earth. I would like, in absolute truth, for
everything to not have happened. And also I'd like
some new foundation and more electric-pink hair
dye. And maybe some vouchers for Top Shop.*

Yours sincerely,

*Reva Marsalis
(Old before her time)*

I've lost track of days, but in the not-too-distant-past me and a group of misfit teenagers were transported from our world to this one. A world that looks, smells and feels exactly like our own but, to put it bluntly, just isn't. It's empty of all life, animal and human, but the buildings and the towns and everything else you can imagine are exactly the same as they are on our version of Earth. All thanks to a yet-to-be-explained flash of light during an after-school detention. After the shock of being transported here, I did momentarily wonder if this new world was a sort of

4

paradise. Until seriously antisocial creatures turned up and tried to kill everyone they came across. Creatures that looked just like us, in truth were us, but with subtle differences, like having talons and steel teeth and powers that I would call super until you're on the receiving end of them.

Us being me, Rev, sixteen-year-old female of the electric-pink hair and questionable heroism; Billie, my former (given the turn of events) forever best friend; Carrie, the girl who has always hated me for no apparent reason (so definitely not someone I wanted to be stuck with in a world populated by just seven other people – excluding our doppels, of course); the Moth, a brainbox in a wheelchair who has surprised us all with his steely resolve; Darren aka, the Ape, the boy who has repeated school year after school year and in this empty world has become my fearless, hairy-backed protector; GG, gay, forever loyal and as ultra-heroic as he is fashion-conscious; Lucas, the very model of teenage perfection who didn't survive very long in this world; and finally Johnson, the casual rebel who makes my heart thump.

There are only three of us left now. Me, Johnson and the Ape. The Moth is nowhere to be found; Lucas is dead after hanging himself. Carrie was killed by one of our dopplegangers and GG fell off a speeding train so, even though we don't know for sure, the likelihood is that he didn't make it either. And Billie may be standing in front of me, but she's not the Billie we all know, not now she's mutated into something spectacularly cruel.

The Ape is still trying to get to his feet, despite his laboured breathing and the death sweat pouring from him.

He wants to keep fighting, because the big buffoon has no idea how to give up.

'I got this.' He pants the catchphrase I've come to love, as he slips and slides in his own blood.

Billie wants to trade his life in return for Johnson eloping with her. She firmly believes that Johnson and she are star-crossed lovers after creating a reality where the two of them had been trapped for months together in this empty world. In her mind they had reached out to each other in their darkest, loneliest hours. She could even describe the romantic walks they went on, the raindrop that hit the back of her neck when they were sheltering from a rainstorm under a large oak tree. She didn't know, at least I don't think she did, that it was actually her newfound powers imagining what she wished to be true into reality. But she now blames me for tearing down her dream romance and smashing it to smithereens right in front of her. She has remembered that I also like Johnson and that has added to her anger at me. Basically she can no longer tell what's real and what's fantasy any more.

'Who's it going to be, Rev?' Billie says. The sinking boat is going to drag us down into the murky brown depths of the river if I don't make the biggest decision of my young and previously non-dramatic life soon.

Johnson already told Billie that he'd stay with her in this empty world. He knew she would kill us all if he didn't. But Billie wants to hear it from me. I have to let Johnson go and I have to say it to his face, breaking any and every connection I have with him.

What makes it all the more insidious is that Billie knows which Johnson I want to be with. Thanks to the fact we've been faced with our dopplegangers from another universe, there are two Johnsons and both are standing on the deck of the sinking boat. They look the same, they sound the same, although Other-Johnson's voice can sometimes be deeper and richer, especially when he's got me fixed in his black-eyed gaze. They even dress the same, apart from the fact that Other-Johnson likes hats.

It's not Billie's fault that this is happening. After being attacked by Lucas's doppelganger, she was transformed into something half human, half talon and all mean. I know this is selling it a bit short, but to sum up, she isn't quite herself any more.

Billie points at the Ape who slips and slides on the ever-reddening deck. 'The gorilla's going to be extinct soon. Look at him,' she says.

'I'm coming, Rev,' the Ape boasts, but his words are mumbled and faded.

'Rev, pick the Ape,' Johnson says. He's standing beside Billie on the opposite side of the boat. Brown river water pours into the holed hull, pulling us down further and further by the second.

'*You hear that, Rev? He's giving you up,*' Other-Johnson whispers into my mind. This once doppelganger turned out to be more of a lover than a fighter and can talk to me telepathically. He can also swap people's minds into different bodies and take control of anyone he likes. But since kissing me in the town square he's been on our side, helping to keep us – well, me more than anyone – alive.

He claims I'm like no other girl he's ever met, including the version of me he's currently dating from his version of earth. Confused yet? This is just for starters: it gets more complicated, trust me.

7

'You have to save the Ape.' Other-Johnson knows me better than I do myself. I can't let the Ape die.

I look across the deck and can tell Billie is becoming impatient; she wants an answer. The seconds are bleeding away almost as fast as the Ape's life is.

How did this happen?

Over and over those four words keep galloping round my head, like the Four Horsemen of the Apocalypse, but these horsemen are bringing Horror, Fear, Loathing and Panic instead of their infinitely more acceptable War, Pestilence and whatever the other two are.

All I did was turn up for a school detention and somehow got flung into another universe alongside seven other kids.

One minute I was in a classroom, enduring the mindless waste of time that is detention, then a white light came and swept us all to Neverland.

That identical, empty world should have been Eden. Nirvana. El Dorado. Or is that a city of gold rather than a heavenly paradise? Whatever, it should have been beautiful rather than the vicious arena of death and mayhem that it turned out to be.

Of course it wasn't as empty as we first imagined; that would've been too much to ask. And I'm not just talking about the replicas of ourselves that we met. No. There was something far worse than them. Something that had the power to destroy everyone, friend and doppelganger alike.

And still the liar and the woman can't stop laughing. After twelve years apart, I can understand how their happiness has turned into a euphoric delirium. That every time they set eyes on one another – and on me, I suppose – they practically have to pinch themselves because surely it can't possibly be real. We can't be together again after all this time.

'Hey, you,' the liar says to the woman at breakfast.

'Hey, you, right back,' she says in return.

The same words every morning.

Every.

Single.

Morning.

'Toast?'

'You sit there, I'll make it.'

'How about we make it together?'

Their voices blend into one another in a harmony of eyes meeting eyes and lips turning up at the corners.

'I'll get the butter, you get the bread.'

Every.

Single.

Morning.

'Reva, would you like some?'

I always nod. I mean, I have to eat, right?

'Toast for three coming right up.' The woman opens the freezer compartment of the fridge because that's where she keeps the bread. It's rock hard and the cellophane wrapper has tiny icy crystals on it, but they melt with the warmth of her hand as she opens the bag and snaps out the frozen slices.

'Toast and butter and jam,' she says. 'You can't beat it.'

Since I arrived here, I've been roaming from lounge to bedroom to bathroom, trying to shut out the sound of their undiluted happiness. I sometimes peer out of my small bedroom window that looks out on to a street of terraced houses. I have yet to see anyone who happens to wander past look remotely happy. But the handsome liar and his wife make up for that in spades. I don't know if it's just because I'm going stir-crazy stuck inside, but it feels like I could set my watch by the comings and goings of the people outside my window.

I badly need to get out of this flat. I have to go and meet the life that's waiting for me out there.

You see this is it for me now. This is the end of my adventure. There's no need to run any more.

Because, according to the liar, he has brought me home.

And that makes every tragic thing that happened to my friends all my fault.

ANSWER THE *%!?ˆ& QUESTION!

Billie stares at the Ape. Her eyes, once a bright sparkling blue, have turned as black as Other-Johnson's. In the doppelganger world everyone has coal-black eyes. Though I'd venture to say Billie's are blacker than anyone's. It's like looking into the darkness of space, and they're just as empty of humanity.

'Time's up, Rev.'

She doesn't bother looking at me when she says this. I don't warrant a glance, just a barely heard whisper crossing the width of the boat as it keels to one side and slumps towards the river's cold currents. I slip on the wet wooden deck and Other-Johnson snakes out a hand to help me keep my balance.

'Make the call. End this.' His hypnotic tones fill my head. *'Let that Johnson go. You've still got me.'* I wish I knew why he likes me so much when he's got the exact equivalent of me in the shape of Rev Two. He did try to explain it but I never know if anything he says is true, or just a manipulation.

'Let him go and you'll find out.' Other-Johnson transmits, always reading my mind and always ready with an answer.

There shouldn't be a difference; both Johnsons are everything I could want: a rock star, a movie star, a star amongst all the stars. But in the same way that Rev Two isn't the same as me for Other-Johnson, he's not the Johnson I truly want either. As heroic and dark as he is, he's just not the one.

'I got this,' the Ape pants as beads of sweat mingle with the gathering pool of his lost blood. Even he, the world-champion fighter of every world, can't win this one. Billie is super strong and faster and more lethal than most in her souped-up, hybrid body.

'You've got a Johnson, I've got a Johnson,' Billie mocks. 'We both win. We both get the boy. C'mon, Rev, they're the same person.' She absolutely knows they aren't.

I start to hope that Non-Ape, the bruising, monstrous version of the Ape, makes a miraculous appearance and saves us all. He's somewhere at the bottom of the Thames, drowning or even drowned by now. Billie's reality-bending power has conjured some unseen *thing* that has dragged Non-Ape to a watery grave.

Or has it? Can anything be more powerful than the Non-Ape?

'Can you read for Non-Ape?' I transmit to Other-Johnson. *'Can you hear his thoughts? Is he still alive?'*

'Nothing,' he sighs after a moment.

I refuse to believe it. Non-Ape and the Ape are the same. So he won't give up, won't ever be beaten; he knows only one way, and that's to win. Any second now he will explode from the Thames and end this horror.

Yes.

Any second . . . now!

Make that ten seconds.

Twenty?

Billie's new metal teeth glint as a sliver of sun squeezes between the grey September clouds. 'Johnson or the Ape?' she says. 'This is getting boring now.'

I look at my dying Ape, the best friend I never knew I had. My greatest protector trying to hold what's left of his life together just so he can launch one final attack.

'I'm coming for you,' he splutters at Billie.

I look at Johnson and he knows what's about to happen. I can see him tensing, ready to make the sacrifice and disappear with Billie. He hasn't got any mind-reading telepathic powers, but even from where I'm standing, some five metres away, I know what he's thinking.

He's telling me to forget him.

The man and the woman stop laughing for a moment and the apocalyptic migraine in my head eases a little. Until they look at one another and start laughing all over again.

'Cup of tea?'

'I'd love one.'

'Reva?'

'Sure,' I nod.

'I'll be two minutes,' she says.

'Make it one,' he says with a loving glint in his eye.

My head is going to explode. And I wish it would. I don't want to have any memories or thoughts or feelings. I can't shut my eyes at night because that's when I see all of the very worst things that happened on the empty earth. Replaying over and over.

The woman returns with a scratched and dented tray carrying three mugs and an open packet of Rich Tea biscuits.

'Drink up,' she smiles.

15

'And eat up,' the liar smiles, crunching into a Rich Tea.

'Please,' I try again. *'I'm going crazy. You can't do this to me. Neither of you can.'*

They stop laughing. Finally. And my mum and dad look at me.

That's right. The liar and the woman are my parents. At least they look like them.

My mum gestures to the half-fallen down homecoming banner – the one she put up for me and my dad.

She smiles. 'Let me say it one more time because it sounds so good. Welcome home, Reva.'

My dad continues to clutch my mum's hand and they laugh again. More fires explode in my head as I fall to my knees, and let out all the melodramatic diva I can muster. 'PLEASE STOP LAUGHING!'

Don't they care that all of my friends are dead?

THE END OF THE END

I brace myself.

'Billie!' I call out.

I suck in a deep breath, but find I can't look at Johnson. I just can't do it. My voice is going to crack and I might even cry.

The Ape is rising as best he can. 'Dazza's all over this,' he coughs.

'Want me to swap?' Other-Johnson's voice booms in my head and it catches me completely off guard.

'With Johnson? You'd do that?' I splutter out loud without thinking, so shocked by the suggestion.

'This was meant to be a private conversation,' he quickly transmits.

'Oh . . .' I again speak out loud and can see that Billie is already looking suspicious.

'You'd do that?' I repeat, this time over our private wavelength.

'For you – anything.'

Other-Johnson is not made of dark materials; he can't be. Not when he's ready to make a sacrifice like this.

'*I can't let you do that—*' I transmit again only for him to interrupt me.

'*You want him and not me. I get that. So what's a world without you in it, Rev? Either way I don't win.*'

'*You've got your Reva. You can't let her go.*'

'*I let her go when I kissed Billie.*'

He means Another-Billie, the would-be supermodel from his version of earth who has the power to heal. He kissed her and stole her heart too. That's what I mean about his dark side. He can't resist girls.

'*My Reva deserves better. And you probably do too.*' He adds his thoughts to mine. '*But at least I gave it a whirl, right? I mean, I almost got you, yeah?*'

Our eyes meet and we both know that there's no time for a discussion.

'*You whirled like no other,*' I transmit and cringe at the hideous words I just conjured. He deserves so much better than that.

'*This decision isn't about your Johnson or the Ape. It's about me and you. I can give you what you really want. And I promise you, Billie will never know that I'm not the right Johnson. Not ever.*'

'*She'll keep you here forever,*' I say, thinking of them stranded in a completely empty world.

But he's made up his mind.

'*This is my exit, Rev.*'

'*Wait!*' I yell telepathically. '*Hold your big hero horses. I still need to find the Moth. He's the only one who read and understood my dad's papers. We need your mind-scanning thing to work out where he is.*'

The papers explain how my dad crossed into alternate

18

worlds. The Moth is the only one of us who has the brains to understand them. And, if he can do that, he can get us all back home. The only problem is that we have no idea where he is after several Black Moths kidnapped him from a speeding train.

Billie summoned a hundred Moths to try and kill us. Not the butterfly type of moth, sadly, rather a doppelganger of our own Moth. The Black Moths appeared from thin air; monstrous panther-like versions of the original.

'I'll scan for him and try and contact you if I locate him.'

'And GG?' I still can't face the fact that GG might be dead.

'Rev ... Let me end this.'

I have no choice. We started worlds apart and it looks like we'll finish the same way.

'Then do it.'

Other-Johnson stands a little taller and summons all the willpower he has. *'See you in another universe.'* But even his telepathic voice is cracking.

And, with that amazing power of his, Other-Johnson swaps minds and bodies with Johnson. No one can see it, or even sense it, but it has happened and I know I'll never see Other-Johnson again.

As soon as the switch is made, the Johnson next to me staggers a little, lurching as my Johnson finds himself suddenly in the wrong body. I snap out a hand and drag him upright on the dangerously tipping boat. He turns to me, but I silence any stunned reaction with a determined look that says: *Don't breathe a word, don't say one thing.*

To his credit Johnson sucks up the shock and barely lets a breath escape.

'Save the Ape,' I finally tell Billie. 'There. I said it. Take Johnson, save the Ape!'

'It's Dazza,' the Ape pants, slipping and sliding on the sinking, tipping boat.

But Billie has sensed something's changed. She looks from one Johnson to the other. Her eyes narrow.

A long sleek talon slips soundlessly from the tip of her index finger. An involuntary instinctive reaction to the sense of threat.

My breath stalls in the back of my throat.

Billie looks again from Johnson to Other-Johnson.

She knows there's something wrong. And I realise the longer I don't say anything then the longer she will have to work out what's just happened.

'Save the Ape,' I call to her, my voice a croak as I try to distract her. 'Save him – please! I've made my call. I choose the Ape.'

Billie continues to hesitate, but the Ape pulls himself on to all fours, one hand going to his bleeding stomach as he lifts his great square block of a head. He fixes Billie with all the deadly intent he can muster. If nothing else I'm praying he can distract her.

'I'm so coming for you . . .' he pants.

Billie doesn't even hear him. It's as if the wind has changed or there's a subtle new scent in the air; things have shifted for her, imperceptibly, but enough for more dangerous talons to slide silently from her fingers.

The Ape grunts as he pads like a sick and disoriented lion towards Billie, every movement using up more of his life. He probably believes he's making progress but the tragedy is he's barely moved at all. He trembles on uncertain limbs, drained of blood and muscle memory.

'Billie,' I try again. But she's no longer listening, focusing instead on the Johnson standing next to her, trying to decide what's changed. And all the while the boat continues to take on water and pitch slowly into the river.

Billie leans in towards Other-Johnson who is now in Johnson's body. She doesn't sniff him as such, but she does try and get a sense of who he is by pushing her face as close as she can to his.

'Who are you?' she asks quietly. And with those words I know the ruse is up. What I thought was an outstanding moment of true heroism is going to be our total undoing. She will – literally – slice through the lie.

But Other-Johnson stays calm. Meets her black soulless eyes with his sparkling blue orbs. He doesn't miss a beat. 'Me? I'm the one you're meant to be with.'

Billie's arm rises, the talons are hit by that lone sliver of sunlight that seems to have hung around just so it can glint and highlight the death-dealing nature of her claws.

'So got you ...' I turn back to the Ape and see he's starting to make headway. I can't believe my eyes. 'Used to like you, Billie ...' he pants, as he throws one hand out after the other, one knee following with the second one close behind. 'Not any more ...'

Billie can't help herself; the Ape has drawn her attention for a moment, and even she, as much as she loathes him, is quietly stunned by his resilience.

'What the hell is wrong with you?' she asks him, momentarily forgetting her Johnson dilemma, as she turns full on to the Ape. 'You're dying, you imbecile!'

'Not before you do.' He stops and pulls himself to his knees, completely short of breath, and possibly minus two litres of blood.

Billie is incredulous. 'You saw what I can do.'

'And you've seen what I can do,' the Ape says as he tries to force himself upright.

As ever he's got it bang on; maybe fighting is the only way forward, that Billie's impossible question was one I shouldn't have even attempted answering because the solution was always option three . . . I need to take Billie on and I need to beat her. I scan the ship for something sharp to use as a weapon. If she really is half human and half alien then shoving something into her throat will kill her. The Ape found that out when their version of Lucas attacked him. It's their soft spot, the only place of vulnerability. The Ape had a weapon earlier, some sort of snapped-off boat hook with a jagged edge, if I can just find that.

The boat sinks lower and pitches towards its port side. Or starboard side. One of the sides, I don't know which, and I don't really care. The roll sends the Ape slumping back down.

Billie laughs. 'Look at him, back on all fours. Evolution in reverse.'

But incredibly enough the sudden movement of the boat has sent the weapon the Ape made rolling into clear view. It makes a rattling sound and my eyes find it – the moment Billie's eyes lock on mine. She reads in a heartbeat what my intention is and it's now a matter of speed and luck.

I'm closer but she's faster. She can leap through the air because her hybrid legs are sinewy and strong. She might get to the weapon first – and then again she might not. I could grab the sharp, snapped-off pole, twist as she lands on me and thrust it deep into her throat, saving the day at the last minute like in every movie when the good guy desperately needs to get ridiculously lucky.

And I am the good guy here. Billie is not the friend she was. I'm fighting on the right side and the universe knows that, it must do to so coincidentally roll the weapon my way. I go for the pole – and can't move a muscle.

'No!' Other-Johnson's voice shouts into my mind and I realise he's taken control of my body.

'Let me go!' I yell across our secret airwave.

'No,' he repeats as I try to break free of his hold. He did this before, when I went to find my dad in a private hospital and he forced me to walk up the stairs. My Non-Mum from the doppelganger world could use mind control to freeze people. She even took the whole town hostage to help us escape, but, unlike her, I think Other-Johnson is using the power of suggestion to trick my body into thinking I can't move. If I can just break through that lie ...

The weapon keeps rolling across the deck and Billie looks like she's waiting for the starter's gun at the beginning of a race. She wants me to think I have a chance and then she wants to crush that chance, obliterate it. Johnson's eyes are watching the rolling boat hook, now he's in Other-Johnson's alien body he knows he can reach it five times quicker than I can.

'Rev.' Other-Johnson stays as calm as he can. He knows Billie will kill me. *'Don't take her on. Don't give her that excuse.'*

The weapon keeps rolling and the Ape has seen it as well. His near-dead eyes brighten considerably. It's not his legendary three-pointer but enough to have something to fight with. The boat pitches further and the weapon trundles faster towards me. I need to break free of Other-Johnson's mental control. I strain with all I've got as my shoulders bunch, and my foot finally slips forward. Billie is grinning; she is prepared to let the weapon roll ever closer to me, she's that confident. My arm pushes through the fog of Other-Johnson's auto-suggestion. The other arm follows and I'm suddenly moving.

'You'll never beat her,' Other-Johnson all but begs me.

But nothing is going to stop me grabbing it. I've been fighting for days on end and so far I've come out on top. Why should that change now? I lurch forward.

But Johnson is quicker, and seeing me move he jumps forward, like the super-alien he is now, snatching up the weapon and turning on Billie. He only has a fleeting second to do this. And the fleeting second is so fleeting that even thinking about how fleeting it is means the moment is already lost. If he'd acted first and thought later, he could have, perhaps, maybe, got to Billie, driven her back, somehow defeated her. But the chance is gone.

Then he hurls the weapon into the river. And I realise that attacking Billie was never his intention.

The Ape howls, furious and bewildered. 'Are you stupid?' he wails with a raspy pained breath as lifelessness gets ready to claim him.

Johnson looms large in Billie's eyeline. 'You've got what you wanted. You won. Now save the Ape.'

A flicker races from Johnson to Other-Johnson, an invisible ripple. Ever since they met, Johnson has wanted nothing more than for Other-Johnson to disappear forever. And right now he basically has to do very little to ensure that happens.

Other-Johnson mentally lets go of me and I almost fall flat on my face because I'm straining so hard to escape his bonds.

24

Billie is about to respond when Other-Johnson pulls her towards him. 'Come here.' Other-Johnson kisses her with all the passion he has. Time freezes as his kiss marches upon her defences and lays waste to them. The kiss enters her veins and rides the blood canals to her heart. I know it because I've felt it twice now. The kiss that can fuse lives. Other-Johnson pulls back and Billie looks breathless and lost. She is transfixed as he gazes into her eyes.

'Save the Ape!' I bellow.

Billie blinks a few times and emerges from her kiss-induced trance before looking directly at me.

'Apologise.'

'What?'

'Apologise. You need to say you're sorry to Carrie and GG and Lucas and the Moth,' Her black eyes glint at me. 'And say you're sorry to me. Because all of this, Rev, everything that's happened to the rest of us, it's all your fault.'

I'm thrown. Where did that come from? Carrie was cut down by Evil-GG, sliced to ribbons, and now that's my fault? GG being thrown from the train, the Moth disappearing, Billie mutating into this monster? It's all on me?

'I'm waiting,' she sneers.

There's no time to argue.

'I'm sorry, Carrie! I'm sorry, GG! I'm sorry, Moth! I'm sorry!' I yell. 'I'm sorry for everything! It's my fault!' I scream, because I need this to be over, for her to save the Ape and leave us alone, but also deep down because part of me thinks it's true.

Billie lets a smile spread along her wide mouth. Finally she's happy.

'Now, please! Don't let him die!' I beg her.

Billie slips an arm round Other-Johnson's waist. 'I'm not letting him die. You are,' she says. 'You said yourself this is your fault. Carrie, GG, the Moth, Lucas and now the Ape. All gone, and all because of you.' And with that she grabs Other-Johnson and leaps from the sinking boat towards the bank of the river. Despite the distance, she lands effortlessly on the paved pathway running alongside the Thames, before turning to take in the jaw-dropping shock on my face.

'Billie, we had a deal!' I yell.

'We also had a friendship. Look how that panned out.'

SCHOOL'S IN

It's my first day back at school and I'm nervous. I'm wearing a brand-new school blazer and a pristine white blouse. I have shiny brogues and knee-length socks. I feel overdressed and ridiculous. No one wears the exact school uniform, no one I know can afford to, but here I am, decked out like some posh kid who has a butler lay out their clothes for them.

The school in front of me is identical to the one we were so cruelly kidnapped from.

But you already know it had to be. Because the world copies keep coming like a rampant photocopier has gone rogue and is spewing facsimiles of earth all over the office floor.

I mean, you know the routine, right?

That's right. I'm on yet another earth.

Mum smiles – I've started to refer to her as Mum because she may as well be my mum, but I can't be totally sure. Every time her or my dad comes near me, my personal alarm system, the spider-sense samba, dances across my shoulders in a frinkly tingle. These two people can't be my real parents. My inbuilt warning system is convinced of it.

As part of the deal for me going back to school, I asked Mum to go out and buy me some hair dye. Electric-pink. My original colour, chestnut brown, had started to show through at the roots and that is not where I am in my life right now. As soon as I applied the colouring, I felt more like me again. The pink hair is my battle colour, the thing that sets me apart, and makes me feel more formidable. The reason I was thrown into detention in the first place was because of the hair. My pink hair is two fingers to the world. And that's any world you care to mention.

Thirteen days I spent in the flat they call home. But on the morning of the fourteenth day they presented me with my new school uniform and told me it was time to rejoin the human race.

Assuming, of course, they are human.

Despite the deal I made about the hair dye I still tried to squirm out of it, to say I wasn't ready yet. But my dad said he'd signed me up and that the school was expecting me. Then Mum handed me the hair dye.

'It's time,' is all Dad said.

'It's not time,' I replied.

'Your father needs to go back to work.' Mum stepped in.

'Good for him, but what difference does that make to me?' I was channelling every ounce of petulant teenager and only stopped short of slamming my bedroom door in their faces.

'He wants to know everything is as it should be,' she told me in her soothing tones. 'He wants to be able to go to work knowing that you're happy.'

'He can't guess that I'm not? He's meant to be a genius and he can't see that?'

We – Mum and I – were talking about Dad like he wasn't there, but of course he was, he just didn't know how to get involved. Twelve years ago I was a caterpillar-obsessed four-year-old, but now he's got a moody teenager to deal with. Both him and Mum have, and they're doing their best to stay calm and reasonable.

Well, not Mum really.

Not even Non-Mum.

Because this is New-Mum. My third female parent in as many weeks. A woman who is identical to my real mum right down to having the same worry lines. Though this New-Mum is more emotionally unhinged. Who wouldn't be when your missing husband and daughter suddenly turn up out of the blue?

'School will be fun,' she assured me.

School is only ever fun when you're not there. The only bits I've ever enjoyed are between lessons. Though eventually it dawned on me that being at school would at least get me away from their mind-numbing happiness.

'There's nothing to worry about.' *My dad finally spoke.* 'Nothing at all. It's all perfectly fine.'

We haven't said one word about the empty world that we were both trapped in. It's as if it never happened. I'd tried a few times to bring up the subject, as in – what the mother-loving hell was all that about? But he shushes me, closing it down as quickly as he can. He tells me that he doesn't want to upset New-Mum.

But I know that he doesn't want to talk about the empty world and what happened there for a very good reason. He knows as well as I do what he did to my friends. He also knows I'm constantly on the verge of tears and is desperate to avoid watching me dissolve into a total heap. He wants a perfect world without tears. He's come a long way to get that, but I wonder how much further he'll go to keep it.

GOOD TIDALS WE BRING

Billie takes a run and leaps into the air, still gripping Other-Johnson like he's her favourite rag doll. She bounds along the river walkway, heading past the bridge that Non-Ape uprooted barely more than a minute ago.

The pleasure boat lurches violently; it's going to flip onto its side at any moment. We slip and slide and all three of us, Johnson, the dying Ape and me, go crashing against the far railing.

'Agh!' The Ape groans mightily when my feet smack into his gutted stomach.

Johnson, in his souped-up body, drags himself to his feet, but even as he does he spots something that freezes him. 'Are you kidding me?'

'What? What is it?' I try to grasp the rail and Johnson grabs my elbow, easily hefting me to a precarious standing position. I look back down the river. I think it's to the east, heading towards the coast, but that doesn't really matter.

Because coming our way is a tidal wave.

Yes.

A tidal wave.

In London.

This world truly despises me and its favourite method of torture is using the elements against me. It's already burned me in a fire. It tried to freeze me in icy waters, and then conjured a snowstorm. I thought I'd pretty much beaten everything it could conjure up for me, but it's left me a leaving present. A nice big wet kiss goodbye.

The wave is coming fast, growing taller and speedier by the second. I have no defence, no ideas, no escape plan.

'Johnson,' I whisper.

Now he's in the body of Other-Johnson he might survive, but the Ape won't. He won't be able to swim in his condition and I make a silent pact to not let him die alone.

The tidal wave rises higher and higher, gathering momentum.

'Johnson,' I whisper again. 'Listen to me. Get to shore. Find the Moth or even my dad and the other Rev. Then get home. Get home and be safe.'

'I can jump you both off the boat.'

'There's no time.' I glance at the Ape. 'And I can't leave him.'

The tidal wave is enormous by now, rising level with the buildings, both ancient and new, that line the river.

Johnson slips his hand into mine. He's not going anywhere either. 'Like I'd leave you.'

The enormous wave is going to smash down on us so I reach for the fallen Ape's mighty paw and, even though it's slippery with his blood, I cling on as we make a tiny human chain in the face of a thousand tons of Thames.

'Dazza,' I whisper to him, my eyes meeting his. This could be the last word I ever say to him.

The river rises like a giant's fist, curling to crush us.

The boat lurches.

And then rises sharply and steeply into the air, sending us tumbling back across the deck, sliding and skidding towards the bankside railings.

A mighty bellow accompanies the violent lurch as the boat floats in the air. That bellow is something I grew to fear before truly appreciating it for its sonorous beauty.

It's the bellow of the Non-Ape.

The boat rises higher as the Non-Ape starts pushing it towards the bank.

The tidal wave closes faster and faster.

Non-Ape's mighty legs and arms propel the boat through the ever-shallowing waters as we're sucked towards the tidal wave which is now only fifty metres away now.

But the riverbank is closer.

Non-Ape bellows again.

The tidal wave closes on us, casting an enormous shadow as it blocks out the sky.

The boat is within metres of the bank.

'C'mon, Ape!' Johnson adds his bellow to Non-Ape's.

'Throw it!' I yell. 'Throw the boat!' Nop-Ape will survive any tidal wave because he's stronger than an ocean.

'Throw it!' Johnson yells.

The boat rises higher and then arcs backwards as Non-Ape's strength defies the wildest imagination and he gets ready to hurl the boat out of the Thames. I swear I can feel his colossal muscles bunching through the timbers of the broken pleasure cruiser.

He's going to do it. Just like every Ape in every universe, he will save the day, because that is what every single one of them was born to do.

But then the tidal wave hits, pounding down on us before Non-Ape gets the chance to launch us.

The Thames smashes into the boat and wipes us out in a stained brown hurricane of water and abandoned shopping trolleys. Then, in one of this world's crueller mocking coincidences, I see Carrie's dead body coming straight for me.

It's impossible. Carrie's body cannot possibly have found its way back to me. But then in this world the impossible has become the norm.

SIGNED UP, SHIPPED OFF

We live about half a mile from the school so I could have walked it in ten minutes, but New-Mum and Dad insisted on driving me.

'Soon be there,' my dad said from the back seat.

'Two minutes,' New-Mum smiled.

She drove straight into the school grounds; usually that's strictly forbidden, at least it is in my world, only teachers and official visitors can drive into the school. But New-Mum is keen to get me as close as she possibly can so there's no chance of me not showing up for lessons.

'We're here,' New-Mum says in her gentle, soothing voice. 'And I know you'll love it.'

'Love it,' Dad echoes.

'I hate school,' I tell them. But they aren't listening to anything I say.

'Only thing you need to think about—'

'—and it's a good thought—'

'—is that we're all back together.' New-Mum pats my knee.

Dad rubs my shoulder. 'That's all that matters,' he tells me.

It's almost as if they have to touch me to make sure I'm real. That I'm actually there.

'And listen, any problems call us,' he adds.

'We'll be here in seconds,' New-Mum says as she offers me a brand-new mobile phone. It's still boxed though the seal has been broken.

'Open it then,' Dad says.

They're very excited. It's the only state they've been in since he brought me here. Pure unadulterated excitement for two whole weeks now.

I'm not worried about the passing of time because the Moth had a theory that time happens differently on different earths. So even if it is two weeks here it can still be a microsecond in my real world. I could go back there and arrive just a moment after I left.

My real world. Going home. It sounds so good I think it twice.

'We already opened it and charged the phone for you.' New-Mum's smile is very similar to my real mum's smile. The deeply protective and loving, yet perennially lost, mother who I'm determined to see again. New-Mum is much more fragile emotionally, more of a deep brittle than anything. She might look the same, but she isn't and, more than anything, she is not someone I can see myself growing to love. So I'm going to wait until I can find an opening, a gap in the fabric of what's real and what's false. Soon as I do, I'm waltzing straight through it, no looking back, no getting hung up on a fragile mother whose life has just been made complete again. New-Mum is not my worry. So *if I have to play games, to behave like everything is hunky-dory, I'll do it to buy myself time until I can figure out exactly where I am and how to escape.*

Back in the empty world the liar had told me that he would fix everything. And I fought tooth and nail to keep him safe while he did that. We all did, human and doppelganger. We battled with everything we had just so he could send us all back to where we came from. He yelled at us to keep him alive while he opened the proper portal. Keep me safe, *he shouted,* I can fix this. I can fix it all. *So the Apes found themselves in their greatest ever battle and they fought and fought. Our doppelgangers buried their grudges against us and joined the war, and even if some did fall, their healer, Another-Billie, was on hand to reanimate them. Although they were being overwhelmed, no one ever gave up hope. The threat came from everywhere, surging forth with only one intention. To stop us, to cut us down. But the battle distracted us and we were all far too slow to see what my father was really doing.*

He had no intention of sending anyone but him and me home. All he ever wanted from the others for was to keep us safe. He whisked me away at the worst possible moment. They were dying in front of my eyes and he stole me away before I could stop him.

I'll never forgive him for that.

Never.

ONE MUDDY RIVER TO CROSS

I'm underwater and I don't know if I'm upside down or which way the surface is. I'm spinning in an endless cycle as if gravity no longer exists.

I also have company.

Carrie's body has become entwined with mine. Her dead arms have bent and locked round my body. Her face is centimetres from mine and we are dancing underwater, twisting and turning, locked in an embrace like old friends reunited. But there's something about this embrace that tells me Carrie would like to hang onto me so she can drag me down to the depths. Even in death she wants to kill me.

I struggle to break free of her grip because I am not going to drown. Not today or any other day. I have a few seconds of air left and at some stage I'm going to work out where the surface is and I'm going to kick like a mule for it.

The last five or so days have hardened me to everything. Even while I'm tumbling at fifty miles an hour as the tidal wave hurls me this way and that, I will not let it defeat me. I have a home somewhere; I have friends and family and a life. I can't disappear; I can't not be. This is not how my story is going to end.

I shove hard at Carrie, desperate to untangle myself, when her eyes spring open.

It takes my breath away – literally – as I open my mouth in astonishment and swallow a gutful of Thames. Her eyes are dark brown and very much alive.

And now I remember. This isn't really Carrie. She's inside Evil-GG's body, and Evil-GG is inside hers because Other-Johnson switched them after Evil-GG attacked us in a five-star luxury hotel.

How he has survived inside Carrie's dead, eviscerated body I don't know. He was the one who cut her to ribbons in the first place. He was also the one who had a hotel crash down on him not long afterwards. But when Non-Ape was clearing away the rubble of the demolished hotel he accidentally grabbed Carrie's body and tossed it into the river.

The eyes stare at me with intensity. He can't speak, he can't move, but it's definitely Evil-GG.

Evil-GG was the worst of the doppelgangers by a mile. An outrageously bitchy killer who mocked and belittled us at every turn. Whip smart and more deadly than the rest of the doppels combined.

Despite those awful staring brown eyes I force myself to grab for Carrie's body and hold on as tight as I can. I can right this wrong, I think. I can hunt down Other-Johnson, rope Another-Billie in and hold some sort of healing-stroke-mind-swapping afternoon tea party to bring Carrie back. I can find GG somehow, the Moth as well. I can do all of these things as long as I don't drown. That's the one thing I mustn't do.

I cling on to Carrie's stick-thin body and can't get any bearing on what's up or down and my lungs are already bursting. I read that when the Japanese tsunami hit, a survivor said he'd remembered reading that if you're ever trapped in a water-related disaster that you usually surface twice, but if you go under a third time you never come back up. It's a sort of universal law. Three strikes and you're in for a watery grave. I haven't been to the surface once so I'm pretty sure I have two lives left. See, there's always a positive, you just need to look for it.

I have no idea where Johnson has gone, or the Apes, for that matter. I don't know if Non-Ape could have withstood the force of the tidal wave, but he seems to have a massive lung capacity because he was underwater for a long time while we were all on the boat. So I'm hoping he could probably ride this wave out and then stomp his way to the riverbank.

Johnson might survive because he's stronger now in his alien body; he could have the power to break to the surface and the speed to avoid being hit by debris. The wave will eventually peter out, so if he can just find a way.

But the Ape . . .

Suddenly my spinning, tumbling progress is halted by a sickening thud as Carrie and I slam into an ancient thick stone leg that holds up one of London's many bridges. The impact is back-breaking but I'm cushioned by Carrie as she hits the bridge first. I follow and headbutt her so hard I almost knock myself out. My teeth jar and my neck is whiplashed back and forth as I give her the Glasgow kiss to end all Glasgow kisses. The torrent tries to drag us away from the bridge, but this is my one chance and I grab for anything that I can hold on to. I can't see much beyond Carrie, but I find a metal loop, a rusted ring of steel embedded in the leg of the bridge, and I quickly slide my fingers in and hold on as tight as I possibly can. But I have no air left and begin to convulse. I haven't ever felt pain like this, it's agony and bleeds panic throughout me. I'm going to drown.

I am at minus air now and every bit of me wants to open my mouth and breathe, even knowing that I'll only breathe in water, the urge to try and gasp is overwhelming. Black spots are appearing in front of my eyes, but I locate another steel ring, higher this time and wrench myself upwards. Carrie comes with me. I could easily be heading downwards, but there's a third ring and I heave on that as the tidal wave tears at me. Carrie is clinging on in her cruel embrace of skinny, dangerously pointed limbs, and I thank God it's not the meaty Ape I have to carry with me.

But then I hate God in the next non-breath because I so dearly wish it was him.

Another rung and more black spots dot in and out of my vision; now they're mingling and fusing, turning into small blinding clouds like oxygen-starved blinkers. How do you syphon oxygen from water? What if I purse my lips and suck the water through my teeth? Would that separate the molecules? Everything is turning dizzy, my brain is demanding that I take a breath and my lungs are screaming at me to do the same. Agony and panic are filling my brain, blotting out sanity and logic. They're yelling at me, over and over.

Another steel ring, another crash and the swell of thunderous river water smashes us hard against the leg

41

of the bridge again. But Carrie is my saviour, my impact-cushioning saviour, whose brittle bones I'm probably snapping with each collision. Over and over she is crushed between me and the thick stone leg. A surge of river wrenches my hand away and for a second we're lost again, swirling away from the great stone leg, and I can only see blackness. I flail out a desperately weak arm and somehow grab the steel ring again. I heave with all I've got. I'm blacking out and I desperately, desperately want to breathe. I don't care that it's water, I just want something, anything, to inhale.

The waves keeping coming, following the worst of the tidal wave with their snide little reminders, crashing into us, but now lifting us . . .

We rise sharply and I find another steel rung. They're not rings, they're a form of ancient ladder, I think. We slip down again, torn away by the thundering, swollen river. My lungs are dead; they are preparing for their funeral.

I snake a hand out.

I can't find the rung.

Where the hell is it?

I've got to try and breathe. Just let me have one tiny breath. Everything is black now, inside and out. I can't find the rung, and I don't even know if we were being lifted. I just can't tell. Maybe I've dragged us to the depths because I can't see a thing. A darkness is reaching round us, urging me to take that breath because, yes, of course it's entirely feasible to syphon oxygen from water through your gritted teeth.

I take a breath and fill my throat and lungs with water. I spasm. It's like I've been knifed in the chest and I try to close my mouth, but the knifing pain makes me gag and I start to choke to death on river water. Carrie's eyes bore into mine and even in the darkness I'm pretty sure there's a vindictive smirk behind them.

I'm putting the Rev in revenge, she seems to be saying.

A wave hits again, harder than the ones before, but it squeezes us like a giant spot and we squirt upwards . . .

. . . and hit the surface.

London air is a different sort of air. I always think it must be some of the most used and abused air in the world. Millions of people breathing it in and out, at least in my real world. It's usually a tired air, exhausted and limp and still, and laced with the dust of endless building and regeneration. But I suck it in now like it's from the Garden of Eden. I gulp it. I eat it. I swallow it and then bite more great chunks of it. I'm panting while I dine on it. Feasting on it. No one has ever digested so much air in such a short space of time.

I clutch on to the iron rung, not steel. How could it be steel if it's rusted. The black spots are turning into crows; they're spreading their wings and flying away. My vision is clearing as I cling on with everything I've got. Carrie continues to stare at me. I can't help myself and I am so elated I lean forward and kiss her hard on the cheek.

Another wave slams into us. But I'm better than that wave. I'm tougher and I'm stronger and I hold firm. The knifing pains are still making me want to curl up, but that's not going to happen, not now, not ever.

Waves continue to hit us, some threatening to send us under again, some pouring over our heads and thumping down on us as hard as they can.

That iron rung is cold and slippery, but nothing is going to break my grip.

Each time a wave hits, I ride it out and then take the chance to look for any sign of the broken pleasure boat.

The Thames has risen so high I no longer recognise London. Familiar streets and landmarks have been submerged in the torrent. The taller buildings look shorter, as if the architects started halfway up and forgot about lobbies and entrances. Some buildings have cracked and broken and then fallen under the thunderous impact. Weirdly enough *HMS Belfast* is now on land, having been thrown on to what's left of the Strand, and is now wedged into the side of a modern office building.

But as for humans?

There's no one.

No Johnson.

No Non-Ape.

And definitely no Ape.

SMARTER THAN THE AVERAGE PHONE

We're still in the car at the school, and as much as they want me to be 'normal' and go into the building, somehow Dad and New-Mum can't bring themselves to let me out of their sight. She, especially, seems scared rigid. That part I do understand. My dad opened doors to new universes and walked through one of them, disappearing for twelve years, so I get her fear. But not his. I know he was desperate, driven near insane on his quest to find a daughter he thought he'd lost, but he won't get one drop of mercy or understanding from me.

I have opened the box with the phone and there's already a text message for me.

It's from New-Mum.

Have a gr8 day hon

She's sitting beside me, staring at me, willing me to smile at the message, which I do, but just for her sake. They mustn't ever know that I'm planning to ditch this world just as soon as I find a way out.

But who calls their kid **hon***?*

45

'Both our numbers are in there,' she tells me.

They've even put a photograph of them holding hands together and smiling on as the screen background.

'That's us,' my dad says unnecessarily.

'Thanks for clearing that up, I'd never have guessed,' I mumble.

I stare out through the windscreen and watch kids wandering into school. I recognise most of them from my original world. They look the same, but something feels odd. All of them seem quiet and subdued somehow. There's no running or noise, even the younger boys who usually spend all their time bombing around jumping all over each other seem blank and vacant.

Into school they trudge and I know exactly how they feel.

I turn and look at New-Mum.

'Do I have to go?' I ask.

'Learning is everything,' my dad responds. 'There is nothing more valuable than knowledge.'

It's still strange to see his face, hear his voice, be around him after all this time. He's not quite how I thought my dad would be. He seems like a copy of a dad; he's got the look right, and the sense of the fatherly off to a tee, but I can't detect a soul inside him. All the things that make a person a person, the dreams, the fears, the natural essences of whatever it is that makes us tick, in him they seem forced, unreal. Maybe that's what happens when you cross dimension after dimension after dimension. You leave a piece of yourself behind in every world you visit.

For the last two weeks he's been deliriously happy and yet I know there is something missing, something less than human about him.

'Do her proud,' New-Mum suddenly says.

Which stops me for a moment. 'Her?' I ask. 'Who's her?'

'You,' Dad whispers.

'The you I lost,' New-Mum says, and her eyes suddenly moisten.

Is she talking about her real Rev?

Dad again whispers in my ear. 'Bear with her,' he says quietly.

I immediately disobey his instructions. 'Are you saying I'm not your Rev?' I ask New-Mum.

'Of course you are.' New-Mum wipes her eyes. She's trying not to get too emotional. 'Of course you are.'

Dad whispers in my ear again. 'She gets confused. But it's understandable. Lots of shocks and surprises these past two weeks.'

If I didn't want to get out of the car before, I am now ready to smash through the windscreen. They are weirding me out big time.

New-Mum seems to be talking as if she knows there are more Rev's than just me. Did this dad tell her he'd go and find me and, if he couldn't find their original daughter, did he promise he'd bring back something similar?

'Am I or am I not her?' I ask.

New-Mum smiles through her reddening eyes. 'You are my Rev and I still can't believe it,' she offers. 'So do her proud,' she then repeats confusingly.

I'm no psychiatrist but even I can see that New-Mum is scarily unhinged.

'Her little Rev never grew up in front of her, so she thinks of you as being different, even though you are the same person,' Dad whispers. 'But don't worry, your mum is working through it all. One day at a time.'

When people tell so many lies, there is absolutely no way of knowing where the truth is hiding. But every lie starts in fact. So somewhere in this deeply disturbing conversation is a truth. But I just can't figure out what it is. Through the windscreen I spot GG. For a split second I imagine that it's really him. That he is still alive. I almost call his name. But the thud of hope crashes quickly down around my ears. It might look like GG, it might walk and talk and dance a little happy jig like GG, but it's not him. My GG is long gone. But the sight of someone who looks so much like one of my friends is enough for me to reach for the door handle. If there's a GG version, the others could be here as well.

My parents see me make what they obviously think is a very sudden move and New-Mum's hand darts out and grabs my bicep through the material of my new blazer.

'Hon.'

'Don't want to be late,' I say. I can already see GG leaping on the back of a large boy. It's not the Ape, but this GG clings on, riding him like a horse and laughing hysterically. He's the only person I've seen so far who is remotely animated.

'We'll be right outside when the end-of-school bell goes.' New-Mum pats my knee again.

'You really don't need to.' If only they knew how capable I have become.

'We want to,' she tells me warmly.

'So we will be,' Dad offers. And I sneak a look at him in the rear-view mirror and I'm not sure but something starkly sad crosses his face. 'Promise you.'

'*Off you go,*' New-Mum smiles. *My shoulders are tingling like crazy. It's not both of them it's warning me about, it's her. When she kissed me on the cheek, my shoulders turned electric. She might be more of a problem than I first realised.*

MY OWN PRIVATE EVEREST

I'm hanging on for dear life to the iron rung, but I need to start climbing again before all of my strength bleeds away and we are torn back down into the swirling, violent river. Above us are more iron rungs driven deep into the leg of a bridge that rises high above the Thames. I am still eating air like it's the best steak bake ever made. And, as I breathe in, the Thames squirts out of my nose. I cough hard, retching up more river, and most of it projectile – vomits into Carrie's bruised face. I must have swallowed litres of it as the knifing pain accompanies every rasping heave.

My vision has cleared enough for me to see that the iron rungs lead all the way to the top of the bridge. I can't imagine they are an actual ladder so they definitely must be there to reinforce. Either way I am climbing up them. My arms will give out if I don't get moving.

'I don't know if you're in there or not, but I need you to cling on to me,' I tell Carrie, who is really Evil-GG. 'I could try swimming for the bank but I'm a rotten swimmer. I can barely keep myself afloat, let alone the two of us.' I cough more Thames into her face just for good luck. 'The torrent will sweep us away.' I cough again, and wonder why I'm bothering to explain.

Carrie doesn't nod or show any sign of understanding. Her eyes remain open though and I'd swear on my life that there is definitely something behind them.

'Hang on,' I whisper. 'Just hang on tight.'

I try and wedge Carrie's skinny arms and legs around me and reach for the rung above my head. But she has no grip or purchase and I almost lose her. I hate myself, but with my free hand I drag her right arm around my neck and wrench as hard as I can, dislocating her left shoulder so that I can shove that arm down into the back of my collar. I wince. This is not a good moment for me.

With Carrie 'tied' around me, I steady my foot on a slippery rung below the waterline and push upwards.

The climb is exhausting. I think the bridge must be fifteen metres or more above us and it doesn't help that we're both soaked through, meaning our clothes feel like chain mail.

I keep going, one slow rung at a time. Telling myself I'm not in a race and that we have all the time in the world. My arms grow weaker and number by the second until I can't feel my fingers any more. I blow on them, gnaw on them, bite deep into them, anything to keep the blood pumping through them. One slip and we're back in that deadly river.

I don't think of anything but the climb. All other thoughts and thinking can be done once we're safely on solid ground.

One rung after another, slow as slow can be.

Up we go.

I don't look down, just up.

Down is where death is and I'm all about life.

I have no feeling in my fingers and hands and the numbness is starting to creep along my wrists. Every single last drop of strength has been used up.

The grey clouds seem to hang lower and the warm September day has disappeared as a chill sets into my bones from the damp clothes I'm wearing. But there are thousands of empty shops with dry clothes. Assuming the tidal wave didn't reach all the way into the centre of London. There are cafes with food and drink. The city is a paradise of free offerings just ripe for the taking. All I need to do is reach the top and the thought of that gives me strength.

One rung after another.

I try not to look at Carrie's staring eyes.

But I do talk to her. 'This is going to make us even,' I pant. 'This will undo all the bad I did to you.' Not that I actually did anything bad, despite what Billie made me yell.

I mean, I was totally unaware of Carrie's crush on my boyfriend Kyle back in our world. We'd pretty much cleared that up anyway so Billie was way out of order making those insane demands.

'You'll thank for me this,' I tell Carrie.

The top of the bridge is coming into view.

'We'll laugh about this one day.' I say, even though I only ever remember her laughing cynically. Usually at people rather than with them.

'You won't be the same,' I pant. 'None of us will be. But we will be alive. I guarantee that. That's a Reva Marsalis promise.'

There are no more iron rungs.

I have reached the top.

Mount Everest has been conquered.

My arms are numb all the way to my shoulders, but I give one last heave and together we topple over the bridge wall and fall over a metre on to stone paving slabs. I land hard on top of Carrie and I think I hear one of her ribs crack. I disentangle myself from her and roll away, glad to be free of those deadly eyes, and press my forehead into a paving slab as I lie there, drenched, but so grateful to be touching land again.

Carrie lies on her back beside me. Still very much dead but that's OK. That's good. There's a healer thirty miles north of here. She can fix Carrie and she can fix the Ape.

All I've got to do is find him again.

Which is going to be impossible. I can't dredge the entire Thames.

I get to my feet and peer over the wall and watch the furious river churning violently underneath me. I hate it with all my heart as I glance back at Carrie, and see her big brown eyes locked on to mine.

'What are you looking at?' I scowl.

But really I just want to cry.

I'm sitting in a classroom, zoning out of a maths lesson because I'm working on a theory.

Imagine this scenario for a second. Imagine that you are four-year-old me and you are watching your handsome young father with his sleek black hair and finely chiselled features. He is excited. He has been working on a theory, writing notes on a whiteboard, maybe jotting them down or even dictating them into a recording device. He's discovered something. The eighth wonder of the world. He's opened a portal into new earths. A white light beckons to him, maybe pulls at him, and the hair on his forearms stands on end because this white light has the tug of a small black hole. It calls to him, but because he's a scientist he knows he can't just blindly walk through it. He needs to run tests; he needs to make calculations and record his observations in a notebook before anything else can happen. A notebook that will come to be the scientific papers that the Moth eventually ends up reading and, incredibly enough, understanding. My father jots it all down because that's what scientists do, and maybe he puts a heavy weight on those papers because the portal is still tugging at the world that has opened before it.

My dad has a problem though. He's opened the portal, but how does he close it? And if he can't manage to do that how does he make it safe? Does he leave the room and lock the door behind him? I have no idea where the portal is, it might be in a laboratory; or it might be in the tiny cramped flat that he shares with his wife and four-year-old daughter. You see the girl is a bit of a wimp and has made a bed on the floor at the foot of her parents' queen-size-bed because she's scared of sleeping on her own in the dark. Little Reva has been pretty stubborn about this and her mum and dad indulge her. So maybe her dad is in Reva's bedroom because it's the only spare room in their tiny cramped flat, and he's so close to making a discovery he often goes in there and works at night while Reva and her mum are sleeping in the the main bedroom.

These are exciting times and little Reva's bedroom, with its electric-pink walls and all her piled-up toys, has become a sort of laboratory. Little Reva's dad only works on paper, he's not boiling liquids in test tubes or sending photons through a home-made hadron collider; almost all of it is words and numbers and calculations. I'm guessing here, but just say he creates the magic formula that opens a portal, a blueprint for building a device. I'm not sure if it's an actual thing or something that exists outside the laws of ordinary physics, but it works. My dad builds a key on a molecular scale and it's as much a shock to him as it would be to anyone. He's discovered that the universe is a multiverse. He creates some form of key and finds that it doesn't just unlock one door, but loads and loads of other doors. And the mind-boggling thing is, the portal opens and the white light pulls things towards it. Millimetre by millimetre.

Can you see where this is heading? Wimpy daughter is scared of the dark so in the night, when she thinks she needs her favourite stuffed caterpillar toy, she opens the door to her bedroom and sees the white light. And she thinks to herself, I like that light. That's so much better than the dark. *There was a moment I'd imagined my dad had used little Reva as a guinea pig, sending her through the portal with a rope tied round her waist. But you wouldn't travel through dimensions to find a daughter if you were so careless with her life in the first place, would you? So instead I think this little Reva, who is scared of the dark, sees a white light and thinks to herself dark is not nice, but white is.* I like white.

I don't remember any white light in my bedroom, but I do recall sleeping on my mum and dad's bedroom floor, in a nest of blankets and pillows, but without my favourite toy for a reason I can't recall now. I also remember my father suddenly not being around and spending twelve years with an overprotective mum who could barely make ends meet. But does any of that make sense?

Wouldn't I remember leaving my world? Did my dad make a mistake and hurry after me when he didn't need to? Or does my theory suck?

'*Reva, perhaps you can answer?*' *A teacher, female and butch, stands at the front of the classroom with a large whiteboard looming behind her. She holds a black Sharpie and uses it to point to the large writing on the board.*

56

The equation she has written on the whiteboard is simple beyond measure.

1 + 1 =

One plus one. Is she kidding me?

The rest of the class sit quietly, more subdued than you'd expect over twenty teenagers to be. Even the teacher looks like she's filling time before the bell rings for the next lesson.

'Anything?' The teacher, Miss Matson, emphasis on the Miss – in my world anyway – is a known and forthright lesbian who is usually very witty and confident. But this Miss Matson is resigned and tired-looking.

'One plus one?' I ask her.

'Take a wild guess,' she says without any inflection or sign of humour in her voice.

At first I think it's a joke, like the answer must be eleven as in 1+1 = 11. A tricksy little joke that was only ever clever when you were five years old.

'Go on,' Miss Matson cajoles. 'See if you can get it right. Let the class see how smart the new girl is.'

No one in the class is paying any attention to me or Miss Matson or the equation on the whiteboard. They're not ignoring her, they're just putting up with the day. Waiting until they can crawl to the next lesson.

'Three,' I answer.

Miss Matson writes a big three on the whiteboard and nods her appreciation.

'What a star. Brilliant. Shall we applaud?'

The class give me a small dull round of applause. I 'know' all of them, at least I know them from my real world, though I have to pretend not to because I'm meant to be new in school.

Miss Matson wipes the calculation from the whiteboard. 'OK, let's do a harder one this time.' She's trying to sound cheery and positive like the real Miss Matson would, but her writing gives it away. Her usual strident swishes of marker pen on whiteboard often bring a squeal of protest from the board, a sound that attacks your teeth every time. But these strokes are light, barely registering, and the black Sharpie pen stays silent.

She finishes writing a new equation on the board.

1 + 1 =

I fall silent just like the rest of the class.

BILLIE MADE US LOOK SILLY

I think I must be delirious. Swallowing all that river water has affected my brain. I've been searching for any sign of life for more than half an hour now when I hear the Ape's voice.

'You were down there hours,' the Ape tells Non-Ape.

'I can go days underwater.'

'I've got to try that,' the Ape decides.

They are talking as if nothing – and I mean absolutely nothing – has happened.

He is wedged into a shopping trolley while Non-Ape pushes him towards me and the dead, unmoving Carrie. They are lost in one of their never-ending, roundabout conversations that only they will ever understand. There is no sign of the Ape's injuries. He seems to be completely unharmed. My jaw literally hits the floor.

'So what was down there?' the Ape asks.

'Dunno. Something wrapped round me then I bit it.'

'Teeth!' The Ape exclaims.

They still haven't noticed me. I want to intervene, to

explain that Billie probably conjured some monster out of thin air to drag Non-Ape down. She made it so strong it held him there until she had *eloped* with Other-Johnson. But it would be like trying to explain the Theory of Relativity to a Dobermann and I decide to let it go. Besides I'm too ecstatic at seeing the Ape again.

'Dazza!' I all but scream and run towards them.

'Boob Girl!' Ape shouts, finally noticing me. 'It's Boob Girl.' Of all the superhero names, that has got to be the worst one ever.

There is no sign of a wound or a cut or any blood loss on him.

And then it dawns.

I am so stupid. The Ape wasn't hurt at all; Billie only made it seem that way. She used my own worst fear against me. She must have been laughing her socks off inside. She created a horrible fantasy just to get me to admit I didn't want Johnson.

Non-Ape shoves the Ape towards me, but the trolley has a left bias and he shoots straight into the stone wall of the bridge before crashing and toppling over with a hefty *whump*. The Ape laughs as his still wet T-shirt rides up and reveals a perfectly normal, perfectly flabby, stomach. He points to his hairy belly.

'I'm a healer!' he declares.

'He's a healer!' Non-Ape lumbers up, echoing the best friend he ever met.

'Let me touch you.' The Ape reaches out for me, his slab of a hand gripping my sinewy arm.

I try to avoid his big meaty hand. 'No need, there's nothing wrong with me.'

But he grabs my arm regardless. 'Not any more!' he declares.

'He's better than Billie!' Non-Ape towers over us, casting a giant shadow. He knows his version of Billie can heal people, but hasn't yet worked out that there's now two of them on this planet. He thinks my Billie is his Billie and there is no way I'm wasting what will end up being the best part of a year explaining that he's got it wrong.

The Ape touches me again. 'Healed!'

I have nothing that needs healing. A few scratches, some burns, the odd loose tooth and all manner of bruises. But when he touches me nothing changes. All the aches and pains remain.

'I'm not hurt.' I tell them.

'Not any more.' Non-Ape repeats.

The Ape gets to his feet, looks around and then touches Non-Ape's massive forearm. 'Healed!'

Non-Ape looks down at his forearm and laughs in huge delight. 'Yowza!'

There was absolutely nothing that needed healing on Non-Ape either.

The Ape touches the stone wall. 'Healed!'

'Bridges aren't alive,' I laugh.

He bends and touches the paving slabs. 'Healed!'

'Neither are paving slabs.'

But he's not listening as he steps into the road and touches the tarmac. 'Healed!'

Non-Ape pulls at his drenched, home-made toga. A bedsheet was the only thing we could find to fit him after he lost all of his clothes when the Black Moths attacked the train. 'Heal this.'

The Ape takes a moment as if summoning some inner chi and then touches the toga.

'Healed!' Non-Ape laughs.

If there's one thing that's bound to drive a person totally and irrevocably insane, it's two Apes having a good time.

I don't know if I should try and explain that the Ape is not a healer or just let them enjoy themselves. In truth it doesn't really matter. Billie made us all believe the absolute worst. For a while now I'd been imagining that this world, this empty, deserted earth, didn't want me in it, so it set about attacking me. But Billie has been behind all of it. She wanted to be with Johnson, and she was ready to do anything to ensure that happened. She manipulates the biggest fears you have and makes you believe they are real. When the train was attacked by the swarm of rampaging and deadly Black Moths, they were just our imaginings. But the more we believed in them and the more we fought them, the more real they became. Just like the snowstorm back in town, and the tidal wave of course. If you see it and feel it, then you immediately believe it. And worst of all you fear it.

And she was the one who thought I should apologise? I should have seen through her lie and the fact that I didn't hurt just as much as anything. She took me for the complete and utter idiot that I am.

The Ape touches Carrie's lifeless body. 'Healed!'

Billie did nothing but present me with my biggest mortal fear. That the Ape would die. And she knew I'd choose him over Johnson. She played me perfectly. It's a strange thing when you realise your best friend is also your worst enemy.

I watch the Ape prodding and poking Carrie with his

thick, stubby finger, bewildered that she hasn't sprung dramatically to life.

'You're healed!' he tells her. 'Get up!'

Non-Ape prods her with his foot. 'Hey! You're all better.'

'Hey!' The Ape nudges her with his soaking shoe.

'C'mon!' Non-Ape bellows. 'You're not dead.'

'No one dies.'

'It's just a video game.'

'Reset.' The Ape keeps touching Carrie's thin arm. 'Reset. New life.'

I remember now that the Ape told me he thought this world was like a video game and that he and Non-Ape never wanted to go home. Which is another hurdle I'll need to ... hurdle. Tearing them apart after they have become such great friends will be awful. Back in the real world the Ape wasn't exactly popular. None of us really liked him until he showed us that for all his flaws he's always the one to stand the tallest and fight until the bitter end. So, if I do find my dad and get out of here, I can't leave the Ape behind.

I right the shopping trolley and wheel it towards the Apes and Carrie.

'Maybe you need to recharge,' I tell the Ape.

'Billie has to do that,' Non-Ape agrees. 'Always fainting.'

The Ape presses his finger into his own forehead. 'Yeah. Not getting nothing.' He presses his finger into Non-Ape's lowered forehead. 'Anything?'

Non-Ape waits for a second that turns into the slowest minute ever endured before shaking his head. 'Nothing.'

The Ape looks a little disappointed. 'I'll save it for GG,' he tells me quietly. 'I'll be all powered up by then.'

The thought winds me. The Ape and GG should never be

friends in any world, but somehow, because of this nightmare we've been thrown into, they formed a close connection. And right now, I wish that the Ape could heal because if we ever do find GG again I'm pretty certain he won't be alive. He was swept from the side of a train doing at least ninety miles an hour. I watched it with my own eyes as he turned and twisted and we saw him *float* away. Those were his words. *I'll just float away.*

I nod to the Ape, 'Yeah, you do that,' I tell him and sadness lingers between us for a long moment.

'That's the plan,' he says softly.

I try and suck it up because we have to get moving. 'We need to find Johnson,' I tell the Apes.

'I'll heal him too.'

'I'm sure he's OK,' I say quietly.

'Will be,' the Ape declares.

'So will be,' Non-Ape agrees.

I need to break through their strange, tortuous dialogue before it repeats for the next twenty years. 'Let's get Carrie into the shopping trolley.' I do my best to try and bump their brains on to another subject.

Barely a second after I've finished speaking, Non-Ape has hoisted Carrie as if she weighed less than a sheet of paper and slung her face first into the trolley. I think he's become confused and believes he's shopping in a supermarket.

'Could you maybe sit her up?' I ask.

Non-Ape looks at Carrie who is face down with her bony body all bent up behind her.

'Butt!' The Ape points at Carrie's almost non-existent rear end as it sticks up.

Non-Ape laughs. 'Butt!'

We haven't got the time for this and I snap at both of them. 'Give her some dignity!' I yell.

The Apes stop sniggering and fall silent.

'She's still a person,' I say in a quieter voice, seeing the hurt on their faces.

'*Moo-dy*,' Non-Ape whispers as he rearranges Carrie in the trolley.

'Always moody,' the Ape agrees with Non-Ape.

'*Mood* Girl not *Boob* Girl.'

'Should never have healed her.' Non-Ape thinks I can't hear him even though I'm standing less than a metre away.

The river has started to recede from the buildings and pavements. The tidal wave was real enough – at least I think it was – but already it's dissipating and at some stage we'll be able to venture from the bridge and into the heart of the city. Either that or we build a raft which I daren't suggest to the Apes because they would destroy the equivalent of the Brazilian rainforest looking for wood.

The ever-gentlemanly Apes allow me to push the trolley carrying Carrie's corpse while they throw anything they can find into the river for no reason at all. As I look down at Carrie, I think about the incredible odds of finding her again. Is it a sign, I think? Is this my cue to go and find everyone else? I've always had a plan of some description – never mind that most of them backfired – but what if I could find the Moth and GG as well? Even poor Lucas. What if we scoop them all into a metaphorical shopping trolley and then take them to Another-Billie so that she can bring them back to life? The thought gives me a new energy. I can make everything better, turn it back to how it was. I quicken my pace and start to believe that we will find Johnson slumped on a riverbank or gamely hanging on to a buoy. If we found Carrie, then we can find him. It's that sort of a world—

'Hey!' A voice breaks through my thoughts. 'Up here!' the voice shouts. It's a soaking-wet Johnson perched on the highest ledge of a ten-storey building. There are a series of puncture marks leading all the way up the face of the nineteenth-century building marking where he's used his talons to climb to safety, sinking them into the brick and mortar.

'I can see my house from here,' he grins.

OK, I think to myself, *just take some breaths and try and accept the implausible.* Or am I dreaming? Imagining him there because I'm so desperate to see him.

Non-Ape hurls a rock at Johnson. 'Johnson!'

Johnson moves like lightning to avoid the small rock and the Apes laugh.

'It's Johnson!' The Ape shoves me hard as Non-Ape picks up another rock.

'What are you doing?' I slap his big meaty paw.

'Throwing stuff,' he responds, looking hurt, as if everyone knows you throw stuff at your friends for no good reason.

'Rev!' Johnson flashes a metal-toothed grin, and starts climbing back down the building, utilising the same puncture marks in the old stone. Even though I know it's the real Johnson, it still feels like Other-Johnson is also somehow present, not in mind but definitely in body.

'You made it,' I manage to stammer.

'You too.' Johnson leaps the last five metres and lands with a light and beguiling grace in a deep puddle as more of the Thames seeps back to its banks. His movements, always

66

silky, have taken on a new dynamic, and his tight jeans, even wet and clinging to his long thin legs, don't hinder his snake-hipped progress.

The Ape immediately presses a finger straight into Johnson's forehead. 'Healed!'

'Healed!' Non-Ape backs the Ape up with a look of absolute conviction. He used to hate Johnson (well, Other-Johnson) until Billie told him to be nice to him and luckily Non-Ape doesn't seem to bear any malice, but maybe that's because he doesn't have the room for memories in his tiny brain.

Johnson looks at me, not understanding what's happening. The Ape isn't wounded and Carrie is slumped in a shopping trolley.

'The Ape was all cut up?' he questions.

'Nothing cuts Dazza,' the Ape boasts. 'Nothing.'

Johnson takes a moment to try and think of the hows and whys of what has happened, but he soon gives up and instead his eyes find the dead Carrie wedged into the shopping trolley. 'Been shopping?'

CRINGE

The fourth lesson of the day is history. Carrie sits at the back of the class, but I have been very wary of making myself known to her. Lucas, or at least this version of Lucas, is in the class as well, but again I have had to remind myself that these aren't people that know me.

Our Lucas killed himself in the empty world and out of all the shocking and unbelievable things that have happened this was possibly the most sombre and upsetting. Lucas was the boy with it all, a gorgeous, intelligent sporting god who was being monitored by Premier League football teams. But I guess having it all means you also have much more than the average person to lose. So, when he thought he'd been flung into a world that was absolutely devoid of family, friends and relatives, Lucas couldn't take it. But seeing a version of him is pretty unsettling. There's an instant reaction of relief and happiness and then a millisecond later I'm reminded of what happened to my versions of him. And then I remember all of the others that I lost and have to bite down on my index finger to stop the tears flooding from me.

Our teacher is called Mr Connors, and most girls swoon over him. He's got a square jaw and sparkling mischievous eyes. He's tall, broad-shouldered and used to play rugby before an injury curtailed his career. His blond hair is thick and wavy and sometimes falls over his eyes so he has to keep sweeping it back. He was the same in my world and I never liked him. I knew he was aware that most of the girls at school had a crush on him and he played on that. The sweeping of the hair, the not-so-subtle attentiveness to any pretty girl over the age of sixteen, the offer of private tuition. He may not have acted on any of it, but he sure did enjoy being the object of so many misguided affections.

This Mr Connors sits behind his desk and stares out of the window, watching the world outside. All he can really see is the sports field and then a row of trees that hide the steep path that leads down into town. He sits staring all through the lesson. He doesn't say one word to any of us.

More remarkably the students don't say anything either. Some sit hunched forward with their faces on their desks, others stretch back, fingers laced behind their necks, and the rest just doodle on their jotters. Carrie is writing in hers and I wonder if this version of her also writes the same dreary, clichéd poetry. Lucas looks more lively than everyone else; he shifts in his seat a lot and tries to get Carrie's attention. He whispers to her but in this silent classroom he might as well be talking to her through a megaphone.

'What you writing?'

'Poems,' she whispers back confirming my wonderings.

It's enough for Mr Connors to drag himself away from staring of out the window. I can't be certain, but he looks on the verge of tears.

'Shhh,' he says.

Lucas falls silent. In my world he was a model student, a perfect specimen with a perfect life. In this world he could be the same, but the fact that he was talking hints at something else.

I'm sitting right at the front, the new girl in the worst seat in the classroom. I turn my head and study Carrie and Lucas for a moment.

'Want to read one?' she asks Lucas.

Lucas knows that Mr Connors is staring at him with his red-rimmed eyes.

'Better not,' Lucas eventually tells Carrie. Maybe he's not so different from the original after all.

Hurt by this rejection, Carrie scowls. So this version has at least got some of the well-documented mean Carrie spirit in her.

I return my attention to Mr Connors, but he is already staring back out of the window, gazing into who knows what.

I dare to raise my hand, which he doesn't see.

I clear my throat and feel tension rise around me. Kids look up from their desks; they unlace their fingers from behind their necks, some lean forward. Everyone seems on edge.

'Sir,' I say.

The swell of guardedness from the rest of the class is so palpable it feels as if it could knock me over.

Mr Connors may want to ignore me, but I'm not going to give up that easily. I clear my throat again and he is forced to turn and look at me.

'What?' he asks.

'Are you going to teach us anything?' I say. Which I think is a reasonable question to ask of a teacher.

Apparently not though as the tension in the classroom grows, so much so that it feels like it's pushing at the windows and the door. No one is enjoying this.

Mr Connors takes an age to respond.

I get into a non-conversation that the Apes would enjoy.

'Sir?' I repeat. 'Sir?'

The anxiety in the room is nearly unbearable, but I persist. I don't know what's wrong with the people in this school. They are disinterested to a level I've never encountered before. And that includes the staff. No one seems to want to say or do anything. Can't they see something is seriously off? Someone needs to question it and after all I've been through I'm not about to let it go.

'Sir?'

He stares right through me.

I turn to try and see if any of the class will back me up and I realise they're all looking at me, but not in an impressed way for winding up a teacher, more of a why-don't-you-shut-your-mouth way.

I look back towards the front of the room and a paper plane zips past my nose, landing under Mr Connors' desk. He doesn't give it so much as a glance.

'Sir, shouldn't you be teaching us something?' I press.

Another paper aeroplane swoops past me. I ignore it.

I can hear pages being torn from jotters and notebooks. A paper aeroplane hits the back of my head.

I continue. 'That's why we're here right?'

More paper aeroplanes are aimed my way. They're hastily made and not very aerodynamic so most miss me, veering off at impossible angles. But one hits the back of my neck. It stings. I grab it after it lands on the floor and hurl it back as hard as I can.

I should've known what would happen when I did that.

The paper plane arrows straight for Carrie and hits her in the eye.

'Agh!' she squeals and immediately clutches her eye. 'You cow!'

Lucas tenses; he doesn't like what I've just done to his friend, never mind that I'm being attacked from all angles. Now everyone else has started ripping out pages from their school jotters. They've gone from docile, sloth-like creatures to animated and angry in half a heartbeat.

'I'm blind! I'm blind!' Carrie howls, one hand plastered to her wounded eye while her good eye lasers me with unbridled hatred.

I'm expecting Mr Connors to rise from his slough of disinterest but he doesn't say a word.

Then the rest of the class take the opportunity to start a fully-fledged attack. Not only have I been goading our teacher, but now I've injured Carrie and that apparently is too much.

More paper planes are launched my way, white pieces of paper filling the classroom, quickly. Notebooks are torn apart as paper plane after paper plane is hastily constructed and flung through the air.

Mr Connors watches them piling up on the floor and desks.

'Sir.' Never mind the aeroplanes, I want an answer, a reply, a riposte, anything. I want him to speak, to at least tell me something.

Paper planes zip over and around me. It's like the Battle

of Britain in the classroom. Some hit my skin with their pointy noses so I shield my head and face and try to crouch lower in my seat. Carrie is still wailing about being blind and Lucas is consoling her.

Everywhere I turn there are a stack of paper planes, and it reminds me of the snowstorm I nearly died in. I'm getting sick of everything and everyone attacking me.

I look back at the rest of the class and all of them are staring at me. There's a silent aggression there and most of it is emanating from Carrie who raises her index finger at me.

I guess she isn't blind after all.

I look away and am about to sweep some crashed paper planes from my desk when I see that one of them has writing on its wing.

I pick up the plane and read words that are designed to mock me: **You'll learn**

Which is hysterical considering I haven't learned one single thing today.

The plane with the writing is immaculately made and perfectly aerodynamic which leads me to guess it must be a message from Lucas. Everything he does is perfect and brilliant. If he threw a paper aeroplane, then it would land exactly where he wanted it to.

It's not like the Lucas I know to use irony and I wonder if there's more to the message than I realise.

You'll learn

THE POWER OF SUGGESTION

'I really thought Billie had cut him open,' Johnson tells me. 'Bought it hook, line and sinker.'

We are heading as quickly as we can towards what's left of a hotel that Non-Ape punched to death while he was busy trying to avenge the tragic death of his version of Carrie.

'You were meant to,' I say. 'But what's worse is that we all thought she could do that. We all thought Billie could be that evil. Which says more about us, I think.'

'She did just try and drown us,' he reminds me.

While we've been walking, Johnson and I have decided on a definite plan of action. We're going to find and collect everyone we can, alive or dead, scoop them up and somehow find Another-Billie and hope she can heal all of them. She's back in our hometown some thirty or so miles north of London, making sure my dad is safe. He's the key to our escape and with Billie distracted thinking she's won Johnson, it's time to get out of this increasingly disastrous world. So we round everyone up, make them all better and then my dad sends us all home.

'What about Lucas?' Johnson asks,

'We'll get everyone,' I assure him. 'We are not leaving without them. Another-Billie can heal them all.' I hope that's true but have no real way of knowing.

'And Billie?'

I haven't got an answer to that. I never imagined leaving Billie here, but it feels like she's made her choice.

The Thames is still settling down, more or less moving through the city on its own terms, rather than being bullied by a giant tidal wave.

'How am I going to explain these when I get back?' Johnson says revealing the talons in his fingertips.

'That's all part of the plan. It's not just us that we need to rescue, it's the others as well.'

'The bad versions of us?' Johnson asks.

'I made a promise to Rev Two's mum. I swore I'd send her daughter back home. And if I can work out how to do that then I'm going to trade it for finding our friends and theirs and then getting Another-Billie to heal them as well.'

'That'll go well. I mean, we all get along so amazingly,' he adds wryly. 'But getting everyone home?' Johnson adds. 'You need proof you can do that before you open negotiations.'

'Which is why we're going back to the hotel. My dad's papers are buried there somewhere. All we need to do is find them, take them to my dad and he'll make everything be as it should be.' That was really the Moth's plan, but I'm picking up the baton and running with it now.

Johnson falls silent; he knows that's a long shot at best. The plans are buried under tons of rubble.

'Wait a sec, their Moth is—' he starts.

'Don't say it,' I quickly cut in, remembering that their Moth got run over by a train and his head sort of got separated from the rest of him. It was my fault and I'm still trying to come to terms with it. 'Every plan has a weak spot,' I tell Johnson.

'But the idea is sound,' he reassures me. 'We help them, they help us. Perfect.'

I know he doesn't believe it will be anything like perfect.

'If we can just find everyone, good and evil, or at least as many as we can, then we've got a chance. I know where their Lucas is, in a motorway tunnel, so surely he'll be grateful when we make him live again.'

'Yeah. Deliriously happy.' Johnson decides against saying more in case the plan falls down around our ears, and we walk in silence for a moment.

'Rev,' Johnson starts again after a long pause. 'I'm just going to put something else out there.'

'I was lying,' I quickly tell him. I know what he's thinking, that I was prepared to let him go with Billie. 'You know that, right?'

'Course.' He nods. 'I wanted you to save the Ape.'

'I wanted to save you both,' I tell Johnson. 'I just didn't know how to.'

'Main thing is, it all worked out,' smiles Johnson. He doesn't bother to mention Other-Johnson, but I can't forget what he did. And even if I could, Johnson's metal-toothed smile is a reminder of their switched minds and bodies. I make a mental note: Johnson's teeth will have to be painted white when we do get back.

Another building gets headbutted by Non-Ape.

The Ape immediately touches his forehead.

'Healed!'

'Sealed!'

I wonder what Non-Ape will do without the Ape and vice versa. He's bound to get very distressed when he realises they can't be together and when he loses it he is unstoppable. It'll take what's left of his doppelganger friends to try and make him see sense. Assuming that after we've brought them back from the dead and reunited them that they don't then turn on us and try and wipe us out all over again.

Evil-Carrie is beyond reanimation, flattened by a motorised wheelchair into a puddle of nothing. I think we could find Moth Two, but I can't see how offering his headless corpse for reanimation to Another-Billie will cement our fragile alliance.

'We're going to need a bigger shopper trolley,' I tell Johnson as we wheel Carrie's broken body along. 'By the time we've finished we're not only going to have Carrie, we're also going to have an Evil-GG, the real GG and two Lucases to wheel back to town.'

The front of a London bus caves in under Non-Ape's headbutt. A moment later the Ape touches his forehead.

'Healed!'

'Sealed!'

'Cut that out!' I yell. It comes as much of a surprise to me as it does to Johnson and the Apes. 'Can we just do what we've got to do, and then get out of London?' The last few days have taken their toll and I'm unravelling. Our plan is desperate and mad and stupid, but without it we have nothing. So I'll take the mad and the desperate.

If the Moth is right about how time behaves differently in every conceivable alternate earth, then it may just be that we all arrive back in the classroom without anyone ever knowing. So it's possible we can Narnia it. That's what we'll do. We'll wardrobe it.

'I'm going to quit school,' he jokes. 'Never going back to detention ever again.'

'What, you didn't like the bright light that swept us away?'

'Not as much as you'd imagine.' He rises to my heavy irony. 'Though I did get to spend time with you.' His black eyes glint and for a moment I wonder . . .

Did Other-Johnson really swap? Or is this another of his daring deceits? My eyes narrow as I take Johnson in.

'What?' he asks.

'Just looking,' I tell him. But then transmit a thought. *'If you're playing games again I will never forgive you. Not in any world or dimension.'*

Johnson stares back at me and there isn't the slightest sign that he heard my telepathic challenge.

I try sending another thought. *'I mean it. If you didn't swap then I'll . . . I'll kill you.'*

His eyes don't flicker, but he does frown. 'Why are you staring at me like that?' he asks.

I let the thought go. This has to be the real Johnson. It just has to be.

'After this ends I might join a nunnery,' I tell him. 'Just do good things that no one can punish me for.'

'A nunnery? You can't do that, Rev.' His black eyes find mine and bore deep.

'No? I'm not sure that's up to you,' I play along.

'Well, I'd only come along and break you out of there. I'd blow a hole in the wall and drive through it on my motor

78

bike.' Other-Johnson rescued me on his Harley and, I have to admit, I still swoon a little at the thought of that. He dragged me from a snowstorm and pulled me into the dying heat of summer. From freezing to boiling in two seconds flat. In more ways than one.

'Then what?' I ask.

Johnson squeezes my hand. 'I'd tell you to climb aboard.'

'Even while I was wearing a habit?'

His hand tightens around mine, he's forgotten that he's much stronger again.

'I'd break that habit,' he tells me with a wink.

'That's possibly the worst joke ever,' I say to him, quickening our pace, as the destruction and chaos loom angrily around us.

We really have made a mess of this city.

I'm five minutes into the last lesson before lunch. Music. The teacher is called Mrs Crow and she is a large, wide woman with huge thick glasses that magnify her eyes.

At home, everyone does impressions of Mrs Crow's shrill, shrieking voice. But not, it seems, people in this classroom. Where again they sit in silence, watching as Mrs Crow plays a piece by Beethoven. Well, she attempts to play, but actually she chops down on the piano keys with no rhythm or grace. The wrong notes jar and clang and set my teeth on edge, but on she plays, trapped in a world of her own.

This world's version of GG is in this class too, sitting in the same row as Billie. I beamed at both of them as soon as I saw them, an instinctive reaction, but when they looked back with a total lack of recognition I quickly sat in the only empty seat. Again at the front of the classroom. And the clanging music is especially loud because I am only a few metres away from the piano.

On she plays, murdering Beethoven with her stubby little fingers, and pretty quickly I come to realise that this is it, this is the lesson, listening to a woman who has her big magnified eyes clamped tightly shut as she loses herself to the rickety rhapsody she is creating.

I glance back at Billie and GG, but like the rest of the class they have come prepared and have slipped earphones into their ears.

This is like no school I've ever known. No one teaches anything and the pupils barely say a word. They just sit waiting for the day to end.

GG is now gyrating to whatever music he is listening to, probably something from a musical, an uptempo, sing-a-long sort of a beat. Billie's earphones are plugged into her phone and she is clearly texting someone. The texts she receives in return make her smile, but in one of those mischievous ways that means whoever is texting is writing naughty things. Her lithe and long fingers dance over her phone keyboard.

My parents told me to go and make some friends so while Mrs Crow has her eyes tightly shut I get out of my chair and head to the back of the classroom. I watch people fidget uneasily as I pass them and I can feel their worry accompanying me all the way to Billie's desk. She hasn't noticed because whoever is texting her is making her snigger. It's only when my shadow falls over her that she looks up.

This Billie is identical to the best friend I'll never, ever see again. But she is surlier and less forthcoming. She clearly doesn't like that I've come over to her.

'I'm Rev,' I tell her. The hideous clunk of Beethoven coupled with New-Billie wearing earphones mean she can't make out a word I'm saying. I try again, louder. 'I'm Rev.'

New-Billie's eyes meet mine and I feel GG stop gyrating

in his seat next to her. I glance his way and offer another smile. 'Reva Marsalis,' I tell him. 'Hi.'

My theory is that there has never been a Rev here – well, for at least twelve years. She never went to this school; she never met Billie or any of the others. She can't have done considering my dad – the liar – spent all that time looking for me. But I need to start making friends quickly and I gravitate naturally to the copies of the people I once knew.

New-GG slips his pink headphones from his tiny but perfect ears. His straight-up quiff bounces back to its full height and I still enjoy that any GG you care to mention would never ever wear a school uniform. He has on bright yellow jeans and a faux-fur-lined combat jacket that has the word **WAR(M)** *stitched on to the back of it. My GG wore the exact same jacket and, although it's a small insignificant thing, it could also be a way to build a bridge between me and them. If they are the same as my friends, then surely they'll like me in the same way. His fingernails are painted yellow and eyeshadow highlights his glittering eyes. Yes. He is definitely very similar.*

'I love that jacket,' I tell him, thinking I can appeal to his vanity. 'It's so you.'

New GG takes a moment to digest this then bats the thought away. 'You don't know what's so me, sweetie. You have no idea in that pink fuzzy brain of yours. So back to your seat,' he purrs.

'I'm Rev,' I try again.

'Get lost.' New-Billie's words hit like a punch.

'Wait—'

'No standing room here, just sitting.' New-GG points a long one inch painted nail towards my desk. Mrs Crow

82

continues to blindly plunge her stubby fingers into the black and white keys.

'You don't understand,' I tell Billie. 'I need to talk to you.'

'Sit down,' a boy hisses behind me.

'Yeah, sit down.' A girl's voice echoes the boy's, the same tautness in her tone.

'Read my lips. Get. Lost.' New-Billie eyes me boldly.

'Fly away.' New-GG flutters his fingers at me. 'Fly, fly, fly.'

'Please, give me one minute to explain,' I tell them. 'Talk to me, Billie.' I'm almost begging her when I feel a hand grip my wrist and suddenly I'm being tugged away. The hand is strong and when I turn I realise it's Ella, a tall thug of a girl who bullied me in my previous world.

'Sit!' Ella urges. I allow myself to be bundled back into my seat as she lowers her face towards mine and breathes smoke-stained breath all over me. 'It is what it is,' she hisses before sitting back down at her desk where she grabs her huge earphones and slips them back on her head.

Mrs Crow hasn't noticed a thing and continues to destroy Beethoven until the bell rings.

I've spent two weeks in this world. The first thirteen of those days I stayed at home as New-Mum and Dad's excitement spilled uncontrollably out of them. I was in shock, mourning the loss of my friends, barely able to put one coherent thought together. I cried most nights into my pillow and, as clichés go, it's pretty much spot on. I buried my face in the pillow because I didn't want my dad and New-Mum to hear me. I cried for all of them, all of the people who never made it. I cried for the doppelgangers. I cried for Rev Two's mum because I broke my promise to her and I can picture her sitting alone in her flat as the loneliness and the longing erode her life. She'll be the most hated person in that doppelganger town because of how she stopped them from killing me, GG and the Ape. No one will talk to her again, and she'll spend her days more alone than ever. The only positive thought I consistently hold on to is that maybe time won't have moved on from the moment we fled the violent doppelganger world. That Rev Two's mum will be frozen in the moment along with the rest of the town. But the truth is, I have no earthly idea.

I cried like a baby while Dad and New-Mum laughed their way through the days. Loss is the worst of the worst. But certainty of loss follows it a close second. I know I'll never see any of my friends again.

The Ape, Johnson and the Moth.

Their names and faces swirl in my head alongside Billie's and GG's. Lucas and Carrie are right beside them, beaming into my thoughts.

Friends.

Lost forever.

And, just to rub salt as deep as it can go into a wound, here I am in a school with people who look exactly like the ones I've lost. It's like leafing through a photograph album after a mass funeral. It makes me want to cry all over again.

But I'm not about to give up. I glance back at New-Billie and seeing her with her phone out gives me an idea. I know my Billie's mobile phone number off by heart so I whip out the phone the liar and New-Mum gave me and dial.

It takes a few seconds but New-Billie sits bolt upright when she sees that her phone is ringing. She answers it tentatively, clearly not recognising the number.

'Yes?'

'It's me,' I whisper.

'Who's me?'

'Your best friend,' I tell her. 'Can we meet?'

Billie hesitates. 'I don't know who you are,' she says eventually. 'And don't say stupid things like that.'

'Trust me,' I say. 'You and me are OK individually. But together we are so much stronger.'

'How did you get this number?' she asks. Then hangs up.

But I don't mind. I've made a connection. I'm in her world whether she likes it or not.

I'M AN EXCELLENT DRIVER

Non-Ape had made short work of clearing the rest of the hotel away, tossing it all into the swirling Thames.

He only stopped once to shove handfuls of food that Johnson and I salvaged from a rather damp Fortnum and Mason's. It's hopefully the last time we're going to be in this particular version of earth and I felt we deserved only the finest food and drink it could offer.

We are now standing in a semi-circle, looking at Evil-GG's body lying semi-squished at the bottom of it all. He's been fortunate that he has a super-rubbery and strong physique, and that some of the rubble fell in the right way, creating a mini shelter over his torso. His legs are broken and flattened, but that's not the end of the world. The Moth could tell him as much.

Johnson pulls smaller chunks of rubble from Evil-GG, revealing the lifeless teenage boy – whose body now plays host to the dead Carrie.

'We've got him,' Johnson declares. 'Or is it her? It's Carrie, but she's in this GG's body. Right?' He looks momentarily confused.

I know how he feels and hand him a list I'd written while waiting for Non-Ape to toss the remains of an entire hotel into the swirling Thames. 'Here,' I say. 'This will help.'

1. Evil-GG killed our Carrie. Other-Johnson then swapped them into each other's bodies.
2. Evil-Carrie got flattened by yours truly and is beyond saving. (Sorry Evil-Carrie, but I wouldn't know where to begin when it comes to rescuing you.)
3. Moth Two is on a train track somewhere, minus his head. Again I'd imagine there's not much chance of healing him.
4. Non-Lucas is lying dead in a tunnel on the motorway that leads to my home town. Other-Johnson killed him to save my life.
5. The Moth – our Moth – was kidnapped by Black Moths created by our Billie. We have no idea where he is. Or where she is. Or even where Other-Johnson is.
6. Our brilliant, darling GG fell off the side of a train and hasn't been heard of since.
7. Rev Two, my doppelganger who loathes me, is back in our hometown with Another-Billie while she tries to heal my dad. After he burned to death. Rev Two must not, at any cost, find out that it's my dad not hers. She will get very angry if she does.
8. I will draw pictures to accompany this list.

Johnson nods. 'Clear as mud.' He folds the list and slips it into his back jeans pocket. 'Can you lift that wall?' he asks Non-Ape.

Non-Ape lifts the wall and Johnson drags Evil-GG's mangled legs free. Non-Ape then hurls the side of wall into the Thames where it lands with a resounding splash.

As Johnson pulls Evil-GG from the rubble, some papers are revealed underneath him. I can't believe my eyes. Out of all the collapsed hotels in all the worlds this has to be the most astonishing stroke of luck. These papers, these beautiful, dust-coated and *intact* papers, are my dad's notes on interdimensional travel. The Moth had argued what seemed like ages ago that they would be salvageable from the wrecked hotel. That was the reason we were on the train that was attacked by the swarm of Black Moths. We were coming to London for the papers and – miracle of miracles – we've actually managed to achieve something positive. It's only taken countless battles and deaths and mayhem, but finally – and this feels so good – we have got something positive to hang on to.

Evil-GG's battered, wiry body is broken and shattered in all kinds of ways. But it doesn't stop Non-Ape slinging it into the trolley where it lands on top of Carrie's lifeless body.

'Does he understand that they're real people?' Johnson asks me.

'I don't know if he understands anything,' I reply as Non-Ape steps back and cracks his great neck after the enormous effort he has put in. He's already eaten over half of what we found and still claims to be hungry.

Evil-GG is covered in dust and has a white face and what looks like grey hair. For a second I can see how GG might look if he ever reached old age. But I have to check myself;

my GG might not get to age another second if we don't put the next part of the plan into action and start looking for everyone.

'We need transport,' I tell the Ape.

'What for?' he asks.

'To get us to town. Back home.'

'Not going home,' he says, taking another great chunk out of a roll of expensive salami.

'No home. No way.' Non-Ape joins him.

Johnson watches on carefully, wary in case I upset them. 'But we want to,' he says. 'Me and Rev. You've got to help us do that right?'

'I'm on it.' The Ape turns and heads away. Just like that, not another word from him.

'Maybe a bus,' I call after him. Because we'll need a bus to transport Non-Ape. 'He's way too big for a car.'

When I said he was way too big for a car, I meant it. I meant every single word of it.

But the Ape wasn't listening. He found the first automatic vehicle he came across and screeched up to us a few minutes later. I think it's a Ferrari, but this one's yellow rather than red.

And boy, how we argued.

'That is useless,' I told him.

'It can do two-hundred miles an hour.'

'It's useless.'

'It's fast.'

'It's useless.'

'There aren't any other cars,' the Ape lied. There are cars parked everywhere.

'It's useless.' I was on Ape-style repeat and I was going to be on repeat until he gave in and did what I told him.

'Only one I could find.' He really wanted to drive the Ferrari. It was in his eyes; his face, he reeked of the need for speed.

'It's London.' My eyes narrowed with all the quiet ferocity I could summon.

'It's only got one car in it.'

'Get a bus.'

'Buses are slow. You said we're in a hurry.' He ran his hand along the sleek wing of the gorgeous Ferrari. Like it was a thoroughbred horse.

'What about GG?' he suddenly asked. 'When are we going to find him?'

The question blew me away for several long moments. Johnson saw it knock the wind from my sails, but I shook my head at him as he made to intervene.

'We don't know where he is,' I told the Ape quietly.

'He's on the railway,' he replied.

'We looked for him, remember? He wasn't there.'

The Ape faltered, only marginally, but his shoulders definitely dropped as he stared at the ground.

'We're trying to prioritise,' I told him gently.

'Pri-what?' he asked.

'Make a list of things to do first.'

The Ape weighed up my words, taking an age to process them before bearing his tombstone slabs of teeth in a big grin. 'We'd better be quick then.'

'Exactly.'

'Lucky I found a Ferrari.'

'It's not big enough. Find another vehicle.' And that was that, argument over.

Mainly because I'd already lost it.

So now I'm wedged in the passenger seat, sitting on Johnson's lap, while the Ape roars through London.

Sitting on the roof of the Ferrari is Non-Ape. His great thick fingers are curled round the top of the open window as he grips tightly. He keeps yahooing like a cowboy every time the Ape takes a bend at speed. Wedged in his lap are Carrie and Evil-GG. The roof bowed the minute Non-Ape climbed on top of it, but so far it's holding.

The Ape claims that the Ferrari is almost automatic and all you have to do is keep your foot on the accelerator while you flick at two paddles that are attached either side of the steering wheel. He spends so much time tapping the paddles that he forgets to steer and when a huge stationary dustbin lorry looms worryingly close I yank the steering wheel.

The car turns so quickly and savagely that Carrie's body flies from the car roof and crashes straight through a newsagent's window.

'Ape!' Johnson shouts.

The Ape slams on the brakes and I pitch forward, heading straight for the windscreen until I throw a hand out and manage to stop my momentum. Johnson crashes forward with me though and my hand goes straight through the glass.

I don't cut an artery, but I do scrape half the skin off my wrist.

The Ape's chest bumps hard against the steering wheel and his eyes water. I'm pretty sure he's still carrying a broken rib from days ago, but he'll never admit to it.

'Lost the skinny.' Non-Ape bangs on the roof of the Ferrari and it bows under the blows. 'Lost the skinny,' he repeats as if we didn't know. So much for his mighty grip.

The Ape jams the Ferrari into reverse and speeds back towards the newsagent's where he again slams on the brakes.

'Can't you drive like a normal person?' I bark at him, my wrist stinging like crazy now that there's no skin there.

The Ape turns to me. 'We lost skinny.'

'I heard,' I snap. 'Because of your rubbish driving.'

'You grabbed the wheel.'

'I had to!'

The car creaks and rises when Non-Ape leaps off the roof. He barges into the newsagent's and a few seconds later he drags Carrie's body out by her ankle, not seeming to care when the back of her head thuds down from the pavement on to the road with a nasty crack.

Non-Ape climbs back on top of the Ferrari's roof and again the car sinks down. My bleeding wrist smarts, but I press it into the material of my dress, hoping it will soak up the blood and help it stop. I've become a master of improvisation.

'You OK?' Johnson asks.

'I've never ever been more OK.' My irony is so heavy it comes out like anger.

Practically since the white light, it seems Johnson has spent half his time patching my wounds. If he does quit school, he should maybe think about studying medicine.

'Can I get you something for that?' His voice is close to my ear and it sends a delicate shiver through me.

'Maybe later.' I reach down and pat the side of his thigh as his legs stretch under me.

I settle back in his lap and can feel his breath on my neck as he whispers, 'The doctor will see you now.' Which is just a little bit too knowing. Borderline smarmy even. And I worry that just like the last time he was in Other-Johnson's body he's going to start changing into a much more confident and dangerous version of himself.

I know the name of the road we need to find which will take us north, and while the Ape careers through the empty streets read a street map of London. But every time I try and see what road we're in he's already sped past the sign.

'Slow down,' I tell him.

'Who slows down when they're in a hurry?'

The Ape flicks at the paddles, but I don't know if he truly knows what they do. The Ferrari slows then lurches forward, slows again, misfires, then growls and accelerates, over and over. The roar from the engine that feels like it's sitting right behind my ears is deafening.

'North,' I tell him. 'We want the A1.'

'I'm on it,' he says taking a bend at an outrageous speed but as he does I see a sign.

'Left,' I tell him. 'Go left.'

'Left?' he asks.

'Not right,' I tell him.

'It's one-way,' he points to another road sign up ahead forbidding all traffic to turn left.

'Then we'd better do as we're told,' I say, knowing he won't be able to resist.

He revs the engine. And screeches left. Sounding the horn loudly at the nearest traffic camera as we do.

'Photo bomb!' He yells at it.

In a car this fast on roads without traffic I think we can easily reach my dad in just over half an hour.

'Rev.' My dad's face appears in the wing mirror. I immediately sit bolt upright. The last thing I'd been expecting was to see him. He has done this before, contacting me in a way that comes right out of the blue and is downright spooky. I dig my fingers into Johnson's thighs and he gives a low yelp.

'Rev?' he asks.

I can't answer because I'm staring too hard at my dad's face in the wing mirror. Whenever he appears, I still don't know if it's a dream or a hallucination or some weird power he possesses. If it is a weird power, then he can't be my real dad, because I'm perfectly normal and human to a near mind-numbingly degree. Unless he picked up this trick from the worlds he's been visiting? Or it's a side effect of the dimension crossing? If he can find me from another world, then I imagine he can find me in a mirror.

'Hurry,' he says simply. 'The other Rev knows I'm not her dad.'

I stare at my dad's reflection and I can tell that he is also scared.

'I'm coming,' I tell him.

'What?' Johnson asks.

'Hide,' I tell my dad.

'Who are you talking to?' Johnson asks.

But my dad's eyes are locked on to mine and I can't think of anything but him. 'Run and hide,' I urge him. 'Whatever you do, don't let her find you.'

THIS WAS AN EXIT

It's lunchtime and I've gone to the Tesco that sits on the edge of town.

After enduring a morning of mind-numbing non-lessons, I snuck out of a side entrance of school and took the steep grassy hill into town. A few kids saw me, but they reacted with the same dull indifference as everyone else I have met in this weird alternate world. But then of course I had to go and see Kyle, an ex-boyfriend in my home world. A small large-nosed boy whom I didn't think I was good enough for. But seeing him sitting on a bench, quietly staring into space, I see him for what he really is. Just a boy who liked me and then asked me out. Which is more than Johnson ever managed. I almost go over to this Kyle, but that was an old Rev and I think I've well and truly moved on.

I spotted GG again after our music class, but never got close enough to try and speak to him. I also saw Billie sitting at the back of another class and Carrie was staring at her reflection in the mirror of the loos when I walked in there. She was checking the eye that I had apparently blinded with the paper aeroplane during the morning history class.

'Sorry about that,' I told her.

'I'm blind because of you,' she growled.

'But you're not because you're staring at your reflection.'

'I feel blind,' she spat again. 'That's the difference. I feel like I can't see.'

Despite her obvious hostility, I took a chance and tried to make a connection with her. I took out the paper aeroplane with the words **YOU'LL LEARN** *written on it and showed it to her.*

'Why would someone write that?' I asked her.

Carrie barely gave it a glance. 'Why wouldn't they?'

Which was no answer at all. 'This school,' I pressed. 'It's odd.'

Big understatement. In truth, if I hadn't been to weird and wonderful worlds prior to this, I would have been running screaming for the hills. But I'm more in control now and ready to face whatever comes my way. Oh yeah, Reva Marsalis is a whole other type of animal these days.

'I wouldn't know,' Carrie dabbed her eye with a wet tissue.

'A school where no one teaches anything?'

'You're new.' She scowled. 'What is it? You been home-schooled and your parents get sick of seeing you every day?'

'No . . .'

'I'll take that as a yes.'

'I've just got here,' I told her.

New-Carrie laughed at this. Snorted so hard she needed to wipe her nose afterwards. 'You should've stayed at home, you're weird.'

'I mean it. I am new. Not just to this school, but to this world as well.'

And with that she grabbed her bag and left.

That conversation was the main reason that made me sneak out of school. Thirteen and a half days of this world was more than enough for me. I snuck down the corridors, mainly moving in the opposite direction to everyone else, until I found a fire exit. The sign on the door said **Only To Be Used In An Emergency** *so I burst through it without a moment's hesitation. This definitely constituted an emergency.*

The morning has lasted for what feels like an eternity. The only real distraction, reaching out to Billie. So far there hasn't been any sign of an Ape but I can feel his presence. We're bonded now, and even if it isn't the real him I'm pretty sure our molecules can sense each other. Not seeing him is almost a relief though. I don't think I can face meeting this version of the Ape because thinking about him makes my stomach churn. He's gone. My Ape is no more.

It takes me eight and a half minutes to reach the automatic doors of Tesco.

The last time I was in the equivalent shop it was empty and there was a near dead burned man slithering along the floor. The man turned out to be my dad.

But at this moment I'm interested in where he dragged himself from. Specifically the overheated lorry he emerged from. Even though my dad claims that the world he came from was burning to death, I want to find out for myself. The lorry had to be some kind of portal to the empty world so logic dictates that there could be another portal in this world. I'm counting on my theory that all of the earths keep copying each other, like a stone thrown into a pond, and the resultant *ripple effect flows throughout the multiverse. If there's one portal in the cabin of a lorry parked behind a supermarket, then there's going to be at least a few more of them.*

Of course I won't know where this portal will lead, and am praying it doesn't take me to a world that's completely on fire. I may even end up trapped like my dad was, doomed to roam through the universes but even that seems like a better proposition than anything this apathetically dead world has to offer.

In the empty world I went to investigate the lorry and after climbing into the cabin I was almost burned to death. I thought I could hear voices calling to me, but now I wonder if they were the screams of people who were dying in a world that had been set on fire. If there is a portal here, the danger is that it'll lead to the charred and burned world and then I'm going to feel just a mite stupid. But I need to know there's a way out. And if this doesn't work I'll think of something else.

In my real world we're supposed to stay within the confines of the school grounds during the day. It's to do with stranger danger and all the panic and fear that goes with the thought that if a sixteen-year-old is out on their own then they'll immediately fall prey to a sadist or a killer. It's also to do with the school not getting a bad reputation if, say, one of their pupils does something horrendous while wearing their hallowed uniform. Well, I'm wearing my brand-new shiny blazer and I'll happily take any punishment, but mainly because I don't intend to be here to receive it. Besides, everyone here is so disconnected that I don't suppose they'll notice me anyway.

I pass the exact same rows and shelves of produce that

exist in my hometown. The only good thing about this parallel world is that the people in it seem normal, no superpowers, no unhealthy violent streak. And definitely no talons. But none of them seem interested in anything. They plod through their lives with no real aim or thought. It's unsettling, but I can't afford to stop and dwell on it. These people are not my problem, escaping from them is.

Their disinterest means that no one is questioning me or looking at me in a strange way. I start to relax. I'm not on the run and that comes as a relief. I've been chased more than enough times lately.

I reach the bottom of the supermarket and seek out the long plastic flaps that frame a doorway that leads to the storage area. The fish counter is next to the doorway and I walk up to the man behind it. He wears a white hat and a white lab coat and has sheer pale blue latex gloves on his hands.

'Excuse me,' I say.

'Yeah?' He's monosyllabic but seems pleasant enough.

'I need to get out the back,' I tell him.

His eyes fall on my blazer. 'You're meant to be at school.'

'Running an errand,' I tell him.

'Won't your school be looking for you?' he asks with little interest.

'They sent me,' I lie. I pretend to reach into my inner jacket pocket. 'I've got a note from them. Permission.' My hand lingers under my jacket. All I've got is a paper aeroplane with the words **YOU'LL LEARN** *written across its wings.*

The fishmonger remains in neutral, not giving anything away of an emotional nature. So much so that I wonder if he has any emotions. He's more robotic than anything.

I pull out the paper aeroplane, well enough of it to make it look like I could really have a get-out-of-school note. 'It's my dad,' I say.

'Your dad,' he repeats.

'He's working today, driving a delivery lorry, and he forgot his phone.' I slip the paper aeroplane away and quickly hold up the smart phone New-Mum gave to me. 'My mum's housebound and hates that she can't call him.'

Lying so easily is obviously a family trait.

'He travels long distance, but I know he should be out back around now,' I offer, embellishing the lie as much as I can.

The fishmonger takes me in for a long moment. 'Why would you say something like that?' he asks suddenly.

'I don't understand.' I blink.

'You sick in the head?'

'No,' I tell him.

'You must be broken then,' he says, his eyes looking at me with pity.

'Broken?' I ask.

The fishmonger's eyes echo the eyes of the dead fish lying packed in ice all along his counter. There's something missing from them, even if he has become intrigued by me.

'Everyone breaks. That's what they say. We'll all break one day.'

I plough on. 'I just want to, uh – to hand the phone to my – my dad.'

'Stop. There is no long distance,' he tells me.

'Sorry?'

The fishmonger gazes hard at me. 'Distance isn't long,' he says then turns to a customer, a stick-thin seventy-something with curly brown hair. She has the look of an ancient groupie who can still rock with the best of them. But the look is all she possesses, inside is a husk at best as she points with a leaden finger at some fresh salmon.

'She's broken,' the fishmonger says to her. His voice has gone up an octave. He's either excited or frightened, I can't tell which.

The elderly groupie immediately glances at me and tears fill her eyes. 'You need to hang in there,' she tells me. The tears are real.

'I don't, uh . . . I don't know what you mean.'

'Says her dad drives long distance,' the fishmonger adds.

The elderly groupie wipes her eyes. 'That's crazy talk.'

'It is?'

She starts pointing hard at me, jabbing the air between us. 'Get a grip, girl, before you do something stupid.'

'We've all seen it happen,' the fishmonger says.

'I'm fine,' I tell them both. 'I'm perfectly fine.'

'You wish, you poor thing,' the elderly groupie tells me as I back away and I can feel the eyes of customers turning on me.

Faces turn hostile in a heartbeat.

'Don't let her put ideas in your heads!' the elderly groupie calls to them.

The other customers stare hard at me. Unforgiving and irate. The atmosphere is strangely similar to the classroom where I was pelted with paper aeroplanes. What is it with this world?

I turn and quickly push through the plastic drapes and head into the storage area. There are a few members of staff working there, opening boxes and crates of fresh produce to stock the shelves with. None of them talk much and all of them seem quiet and subdued. Some look my way, but no *one comments. It's like they just can't be bothered. Which works for me because I obviously don't know how to say the right thing. Best to stay quiet until I discover why I've upset these people so much.*

I move deeper into the storage area before finding the exit door that leads out into the grey September chill. It's been raining and I splash through several puddles as fast as I can – because I've already spotted the lorry. It's definitely the same one that my father crawled out of. The memory of following his burned skin trail last time springs into my mind, but I quickly shake away the grim image. The lorry is parked in the exact same spot as it was in the empty world.

My heart is beating hard by the time I reach the lorry. The tall, towering cabin can only be accessed with the aid of steps and a handle to hoist yourself up. It takes me less than a second to climb high enough to be able to open the shiny metallic black door. It's not locked which means the signs are becoming more and more hopeful. I should be wary of what lies inside, but I can't help myself and bundle in behind the wheel, and await the surge of heat that represents a gateway to a burning world.

Which doesn't come.

But that's good, I think, that means the world has stopped burning.

But what do I do now? How do I open this portal?

I sit there for a moment, not knowing what to do next. I was hoping that if there is a portal to another world then surely something will magically happen. The white light that seared through the classroom detention should be happening here as well.

Right about now . . .

But there's nothing.

I scan the dials, the read-outs, the speedometer, everything and anything along the dashboard. Perhaps there's a switch. Stupid as that sounds, I try flicking every switch and lever I can find. I even jar the gearstick back and forth.

Nothing.

'C'mon,' I urge to no one in particular. 'C'mon, c'mon.'

Why didn't I think this through? Just say my dad did create a super-equation so powerful that it opened a door to the omniverse then I need that same equation.

I check my phone. I've still got twenty minutes of lunch break left. Eight and a half of them I'll use to get back to the school. Assuming I do go back there.

'C'mon, portal, show thyself,' I say, channelling my inner Harry Potter. Maybe if I had a wand and garbled some pseudo Latin the portal would magically open up.

'I know you're here,' I tell the air in front of me. 'If it worked in one world it has to work in another.'

Of course it doesn't have to work at all; the Moth would be the first to tell me that the law of portals in lorries on one world doesn't equate to the law of portals in lorries on another. But I'm desperate. I want out of this weird world where people don't talk much and stare with empty, dead-fish eyes.

I check the time again. I've been in the cabin for five minutes and there's no heat, no voices and no interdimensional transportation.

I try the switches and levers again.

Same result.

Nothing.

I sit back, fighting the rising disappointment. If I could,

I'd drive the lorry away from here. That'd scare the hell out of my dad and New-Mum. Though I have no idea where I'd go. There's no long distance according to the weird fishmonger. Whatever that means.

'Hey!'

The voice breaks through my crushing disappointment. It's a voice I know only too well.

Johnson.

'Hey!' he calls again and I turn and look out of the driver's window. New-Johnson is snake-hipping his way towards the lorry. He's smoking a cigarette and his black desert boots glide through the small puddles as if he's walking on water.

I hadn't seen him at school, but then if he's anything like the real Johnson he'll have been cutting classes.

He climbs easily up the steps to the cabin and draws level with the driver's door, his face appearing next to mine. He blows smoke towards me and it bounces off the door window.

'Got a licence to drive that?' New-Johnson asks.

I wind the window down a little. His bright blue eyes take me in. But there's none of the familiar look of the original Johnson, or even Other-Johnson. The one that tears right through me.

Again he's identical in every way. Apart from the one thing that counts above and beyond everything else. He doesn't appear to like me very much.

'You new?'

That same question.

'So what if I am?'

'You can get out of the lorry for starters,' he orders.

'Who are you to tell me what to do?' I counter.

'Doesn't matter who, it just matters that you get out.'

There is nothing beaten down or cowering about this Johnson. Nothing seems to worry any Johnson in any world.

'Make me.'

'You want that?' he asks.

'You wouldn't be able to,' I assure him.

But he moves with grace and speed and, before I know it, the door is open and I'm being dragged out of the cabin. I fall and land hard, which is something I do a lot of these days, in a crumpled heap.

New-Johnson jumps down with little in the way of care or remorse. 'I'm saving you by the way,' *he tells me as he flicks the stub of his dying cigarette over my head.* 'You won't know it but I am.'

He wanders away without another word. My arm is sore and when I move it my elbow feels like it's on fire.

'Johnson,' *I call after him.*

He stops and looks back.

'It's me,' *I tell him.* 'Rev.' *It's a wail more than words and I can already feel how much this world is breaking me down. It's killing me, wearing away my spirit bit by bit.*

'You don't know me but you do,' *I tell him.*

He stays silent, brooding, staring at me.

'I need your help.' *I get to my feet, brush myself down. His cigarette ash speckles my blazer, but I will happily wear it like a badge.* 'You always help me,' *I tell him, my eyes meeting his.* 'Always.'

He touches his chin in thought. I dare to offer a hopeful smile.

'I don't care that you threw me out of that lorry,' *I tell him.* 'I'm not even going to ask why anyone would do that. But you know me, or at least you will know me, and when you do you'll be right there, at my side.'

'That right?' His eyes keep taking me in. The school blazer does nothing for me, but he's looking closer now, peeling it back and working his way into me.

'I guarantee it,' I say.

A new look flashes across his face and his eyes seem even bluer.

'Name?' he asks.

'Already told you,' I hold his look.

The slightest of smiles curls the corners of his mouth. 'Yeah. You did, didn't you?'

This is better, *I think*, this is headway. *I'm reaching out and finally someone is there. And it had to be a Johnson because we echo through time and space and there's nothing anyone or anything can do to stop it.*

'Can we meet?' I ask him.

'Meet?'

'Meet up. You and me. After school.'

New-Johnson considers this for a long moment and I know he's tempted. But, before he can answer, his phone vibrates with a text message and it tears the moment to shreds. He flips out his phone and grins at the message.

Worse follows as he forgets all about me and turns towards the storage-area door while answering the text.

'Later?' I call after him.

But he doesn't answer.

'Hey!' I call. 'Johnson!'

But the text has absorbed him and I doubt he hears me. The tiny connection I managed to forge with him forgotten in an instant.

NO ONE KNOWS BETTER THAN I DO

Carrie slipped from Non-Ape's grip two more times and he claimed it was because she was so skinny he couldn't get a proper hold of her. It's more likely that he saw something and got distracted. Like a cake shop. I felt every sickening jar and smack and crunch for her as she flew from the car roof and ended up lying in the road.

I think we're twelve miles from home. I haven't heard from my dad since he appeared in the wing mirror, but one glance at the Ferrari's speedometer tells me we are hitting a hundred miles an hour as we approach the tunnel Non-Lucas died in, so we'll be there soon enough.

'We might need to stop and pick someone up,' I tell the Ape.

'Yeah?'

'Lucas,' I tell him. 'Their Lucas. The evil one.'

'Want me to run him over?'

'No. I said pick him up.'

'I can run him over.'

'No.'

'Foot down and bam!' The Ape grits his teeth.

'I said we're stopping—'

'—Gotcha!' He laughs. 'So gotcha!'

The Ape veers between infuriating and even more infuriating. There isn't much else to him which is exactly why I hold him in such high esteem. I think I've grown to love that he drives me insane.

'Gotcha!' He sounds the Ferrari's horn.

'We already established that.'

He sounds the car horn again just for good measure. 'Gotcha, gotcha, gotcha.'

I feel Johnson shift under me as he tries to quell a laugh. 'How come you always fall for it?'

'I do it to humour him,' I tell him tetchily.

'Gotcha!' The Ape adds.

'He's smarter than you,' Johnson whispers.

'Oh, yeah?'

'What if I just glance off him?' the Ape asks, thinking I'm going to fall for the same joke.

And just for him I do.

'What did I just say?' I pretend to be at the end of my tether.

'Gotcha again!' The Ape points a big stubby finger at me.

The Ape roars into the mile-long tunnel and I feel Johnson shift under me. His long legs are not designed for a Ferrari.

'Shouldn't be much longer,' I tell him.

'What's the hurry?' he says playfully. 'You can sit here all day long.'

The tunnel flashes past, the lights embedded in the walls hypnotically bouncing off what's left of the broken windscreen.

'The Moth!' I shout. It takes even me by surprise.

'Where?' the Ape asks.

'I don't know!' Something flashes into my head, an image, a thought. It scratches at my brain so hard it hurts.

'Rev?' Johnson puts a hand on my shoulder.

'He's here,' I tell them. 'The Moth is here. Slow down, slow the car.' An image of the Moth's face is battering at my forehead. 'Stop the car!'

'Which one? Stop or slow?' the Ape teases.

'Stop!'

The Ape immediately stands on the brakes and the car fishtails, skidding left and right before he eventually gets it back under control.

As the momentum dies away, I glance in the rear-view mirror and see Carrie's body come rolling to a stop some thirty metres behind us. Non-Ape has once again lost his grip on her.

'Rev?' Johnson asks again.

I try and clear my head, but the Moth's face keeps looming. 'He's around here somewhere,' I tell Johnson. 'The Moth is close.'

My heart is racing. I don't know why I can sense or see him, but who cares? He's got to be within spitting distance, I'm sure of it.

'He's in my head, Johnson.'

'How though?' he asks.

'Hey!' Non-Ape bends into view, his massive head and face staring into the car. 'Why have we stopped?'

'Rev thinks she's found the Moth,' Johnson tells him.

'I don't see him,' Non-Ape says.

'He's in her head,' Johnson explains, and I already know what's about to happen.

'In her head?' Non-Ape sniggers.

'That's a big head,' the Ape adds sniggering as well.

'Or a small Moth.' Non-Ape laughs.

The Ape raps his knuckles on my forehead. 'Hey, Moth! Hey! You in there?'

Non-Ape is laughing so hard the Ferrari is shuddering.

'You need to go and pick up Carrie,' I tell him. 'Again.'

'So you can put her in your head?' the Ape laughs.

'That's a big head!' Non-Ape climbs down from the roof of the Ferrari.

'Who else you got in there?' the Ape asks.

Johnson and I sit for a good minute while the Apes do big head jokes until they decide I've got the rest of the world in there.

'That's where they've all gone,' the Ape decides. 'They're all in your head. The whole world.'

Non-Ape now has his hands on his knees and I swear he's crying with laughter, his huge body shaking so hard the tunnel is rumbling.

'Go and get Carrie!' I snap at him.

Non-Ape straightens and tries to pull himself together, wiping his teary eyes with his huge knuckles. It takes him a few moments until he manages to collect himself. But for some reason the rumbling in the tunnel continues.

And grows louder.

Non-Ape sets off to collect Carrie.

The Ape scans the road, craning his great neck past the steering wheel. 'Is that him?' he asks.

'Who?' I squint.

'Up ahead.' The Ape points to a lone figure standing at the exit to the tunnel. 'Is that the Moth?'

The figure stands like a statue but I already know who it is. This world is on constant repeat. We're about to play out another mutated echo of what has come before.

'Is that . . . ?' Johnson asks.

'Yeah,' I nod. 'It's Non-Lucas. And I don't quite think he's dead any more.'

Up ahead and standing at the exit to the mile-long tunnel is a shimmering, human-shaped blur. The Ape is already instinctively tensing. He's not scared or worried, but I can feel him tightening as his fighting instincts take over. I've seen it happen over and over; he turns into a Mensa candidate the minute there's trouble, weighing all the angles at light speed, scanning for weapons while working out how he's going to smash whatever's coming his way. And all of it happens in the blink of an eye. The boy's a genius when it comes to war. And luckily for us his doppleganger BFF who returns with the eternally broken Carrie is cut from the same cloth.

We're a hundred metres from the blur, but I absolutely know who – and what – it is. Even if he is moving inhumanly fast while standing still, if that makes any sense. Which it doesn't. He's moving but he's not moving.

'I thought he was dead.' Johnson shifts in his seat to get a better look. As he does the blur stops blurring. It settles and achieves a complete stillness. It's definitely Lucas. Their Lucas, complete with claws and skin that turns into armour. 'How can he be alive?' Johnson asks.

'Soon won't be.' The Ape revs the engine hard and the Formula One roar echoes down the sodium-lit tunnel. It's now night outside, but inside the tunnel it's as bright as day.

I place my cut and bloody hand on the Ape's thick hairy

111

wrist. 'We were going to collect him, alive or dead. It's not fair to leave him stranded here. So let me go talk to him.'

The Ape looks at me and for once he studies me, the few cogs in his brain reaching for something profound, and he nods. And then he touches my hand with his stubby finger.

'Healed!'

The car shudders as Non-Ape bellows. His eyes are on Lucas as he raises a huge meaty paw.

'Luke!' he cries. 'Hey Luke!'

Non-Lucas doesn't move. He stands like a statue, just like he did when we first encountered him. The stand-off is almost identical to our previous meeting in this very tunnel. The resonances keep on coming in this world. Ripples of re-happenings, if there is such a word. The same thing, over and over, only slightly twisted and different. And usually deadly. He starts to blur again, moving so fast on the spot that he's like a shimmer on a hot road.

Non-Ape hesitates. 'Where'd he go?' he asks.

'He's still there,' I tell him. Then I try my best to turn to Johnson in the cramped confines of the low-slung sports car. 'You killed him. I mean . . . He thinks you killed him; it was the other Johnson, but he might not understand that. So we need to get out there and explain.'

'That'll work,' Johnson says wryly. 'If he thinks I killed him, then he'll definitely want to listen to me.'

'But the good thing is he's alive, so Other-Johnson didn't get him properly. Maybe he'll turn a blind eye.'

'And maybe he'll take us for tea and cake,' Johnson says.

Non-Lucas was the first doppelganger to attack us but to

be fair that was in self-defence. He was anxious and afraid, couldn't find his friends and didn't know who we were, even though we looked like the people he knew. The Ape didn't help matters by immediately trying to kill him. Non-Lucas has a hair trigger, a fuse so short it isn't a fuse. He does everything at great speed and his body can cloak itself in some sort of rubbery, oily black armour. I haven't seen him turn into a blur before, but somehow or other he has attained a scary new level of velocity.

'Hey!' Non-Ape waves his arm again. 'Luke!'

Non-Ape's voice almost breaks the sound barrier with its echoing boom, magnified tenfold by the tunnel.

But as the echo dies away the rumble continues to grow louder and louder behind us ... There is definitely something approaching.

'Brace yourselves,' Johnson tells us. 'It's coming.' He's learned to know danger when he sees it. Just like we all do. 'Ape, floor it.'

'Hey!' Non-Ape bellows again at the blur. 'Luke!'

I've learned by now that Non-Ape will say one thing over and over until he gets a response. Up ahead the blur moves. It goes so fast we barely see it travel fifty metres towards us in the blink of an eye, as if he's passed through a wormhole in time. Non-Lucas comes to a stop, but remains a shimmering blur.

'Hey!' Non-Ape waves his great arm again.

The Ape revs the engine over and over; the deep throaty roar reverberates.

The tunnel lights flicker on and off, throwing dark shadows one moment and blinding us with a full-on glare the next. Non-Ape has to shield his eyes. A ripple runs from

113

one of my shoulders to the other. Then it comes back again, a slow shiver. A very gentle alarm. But one that is silently screaming at me.

The Ape's eyes find the rear-view and he nods slowly, appreciatively.

'Classic move,' he says.

'What?'

'Classic.' He almost purrs. 'Trapped us.'

I try to look behind me but it's almost impossible to manoeuvre in the tightly packed car.

Johnson is on high alert. 'Ape?'

'It's Dazza.'

'How fast can this car go?'

The Ape reaches forward and turns on the in-car music system. Typically something loud and heavy erupts from the expensive and powerful sound system. 'The Hunter' by Slaves. The song drowns out the jet engine that's purring in the back.

'Glad we didn't take the bus,' he says straight to my face.

Then he slips the car into drive, one hand on the hand-brake, revving the engine in time to the throb of the music. The Non-Ape starts to nod his huge head to the song, a slow measured headbang. But as the song builds so does the intensity of the headbang. Next to me the Ape is moving his head back and forth in perfect synchronisation with his brother-in-arms. It makes me think of the haka that Maoris do before war.

And war is definitely coming.

The blur is still waiting up ahead and I think we should accelerate right for it, like the Ape wanted. My plan to reason with Non-Lucas and bring him with us was just

114

crazy. Why didn't I listen to the Ape in the first place? His instincts are always – always – spot on. The Apes keep rocking back and forth, but the Ape is convinced there is something coming from the other end of the tunnel because he keeps glancing in the rear-view mirror.

Johnson slips an arm round my waist as he breathes in my ear. 'Stay in the car.'

'What?'

Johnson uses his lithe alien body to open the car door and slide out from under me before I can react. 'Johnson!'

He touches his finger to his forehead and cocks it my way, 'We've got this,' he tells me but is already looking past me to the Ape. 'You've got to get her home.'

'No!' I shake my head at Johnson. 'We're in this together.'

'Still are,' he assures me. 'But you've got to get home.' Johnson's eyes meet mine and I know I can't change his mind. 'When you do, take a moment, work it all out with your dad, then come back for us.'

The Ape hesitates; he wants to stay and fight. Johnson can easily read that in him. 'We'll be waiting for you.'

'This wasn't the plan, Johnson,' I urge him.

'Plan's changed,' he says, casually cricking his alien joints, limbering up for battle.

I can hear footsteps thundering down the tunnel from behind us. I say footsteps, but the closer they get, the more it sounds like a stampeding herd of cattle.

'The Hunter' is on repeat. Well, that figures. The opening chords, played in a low, ominous key, sounding the bugle.

'. . . *it does what it needs to, to stay strong and to survive . . .*'

The lyrics echo the moment perfectly.

The Apes again nod their great heads in time to the song.

The stampede is coming fast. The lights in the tunnel keep flickering on and off. The blur waits up ahead.

Non-Ape opens the car door and stuffs Carrie and Evil-GG in with me. There's barely any room in the back, but he squeezes them past me at impossible angles, almost folding Carrie in half as he wedges her in the tight space between my headrest and the massive revving engine in the back. He closes the door and one of Evil-GG's feet sticks up level with my face. He wears cool pointy shoes that are covered in grit and grime from the hotel rubble. The real GG would have a breakdown if he saw the state they were in. But then again the real GG lost a shoe when he fell from the side of the train so if the fall didn't kill him I'm pretty sure the shame would have done.

'Find the Moth. Find GG,' I tell Johnson and Non-Ape. 'We'll wait for you at the hospital.'

'That wasn't the second plan,' Johnson says.

'Plan's changed,' I echo. There is no way I'm leaving this world without him.

But the noise in the tunnel has swelled and I don't know if they hear me over the thundering swarm of Black Moths. They charge along the tarmac, but some dig into the tunnel walls and scramble horizontally towards us, black panthers eating up the ground.

'That's not possible.' My voice is lost in the thunder of noise. 'They shouldn't exist. They're not real.'

Some of them are running upside down along the roof of the tunnel.

The Lucas-blur moves. I catch it in my peripheral vision and try to warn the Ape, but he's seen it way before me and stands on the accelerator. The Ferrari roars forward, but not before Non-Ape tears the passenger door free. The car hurtles towards the blur, hitting sixty in a matter of seconds but the blur is quicker and Non-Lucas comes crashing through what is left of the windscreen.

Behind us Non-Ape hurls the car door like a frisbee and it hits the herd of Black Moths, scything through them before they can react.

'YOWZA!' I hear him bellow as he sets off, taking the fight to the Black Moths who should have blinked out of existence the moment Billie got her heart's desire. They're not real, I keep telling myself; stop believing in them and they'll disappear.

Non-Lucas stops blurring as he lands between the Ape and me. His talons are out and he slides one a few centimetres from my right eye. 'Stop the car, fatboy.'

The Ape glances at him, weighs up his next move. The talon is dangerously close to my eye.

'I'll put this right through her brain,' Non-Lucas warns.

'Yeah?' the Ape dares him.

'Oh, yeah.'

The Ape's eyes meet with Non-Lucas's as the speed climbs and climbs. We are already out of the tunnel.

All I can see is the sharp point of Non-Lucas's talon blurring in my vision it's so close.

'Ape.' My voice cracks.

Non-Lucas enjoys my abject fear.

'Yeah?' The Ape keeps piling on the speed.

'Do as he says.'

The Ape hesitates then starts to slow. Non-Lucas grins. Relaxes. Which is when I make my move. He really thought I'd just give in? After all I've been through? I duck down as fast as I can in my seat and the Ape uses all his might to shove Non-Lucas straight out of the car. There's no door to stop him and he flies from the Ferrari. Even his rubbery armour won't do him much good as he goes into an ugly roll and strips of his dark black skin start to peel and fly off as his body meets with the unyielding road. Over and over.

'Classic,' the Ape purrs as he accelerates again.

'Yeah. Classic,' I agree. We're so in tune now we know each other's moves instinctively. I crane my neck and watch Non-Lucas roll to a halt, smashing into the short metal fencing that lines part of the road.

'Classic,' I repeat, just for good measure.

Behind us Non-Ape's bellow booms from the tunnel. I can't figure any of it out; the Black Moths, the Lucas-blur, it doesn't make any sense.

And then Non-Lucas springs to his feet. Injured and hurting but upright.

He begins to blur on the spot.

'Ape . . .'

The Ape glances in his rear-view and looks impressed. 'Reset,' he says simply.

The music vibrates throughout the car.

'. . . *Oh, it's reckless and pointless, but it's also very fun . . .*'

Non-Lucas starts coming after us.

'Foot down,' I urge the Ape, glancing back to try and see if I can spot Johnson.

The Ape's foot slams down on the accelerator and the

118

mighty car hits one hundred and twenty. But Non-Lucas is already gaining and the inrushing wind through the smashed windscreen is tearing at my face.

One hundred and thirty.

I can see the blur in the wing mirror as Non-Lucas gains more ground. Moth Two was fast when he chased down the train we were all on, but Non-Lucas is faster than light.

One hundred and forty.

We're going to be travelling far too quickly to take the exit lane into town.

Non-Lucas keeps gaining.

One hundred and fifty.

The car judders, but it's more from the onrushing wind pouring through the non-existent windscreen. There is no aerodynamic marvel to the car any more, especially when it's also missing a passenger door.

Non-Lucas is closing on us.

One hundred and sixty.

The Ape's hands remain steady on the wheel, his eyes buffeted viciously and his vision blurring as he blinks as rapidly as he can.

One hundred and seventy.

Signs flash past us.

Non-Lucas continues to draw closer, an insane blur looming in the rear view.

One hundred and seventy.

We're not getting any faster.

'Ape!' I yell. As in, *Over to you, buddy.*

None of this makes sense. Non-Lucas was dead. I saw him die.

The Black Moths must be the ones who kidnapped our

Moth from the train. They have somehow survived even though they don't exist.

This is crazy.

One hundred and seventy-one.

I've never travelled this fast before. Never been in an aeroplane or a helicopter for that matter and I admit I like the feeling of raw speed. I like watching everything shooting past us. If it wasn't for the fact that a murderous doppelganger was chasing us, I'd thoroughly recommend this to anyone. One hundred and seventy-one miles an hour. But then, to my shame, I realise I've been looking at kilometres per hour. The car is Italian made and the speedo has thrown me. I don't know how to work out how fast we're really going, but for a second or two I was travelling at the speed of light.

The Ape coaxes a little more from the screaming engine. We are a mile from our exit point.

Non-Lucas is almost upon us.

When did he get this fast? He's practically at our bumper, blurring through time and space.

'The Hunter'. I'll never forget this song as long as I live, which might not be as long as I'd hoped.

Non-Lucas lands on the roof of the car.

The Ape reacts instinctively and tries to swerve to throw him from the roof. But the car, for all its incredible engineering, starts to lose traction and tip over. We are about to go into a roll that none of us will survive.

But the Ape yanks the wheel – another echo of when we nearly killed Carrie in a tiny Fiat that almost rolled over on its side. The Ape fights all the laws of physics as he flaps the paddles down through the gears, his foot easing off the accelerator, but the car is fighting back and even as the speed bleeds away we go into a frightening, dizzying skid that turns the car in circles. The airbags explode and balloon in our faces and I lose sight of everything as we hit the sickening roll that was always waiting for us. The Ferrari leaps into the air and turns on its head. I have no idea what happens to Non-Lucas because all I know is we're rolling over and over along the road.

The airbags deflate and I look across to the Ape who seems to be in excruciating pain. Evil-GG's pointed shoe is no longer level with my nose and I hate to think of the mess he and Carrie are now in. They've probably been fused together.

I know that people aren't meant to move after car accidents, but I'm almost suffocating because I'm basically caught in a frozen cartwheel, with my legs bent back over the back of my head. I roll as gingerly as I dare and spill out of the open car door. I land hard and manage to get on all fours. Every bone aches and my neck feels like it'll never move again; it's rigid with pain. I cough and blood lands on the road. For a second I'm thinking punctured lung or heart, but when I wipe my mouth I realise I've bitten my tongue. The blood pools in my mouth and I try and spit it out.

'Ape?' I breathe.

'Yowza,' he says but without any of his usual swagger.

'C'mon, move.'

But, even before my words hit his ears, feet land in front of my face.

The blur is back.

Non-Lucas.

'I told you to stop the car.' He grins and what are left

of his metal teeth shine against his loam skin. Half of his armour has been scraped off, but some of his talons are still functional. He has three left, and it's all he needs as he draws his arm back.

'Now where were we?' he grins.

DAZE OF DAYS

I slipped back into school with a minute to spare. But not before phoning New-Billie again. I had to ring three times before she answered. She'd have seen the number on her screen and known it was the weird soft-voiced person who she hung up on earlier in the day.

'What?' she asked.

'Can we meet?'

'I'm not meeting up with a disembodied voice.' She hung up again.

I rang her again. 'It's me ... Reva.'

'Look, I get that you've been home-schooled or whatever and that you're so bored you want a friend. But that friend isn't me.'

'But it is, Billie,' I actually managed to say her name without being overwhelmed with emotion. The last time I saw my Billie she was ... No. I can't and won't think of it. It's too much. 'You're my best friend.'

'You're so weird,' she said.

'I need you,' I told her. There was no point beating about the bush. She'd either go for it or not.

Another longer silence followed.

'How did you know my number? We only just met,' she asked.

'But we haven't,' I told her. 'We've been friends since we were four years old. Your phone number is stuck in my brain I call it so much.'

New-Billie laughed. 'Weirdo.' And hung up again.

The next lesson on my new timetable is drama and it's taught by the only teacher I have ever really had any time for, Mr Balder; as enthusiastic and knowledgeable a teacher as there ever was, he's an inspiration to every pupil who takes his classes. He teaches us about life through the works of the world's greatest dramatists. I'm hoping this world's version of Mr Balder, with his full ginger beard and receding hairline, will have something more than silence to offer.

Moving swiftly down the corridor I look for the main hall where the drama classes are usually held.

My dismay at not finding a portal in the lorry's cabin has been offset by managing to strike up a conversation with New-Johnson. It didn't lead anywhere but I'm convinced it will eventually. Mainly because I'm going to make sure of it.

The new plan is to find my dad's papers and try and use them to escape. I'm not sure why I didn't think of this to begin with but it seems I don't learn from my relentless stupidity.

I reach the door to the main hall and find it's locked.

The door is made from thick old oak and is almost as ancient as the school itself, but it doesn't budge when I shake it as hard as I can. I check my timetable again. I'm definitely supposed to be here. I look around, but already the corridors are empty as the last few pupils find their respective classes.

Only thing for it is to try the school office; maybe there's been a last-minute change. I'm already planning to tell my dad and New-Mum just how much fun I had at school, so much so that I can't wait to go back tomorrow. Deception is the key word until I find my dad's papers. Yet again it's like my life is an eternal groundhog day as I relive something I've already tried to do twice before. Find my dad's blessed papers.

The school office is behind the main reception area, a small room with a perspex window looking out on to the entrance lobby. There is no one behind the perspex window. I get on my tiptoes and peer as close as I can into the small area, but there's no one there.

'Hello?' I call out.

No answer.

I rap on the perspex. 'Hey?' Louder this time.

The door to the school office opens and Miss Hardacre emerges. She's a mousy blonde forty-something and in my world owns two small terriers whom she walks twice a day through town and who once joined a mature dating agency. Her home-made video plea for love was found on a dating website by one of the pupils. She gets phone calls every week from pupils pretending to be her Ideal Man.

But this Miss Hardacre is crying. Her eyes are red-rimmed and she isn't at all interested in talking to me because she pulls a blind down behind the window, blotting me out. I crouch in time with the lowering blind.

'I'm meant to be in Mr Balder's drama class,' I say, squatting lower and lower, trying to be seen and heard.

The blind stops a few centimetres from shutting me out altogether. It doesn't go back up though.

'Mr Balder's class?' I offer again.

The blind remains where it is and I almost bend double trying to see through the gap in the perspex.

'The door to the main hall's locked,' I explain.

Miss Hardacre doesn't respond, but I'm getting used to that by now. No one ever talks. She steps slowly over to the door to the school office and, knowing that I can see just enough, she opens it, pushing it and letting it swing back so I can see some of the way into the room.

The first thing I notice is a fallen chair. It's on its side. Above the fallen chair is a pair of shoes. Soft loafers made from tan-coloured suede with rubber soles. The shoes dangle in the air a metre from the floor. They are attached to a pair of men's legs. Brown corduroy trousers cover the legs.

I've found Mr Balder.

I don't need to look any further to know that he has hanged himself. I've had prior experience spotting people who have hanged themselves, namely poor Lucas, and this is no different. The best teacher in the world has walked into the school office and ended it all. Another heartbreaking echo.

I have no idea what to say, and even if I did I wouldn't know how to speak because I've lost all control of my motor functions. The sight of the brilliant Mr Balder, whether he's the real Mr Balder or not, has turned me completely numb.

My mouth dries as I stand there uselessly, listening to Miss Hardacre sobbing quietly to herself.

It takes a good few minutes until she steps back and pulls the blind down completely. Blotting me out of the hideous tragedy.

I turn away, lurching into the school corridor, head spinning.

TALONS ARE AS TALONS DO

Non-Lucas the blur is as still and as calm as a statue. For someone who moves so fast he's very good at standing still. He is also very good at death. He has no compunction about gutting me.

'Love to know how you got so fast,' I tell him, blood continuing to pool in my mouth.

'I was always fast,' he boasts.

'I can save us all,' I tell him. 'I can fix the whole thing.'

'Sure you can,' he says dismissively. 'Now hold still, this is going to hurt.'

His broken metal teeth try to form a smile, but it's jagged and misshapen and the lack of teeth have given his mouth a cruel slant.

'Kill me and you'll have to stay here forever,' I warn him with my level best look of forthright honesty.

'I'm going to do this slowly,' he continues to boast, completely ignoring me into the bargain. 'Which goes against everything I am.'

He draws his arm back. I won't be fast enough to dodge him.

'You're making a big mistake,' I attempt one last tried and trusted cliché.

'Maybe I'll get detention for it.' Non-Lucas feels around with his tongue. There's something in his mouth and after a moment he spits out a steel tooth that when it lands, echoes on the tarmac.

'Listen to me!' I raise my voice, spitting blood at him as I do.

'While you're lying there, bleeding out, I'm going to go back for Johnson,' he replies calmly.

'I've got the answers! To everything,' I tell him, stalling for time. Which is ironic when you're facing the fastest creature you'll ever witness. 'I can send you home, but only I can do that,' I lie. 'Only I have the answer to making that happen.'

Even from several miles away I can hear Non-Ape bellowing in the tunnel as he and Johnson battle the swarm of Black Moths. While those two are alive, there's hope.

'Then I'm going to bring Johnson back here so he can watch you die.' Non-Lucas grins cruelly.

'We can all go home,' I try again. 'And time isn't like you think; you'll be back in your world as if none of this ever happened. We're talking *Wizard of Oz*, where it's all been some Technicolor dream.'

The Lucas-blur stabs his arm towards me, talons slicing through the air, when for some reason a talon emerges from his throat. He stops dead and pitches forward. He gurgles and black blood fills his mouth before he crashes down face first on the ground next to me.

I look up to see the Ape standing with what I can only presume is one of Evil-GG's fingers gripped in his meaty fist. 'He talks too much.'

'Where the hell did you get that finger from?'

'It broke off in the crash,' the Ape tells me. But I don't believe him and am pretty sure he somehow snapped it off Evil-GG's lifeless hand.

The Ape scratches his cheek with the black and bloody finger. 'I'll heal him,' he says and then yanks me to my feet. My body screams from a thousand more cuts and bruises.

We are stuck with no transport and no way of moving Carrie and Evil-GG let alone the now non-moving Non-Lucas. Our home town is still three miles away.

'If you've got any good ideas . . .' I tell the Ape, knowing that he won't, but that's where I am right now.

He takes a moment to scan the evening gloom, looking at the surrounding road and fields that stretch out around us, undulating for miles in every direction.

'I know a short cut.'

'Seriously?' I ask the Ape.

'Across the fields.'

'How would you know that?'

'I know where home is.' He points in roughly the direction of the town. 'It's that way. And we can go across the fields. So that's a shorcut.'

An inhuman bellow cracks like thunder seven miles back down the road, rippling through the gathering darkness, and I can only imagine it's come from Non-Ape. In an empty world sound carries further than you'd ever believe was possible. I know the real Moth is back there, somewhere. I can still sense him. But do we go back for him or do we stick to the plan to find my dad? I could just about carry Carrie and I'm pretty sure the Ape can hoist Evil-GG. But cutting across endless dark fields in the gathering night won't be much fun. So, if we have to do it, we have to go now.

'OK.' I sigh.

'OK?' he asks.

'Let's take the fields.'

'Was my idea.'

'I'm not saying it wasn't.'

'Get your own ideas.'

From the moment I first got paired with the Ape when we all decided to split up to find out if anyone else had been sent to the empty world, I have found our conversations blunt and circuitous. But as I look into his big brown-cow eyes I think back to when I thought he was dying, that I was about to lose him forever, and I don't care how many nonsensical conversations we have: I'll endure every single one of them if it means he's there by my side.

'Yep.' He peers across the fields, scrunching his eyes to get a better look. 'That's a great plan.'

Echoes of the battle that's happening seven miles away come tumbling on us. If Johnson and Non-Ape fall, then we need to get moving. If they don't, they'll come and find us.

So they better win.

F FOR DETENTION

There's another Ape staring at me.

It's sitting in another stale, musty classroom and it keeps looking at me.

I'm trying to ignore it. But it won't stop staring.

'What?' I ask it.

'What?' it asks back.

'I asked you first.'

I had to get detention. Obviously I did. It's the way things work. Round and round we go and where we stop, well, we pretty much already know. I'm surprised anyone was bothered enough in this school to even hand out punishments, but the teacher who took over Mr Balder's drama class was not happy that I was late, despite my explaining that one of her colleagues had committed suicide.

The thing that broke me was her indifference to Mr Balder's death. All she was really interested in was how late I got to her class, even though it's not like we actually learned anything. It was just another class of sitting around, waiting for it to be over, but apparently even in this world being late gets you detention.

'Why are you staring at me?' I ask the Ape. I couldn't believe it when I sloped into the classroom and saw him sitting there. My heart skipped a couple of beats. He is identical to my Ape: the same stained T-shirt, the same jeans, the same lack of school uniform.

The same unbending stare.

'I'm not,' he tells me.

'You are.'

'He isn't,' New-GG chips in. 'It's his glass eye.'

'His what?'

'A glass eye, as in an eye made of glass, He lost one and someone popped a little old marble in there.' New-GG is sitting three desks away, painting his nails a bright yellow.

'Stop picking on him.' The New-Moth, non-paraplegic and therefore minus his wheelchair and sitting with his face in a book on quantum physics, doesn't even bother looking my way.

'I wasn't.'

'Yeah, you were,' the New-Moth says. He's got the same flat nose and the glasses that keep sliding down it as my Moth has.

'If you make him cry . . .' New-Carrie warns in her brittle voice.

'Cry? The Ape doesn't cry.'

'The Ape cries.' New-Carrie's earlier blindness has miraculously healed. She's writing what I assume is more shocking poetry in her notebook, but has stopped to join in the conversation.

'All the time.' New-Lucas is stretched out at his desk, calm and easy with himself. 'Dontcha, Ape? Ya big crybaby.'

The Sad-Ape doesn't reply and instead tries to curl his huge bulk into a small ball, head bowed forward, hands cupping his face.

'There, look, he's about to get teary again.' New-Lucas points.

Sad-Ape hunches over even further and for someone so large he can make himself seem extremely small.

New-Lucas laughs. 'Go on, show the new girl how you cry.'

'Hey!' New-Billie swans into the classroom, all grace and elegance and beauty. 'Leave the big beastie alone.'

New-Lucas laughs again, but it's not the laugh of before. New-Billie's entrance has taken his breath away and I can tell he likes her – a lot. I spot the New-Moth glance up from his book and try to nonchalantly watch her serene sweep towards the first available desk. Apparently he too has a huge crush on her.

New-Billie sits down at the desk next to mine, takes in my now cigarette-ash-stained blazer and my bright, pristine white blouse then glances at my electric-pink hair. 'Never said earlier, but I like the hair.'

A breakthrough at last.

'Rev.' New-Billie says my name, dragging it out, getting used to it. 'Rev.'

'Short for Reva. Reva Marsalis.'

'Rev,' she says, rolling it around her tongue. 'Rev, Rev, Rev.'

'Vroom, vroom, vroom,' New-GG adds.

'What you in for?' New-Lucas asks.

134

My head is starting to spin. Isn't that the Ape's line? When we – as in the originals – were all back in the first fateful detention, that was definitely what the Ape asked.

I don't know the rules of the many earths, but these copies are like reflections from a house of mirrors. Twisted and warped.

'I turned up late for drama,' I tell him. It feels good to be having a conversation at last. I've spent all day trying to break through to someone. 'I, uh ... I saw Mr Balder. He'd hanged himself.' The image of the soft suede shoes suspended in mid-air comes flashing back. 'And no one's said anything about it. No one's batted an eyelid.'

Looks cross from New-Billie to New-Carrie and New-Lucas. The New-Moth lowers his book and then pushes his glasses back up his nose. I get the feeling they all know something I don't.

'Aren't you going to say anything?'

They all fall silent, so I turn to the one person I think I can rely on.

'Ape?'

Sad-Ape still has his head in his arms, face all but buried on the desk. He doesn't respond.

There isn't a single sign of any Ape-ness from Sad-Ape. I thought the multiverse was packed with their booming voices and massive, unrelenting and unbreakable characters. But this one is barely there. He's a wisp of smoke, a glimpse of a human being at best.

New-Billie's mobile phone pings with a message and when she reads it a smile spreads across that large wide mouth of hers. 'Filth,' she mutters to herself, then turns to the back of the classroom and her eyes settle on

New-Johnson, stretched out, black desert boots up on a desk, phone in one hand, a match in the other.

His eyes meet New-Billie's and the electricity between them buzzes back and forth as he sends another message. Her phone vibrates and she giggles. 'Pure filth,' she mutters. I try to get a look at the text but she is quick to obscure her phone from my view. 'Sorry. My eyes only.'

I don't quite understand how New-Johnson came to be in detention if he wasn't even at school earlier, but he's here and I am determined to make contact with him and force my way into his life. I need as many allies as I can muster if I'm going to escape from this world.

There's no teacher to stop New-Lucas shouting at the back of Sad-Ape's head.

'Cry from your glass eye.'

Which means there's also no one to stop New-GG suddenly leaping up and climbing on top of a desk. 'GG likes that rhyme!' New-GG becomes animated, his eyes widening. 'Cry from your glass eye.'

Sad-Ape tries to shut him out by putting his great hands over his large ears.

'Cry,' New-GG starts singing. 'Cry from your glass eye.' New-GG is now dancing some weird cancan, his pointy, shiny shoes flicking ever closer to Sad-Ape's bowed head and face.

'I thought you told me to leave him alone,' I say.

'I did.' New-GG swings a foot dangerously close to the Ape's head. 'Doesn't mean I have to.'

'You're new. You haven't earned the right to make him cry.' New-Carrie aims a challenging look my way.

'Cry from your glass eye!' New-GG sings, kicking his

feet towards Sad-Ape. New-Lucas starts laughing and New-Billie sets her phone down and stares hard at the outrageous New-GG.

'Leave him alone, GG.'

'But I'm soooooooooo bored!' New-GG tells her, dancing and kicking dangerously close to Sad-Ape's head.

I hate what New-GG is doing but I also hate that their Ape is sitting there accepting it without a fight or even so much as a word or bellow. The New-Moth is pretending to be absorbed in his book, but I can see his eyes shifting back and forth to Sad-Ape. He looks uncomfortable, but he's smart enough – or is it cowardice? – not to speak up.

'You could take his eye out,' I warn New-GG.

'How do you think he lost the other one?' New-GG laughs.

I turn to New-Billie and I can tell she feels awkward. 'You going to stop this?' I ask her.

She weighs me up then lowers her voice. 'You know it makes no difference.'

'That's not how any Ape should be,' I tell her.

'Nothing makes a difference,' she adds solemnly.

'All day long no one does or says a thing,' I plead with her. 'All day it's been like that, but now people are getting animated – and ugly,' I add. 'Why?'

I know all of the people in this room; I've fought and laughed with their exact copies and none of them would behave like this.

'I don't get it,' I tell Billie.

She drops her eyes, won't look at me. 'You've got to find a release,' she mumbles. 'You've got to find something that'll get you animated. Gives you a reason to have a heartbeat.'

'That makes no sense,' I tell her.

'It will when you've been here as long as we have,' she continues to mumble. 'The pressure builds and it keeps on building and building until . . .' She trails off.

'Until what?' I demand.

'Until something gives,' she says simply. Then she glances at New-Johnson, takes him in as he lights another match then lets it drop to the floor. 'Phone me,' she says quietly, rising from her desk before leaving detention. 'Or I'll phone you. Deal?'

New-Billie hustles from the classroom before I can answer.

I glance back at Sad-Ape, a tiny frightened boy lost in a huge body.

'Hey, you, you one-eyed boo-boo,' New-GG sings. 'Hey, you, you animal of the zoo.'

The toes of his pointy shoes are millimetres from taking Sad-Ape's good eye out.

'Hey, you, monkey boy. Hey, you, glass eye. Hey, you, cry baby.'

New-Lucas is now banging out a rapper's beat on the table, like it's a drum, syncing with New-GG's song and his dance steps. 'Hey, you!' he sings.

New-Carrie starts bopping in her seat, her stick-thin stiletto body carves dance shapes that are all angles and sharp edges. 'Hey, you!'

Sad-Ape cowers, but his good eye stays fixed on the swinging shoe. It's as if he's almost welcoming it, hoping it will dig deep into his eye socket and blind him forever.

'Stop it!' I yell.

But no one pays any attention.

'Hey, you!' New-GG sings.

'Yeah, you!' New-Carrie echoes.

'Killa Gorilla.'

'Stop!' I'm on my feet now. New-Carrie tries to grab my arm, but I shake her hand away, giving her a venomous stare. 'You really shouldn't do that,' I tell her. She doesn't know what I've been through, the endless battles to survive, and if she thinks she can grab my arm again she'd better be ready to have her wrist broken. What they're doing to this Ape is killing me.

'Hey, you!' New-Lucas thumps out the rap, harder and faster.

'Cry from your glass eye!' I've no idea how New-GG hasn't kicked Sad-Ape in the face yet.

New-Johnson, relaxing at the back, picks up his phone and starts filming the bullying.

'Guys, c'mon,' I plead.

The rhythmic drumming and dancing are making my head throb. New-Carrie has picked up New-Lucas's beat and slams her tiny feet down on the floor in sync.

The New-Moth has stopped reading and now watches the relentless victimisation. He isn't enjoying it, but he's definitely not brave enough to try and stop them.

New-Lucas moves closer to Sad-Ape by picking up his table and chair and edging it across the classroom. Kangarooing it closer to the Ape.

That's something else my Ape did. That's his move!

New-Carrie picks up her desk and chair and copies New-Lucas as together they pincer themselves towards Sad-Ape. He has no escape as they sing and bang out the rap beat scraping their chairs and desks closer to Sad-Ape. Coming from all angles and hemming him in. Their voices grow louder.

'Hey, you!' they chorus.

I shove my chair back so hard it crashes to the floor.

New-Carrie gives me a dark warning look. But she's nothing compared to what I've had to face recently. She's a puff of air in comparison.

I move quickly, pushing between the converging chairs and desks, and, while one of New-GG's feet is in mid-swing, I swipe his standing leg from under him. He crashes to the classroom floor and the song and the dancing and the kangarooing stop abruptly.

But I'm not stopping. I'm on the move. I grab Sad-Ape's huge hands and try to tug him to his feet. 'Get up!'

Sad-Ape barely reacts.

'I said move it!'

His leaden, scared eyes meet mine. 'It's OK,' he says quietly, resigned to his fate. 'I'm used to it.'

'Get up!' I yell.

New-GG is already getting gingerly to his feet and New-Carrie and New-Lucas are helping him.

'What a bitch,' New-Carrie says.

'Ooh, she's a hot fiery one,' New-GG comments.

'Anything broken?' New-Lucas asks him.

New-GG wiggles his right pinkie finger and he's missing a long nail. He winces in exaggerated agony. 'D'you think I'll live?'

I drag at Sad-Ape's meaty arm. 'Please, I'm getting you out of here.'

Sad-Ape finally rises to his feet, a deep frown on his brow. 'Why?'

'Seriously?' I shout at him.

Behind me I hear a match strike and when I swivel round

140

New-Johnson is showing me a burning match. His eyes meet mine through the flame and I think it's some sort of a warning.

I lead Sad-Ape towards the door, expecting the others to descend upon me, but instead they start singing again.

'Hey, you.'

'Hey, you two.'

'Hey, you two lovers.'

They start banging their desks in unison and stamping their feet. The only ones who don't are the New-Moth and New-Johnson. New-Moth looks awkward, trapped between joining in or being outed as a non-believer. New-Johnson seems to have lost interest in the bullying and instead his mesmerising blue eyes are locked on mine. C'mon, Johnson, *I think.* Be the rebel, be the one who swims against the tide. This isn't you. *This isn't any Johnson in any world. I know it. I can feel it. Inside him is the indomitable spirit of the boy who never obeys. The loner, the wolf, the motorbike king.* C'mon, Johnson, show me you're in there somewhere. Give me a spark.

His eyes drop from mine.

Johnson, don't look away.

He lights a cigarette and stares dolefully out of the window.

No!

I have no choice but to lead the big lump of frightened Sad-Ape out of the classroom and slam the door behind me. I have to stop and take some breaths so I can clear my head.

The singing and drumming echo down the long corridor, chasing us all the way down the four flights of stairs. The empty school reverberates with their bullying, but it gives me the chance to try and collect my thoughts as I walk Sad-Ape down the corridor.

'You OK?' I ask him.

'No,' he answers bluntly. Which shocks me as much as anything else that has just happened. No Ape would ever admit to that, not ever.

'Good,' I reply. 'That's good.'

'It is?' he asks.

'Means it can only get better,' I tell him.

This world is the worst one yet. It may not kill you or swarm with violent, clawed monsters, but it does something different. It takes copies of people you've come to regard as your best friends and twists them into ugly facsimiles. But I've learned one thing from them: they are bitter, they are resentful because something happened. Something dark and bad is lurking or looming in this world. No one cares because, I think – and this is just a theory right now – it's too late. It's too late for everyone in this world. There's no life here, just existence. And that worries me more than anything I have faced so far.

HELL'S A COMING

It takes a lot longer than you'd think to walk across seven fields. From a distance you weigh up those fields and you think that's what, five minutes a field, so it's thirty-five minutes in total. I have fallen over so many times that I doubt I have any skin left on my knees. The fields are mainly grass and crops, but unseen sticks and stones lurk silently and I swear I've tripped over and landed on every single one of them.

The Ape has Evil-GG slung over his right shoulder in a fireman's lift, and Non-Lucas slung over his left. They're weighing him down, but I think he sees it as a test of physical strength so he marches through the fields in defiance of their combined weight and the pressure they're putting on his cracked ribs. He has no quit in him.

It's almost pitch-black by the time we come across the railway line that leads from my town all the way into King's Cross. The Ape is the first to see it and his eyes light up. A train sits alone on the railway track.

Another train?

143

Really?

It can't possibly be there. We didn't pass another one on our way into London and I know for a fact that the line this one is standing on is the same line we rocketed down before we crashed into King's Cross station. That train has to be a hallucination at best.

My shoulders are tingling again.

'That train shouldn't be there,' I tell the Ape.

'It's there,' he confirms.

'That's not what I'm saying.'

'It's there,' he repeats and points to add to his concrete assessment. 'See. Right there.'

Yet again the conversation is going to go around in circles and I need to divert his one-thought-at-a-time mental process.

'Think we could drive it?' I ask.

'Easy,' he decides.

'Then let's get the doors open and load these three into a carriage.'

The Ape lets Evil-GG and Non-Lucas slip from his mighty grasp. They both land on their heads before flopping beside the steel wheels of the train.

I let go of Carrie and almost topple down with her because I'm so tired now. If I let myself, I'd gladly curl up into a ball and spend the rest of the night in a dreamy snooze. I try to listen for any noise coming from the battle in the tunnel. But the sound isn't carrying as strongly as it did before. Either that or the fight is over.

The Ape presses the OPEN button on the nearest carriage door. Nothing happens. He presses it again. Same result.

I march down to the next carriage and try that instead. Still nothing.

The Ape tries the next carriage, but the doors remain firmly closed to us.

I look past the train and down the stretch of railway track that leads to our hometown. If nothing else, it will be easier going if we head straight down the line.

'Let's take five minutes, catch our breath, and then walk the rest of the way,' I tell the Ape.

He presses the fourth carriage door button and it opens. This carriage also houses the driving compartment. He turns back to me.

'You can walk, but I'm taking the train.'

The Ape turns back, collects Non-Lucas and fireman lifts him into the carriage. He does the same with Carrie and Evil-GG. Finally he climbs on board and I follow.

The lights aren't on in the empty, silent train as the Ape tries the door to the driver's compartment, but it won't budge. He wrenches at the handle until it snaps off in his meaty paw.

'Nice work,' I mumble.

He looks at the handle and weighs it before turning on the door and kicking it as hard as he can. His boot rears up and smashes against the lock. Once, twice, three times. But the door doesn't give.

'I'll try the driver's door from the outside,' I say. But he doesn't hear me because all he can think is to batter at the door.

I head for the open carriage exit door only for it to hiss shut in front of me. I try the OPEN button but the door won't budge.

145

This happened before when I found Billie on a Eurostar train. Right at the moment she was transforming into her hybrid self. She was decidedly unhappy when talons sprang from her fingertips and, quite naturally, it tipped her just a tad over the edge.

The Ape keeps hammering at the driver's door while I look for the emergency carriage door release. I have to break open a plastic covering but after what I've been through nothing's going to stop me and I'm through to the door release in a heartbeat. But even after yanking it so hard it almost comes off in my hand the door remains firmly closed.

The Ape is forced to take a breather because the driver's door won't open either. He turns to me and I can tell just from the way he's now listening keenly that he knows there is trouble coming. His eyes find a carriage window, but it's pitch-black outside and the light from inside fades two metres into the darkness. He stands and listens; he has incredible hearing, as he keeps telling me, so I fall silent and wait for him to pinpoint exactly what it is that's bothering him.

His chest rises and falls. I know his ribs must ache, but he still shows no sign of pain.

He just listens.

'What is it?' I whisper.

The Ape holds up a meaty hand, shushing me. He crosses to the window and lays one side of his head against the pane. His breathing calms as he listens.

I go towards him, leaning a hand on the top of a seat, but not realising that I'm actually gripping it tightly. So tightly my knuckles are white.

'Ape?' I barely breathe the word. 'Is there something out there?'

'There's always something out there.' He breathes quietly, his ear still planted up against the reinforced windowpane.

'We need to run?' I ask him. Even though I don't think I can take a single step.

'Or fight.' The Ape isn't keen on running.

'How about we get into the driver's cabin,' I tell him. 'Somehow. Will there be time?'

The Ape takes an age to listen to whatever he thinks he can hear outside in the darkness. Precious seconds are eaten up where we could be tearing through the driver's door. But this is his way; he is the original immovable force.

Finally he climbs away from the window and his skin makes a sucking sound on the glass. I step back, freeing my fingers from the death grip I had on the top of the train seat.

The Ape backs all the way across the carriage and without warning he charges back across the aisle and hurls his entire overweight, flabby body at the train window. He lands with all the might he can muster and crashes out through the window.

I reach the smashed window and for a moment I can't see where he is.

'Dazza?' I scream-whisper into the night. I don't know why I'm trying to be quiet after the racket he's just made. 'Dazza!' I say louder.

I hear movement, a groan, and realise the Ape is still lying on the ground. Even in the dull sodium glare, I can see that his left shoulder has dropped wickedly to level with his chest practically. He's dislocated it badly.

I instinctively pull the end of my sleeves over my hands

147

and, trying my best not to cut them on the jagged pieces of broken glass sticking out from the frame, I launch myself out of the window.

I land awkwardly, go into a stumble, finding myself outside the glow from the carriage and suddenly in the pitch-black. I have to get my bearings and then turn back to the Ape. He is climbing to his feet, cradling his shoulder.

'We're out,' he declares proudly.

'Let me see that arm.'

'Later.' Then he looks round the side of the train before seeking out a large rock. He grimaces with each movement.

'Just tell me what to do,' I quietly hiss at him.

'I got this.'

I grab the rock from him. 'I've got it too.'

A rumble climbs through the night behind us. We both stop. As ever, the Ape was right. There is something out there.

'Smash the driver's window,' the Ape tells me. Quietly. Calmly. All matter-of-fact, as if there's no other reason for holding a rock other than to smash something with it.

I don't need a second invite and race to the driver's window and hurl the rock clean through it. Glass explodes everywhere and showers us in tiny shards.

'Boost me,' I tell the Ape, momentarily forgetting about his dislocated shoulder.

He offers his mighty and meaty good arm.

The rumble is growing louder. If it's the Black Moths, then it means Johnson and Non-Ape have been defeated. So what chance do we stand?

'I won't be able to pull you up,' I say to the Ape. 'I need to fix your shoulder first.'

He shrugs with his good shoulder. 'So fix it.'

I have no idea how to pop a shoulder back into its socket. I think it involves either a sudden yank or maybe some quiet manipulation. It's one of the two – or both.

The rumble is growing somewhere in the darkness. Swarming across the fields we just took ages to navigate.

I won't let myself believe that Johnson and Non-Ape are lost. They can't be.

'Give me your arm.'

He flinches and grits his teeth as he moves his bad arm and I take his wrist as gently as I can.

'Look away.'

'It's dark, stupid. Nothing to see.'

'I don't really know what I'm doing so it might take a while.'

'We haven't got a while.' He can hear the rumble drawing ever closer, just like I can.

I take the Ape's wrist and pull his arm towards me. I've seen this on telly before. I think what they do is stretch the arm to the horizontal and then try and pop the shoulder with a sudden, violent yank. Where's Johnson the doctor when you need him?

I blow out a few times, fully expecting to make a total hash of this. The Ape stares at me. There's a sheen of sweat on his brow which means he's already in great agony so I guess whatever I do won't make it much worse.

'OK . . . On three.' I barely take a breath. 'Three!' I yell, quickly grabbing his wrist and shoving his arm as hard as I can, pushing it upwards, hoping to find the socket, hoping to drive the shoulder back into its original place. He muffles a scream. But it doesn't work; his shoulder remains limp

149

and low. I go again, not bothering to count or warn the Ape. I shove the arm, twisting it, manipulating it as I thrust it upwards – until I hear a definite click. I step back, panting, as the Ape turns away and half bends as he swallows the pain into the pit of his belly, holding it there until he's ready to straighten again.

He rises to his full height and looks down at me, and even in this dull light I can tell he's as white as a sheet from the pain. But he takes one breath and nods.

'Nice,' he says. 'Feels good.'

His shoulder is back where it should be and I know it's still going to be utterly painful for him, but he immediately presents his cupped hands. I step into them and, grimacing hard, he boosts me through the shattered train window.

I land awkwardly, cutting myself on shards of broken glass but there's no time to worry about that as I look at the controls and the strange steering stick and start pressing buttons. The train comes alive and starts to move. I don't know how to stop it and go back to the window.

'Jump!' The Ape coils his powerful legs and leaps at the slow moving train. His hands land on the edge of the smashed window and as we pick up speed I heave as hard as I can, almost dislocating my own shoulders as I drag and pull and yank the great beast of a boy. His feet scrabble and then find purchase and this helps him as he coils again and thrusts upwards. Half of his body is inside and, as the train continues to gather speed, I drag him by the back of his belt until he falls inside the cabin, landing on top of me. This has happened a few times before as he looks down at me and then grins.

'Tickets, please.'

I lie there, knowing the train is heading for our hometown, and for now that's all I care about. The rumble starts to fall away into the distance and for the moment we're safe. I don't know why the train doors closed on us like that, but we've gathered Non-Lucas, Evil-GG and Carrie and right now that feels like a triumph.

The Ape gets to his knees and looks round the cabin. I slide out from under him and manage to get into a sitting position in the cramped, confined space. We stare at each other for a moment, but no words are available to either of us. We're all out of chat.

The Ape rises to his feet, flicks some more controls and the train headlights spring on, full-beaming the onrushing track and the surrounding bushes and trees that line the railway banks. The train moves steadily.

Until the headlights pick up a lone figure on the track.

A figure I recognise immediately.

'Brakes!' I yell at the Ape, but he's seen the figure a fraction of a second before me and is already dragging on what I hope is the brake and not the accelerator.

Because GG is standing on the line.

DAZZA DON'T DAZZLE

I'd almost forgotten that my parents, for want of a better word to describe them, would be outside waiting for me. I can see New-Mum sitting behind the driver's wheel and it's highly likely that she hasn't moved from there all day. The car is parked in the exact same spot. My dad is pacing outside the car, smoking an anxious cigarette. They wouldn't have known about the detention, but skipping out early with Sad-Ape means they haven't yet sent out a search party and sniffer dogs.

The sad, hunched apology that is Sad-Ape is about to push through a side exit door when I hold him back. There was no way I was going to walk past reception after what happened this morning with Mr Balder.

'Wait a sec.'

Sad-Ape immediately does as he's told.

I look at him and know that I can't face this world without a friend.

'Do I look like a liar to you?' I ask.

'No,' he replies, but in such a way that he would probably say anything to agree with anyone.

'Like I'm crazy?' I ask.

He shakes his great jowly head and I wonder what has happened to him in this world. His glass eye is a real worry to me and when I look closer I can see that the false one doesn't even match the brown of his original eye; it's a dark blue.

'There are things that have happened to me that you wouldn't believe,' I tell him.

In the car park my dad finishes his cigarette and goes to light another one straight away, but thinks better of it, instead slipping the cigarette back into its packet. New-Mum is scanning the last of the children leaving school, hoping to see me amid the few who had extra-curricular activities, which would have been extra-curricular non-activities if I've got this school right.

'Things that mean I shouldn't be here,' I tell Sad-Ape.

'OK,' he says quietly.

I don't know how much he will understand or grasp but at this moment it doesn't matter, I have to let someone know the hell I've been dragged into. I suck in a deep breath, and then before I know it, it spills out of me. 'I'm from a different world.'

'OK.' He nods. But without a hint of irony or sarcasm.

'I'm talking a whole different universe.' The words are racing from me. 'It's complicated and I don't think you'd understand if I explained how and why, but the important thing is that you believe me.'

'OK.'

I stare into his good eye. 'You believe that I don't belong here?'

'Yeah.' His glass eye stays fixed in his head but his large

soft brown eye moves to find me and take me in. 'Yeah,' he repeats.

'You also believe me when I say I'm in the wrong world?' I spell it out again just to make sure he does get what I'm telling him. 'My earth looks like this; it has the same people in it. There's a you and a Billie and a Johnson and all the others.'

I catch my breath. Just saying their names almost folds me in half. I feel tears springing to my eyes and I quickly wipe them away, but can't stop a sniffle escaping.

'They were all my friends and . . .' I trail off. I have lost my momentum. How could anyone understand this, let alone an Ape?

I see New-Mum climb from the car and join my dad who offers her a panicky cigarette. But the cigarette doesn't ease her anxieties as she scans the school. I can see them but they can't see me. New-Mum reaches for her mobile phone.

I have to be quick. 'I'm not joking,' I tell Sad-Ape.

'I know.'

I'm not sure if Sad-Ape is so desperate that he'll say anything to make a friend or if he really does believe me.

'I thought it'd take more than that. Some sort of proof, or endless hours of arguing.'

'I get it,' he tells me.

'You can't just get it!' I raise my voice and then immediately wish I hadn't because my voice carries all the way to my parents. New-Mum puts her phone away and touches my dad on his arm. They both turn and see me standing in the side exit to the school.

New-Mum waves and calls my name. 'Reva!'

'Hey, we're right here,' Dad adds.

They can see I'm talking to Sad-Ape so I snatch one last look at him.

'What I'm saying is I've been brought here from another earth.'

'And I'm saying I get it.' Sad-Ape shows a glimmer of the real Ape, that rude beast of a boy. 'How many times you going to tell me the same thing?'

And then I realise that he hasn't a clue what I'm talking about and my heart sinks. 'You're useless,' I say, immediately hating myself for treating him just like the others in detention did. 'I didn't mean that. Sorry,' I tell him hastily. 'It's not easy being from another world.'

'You'll wish you were still there,' he mumbles, head bowed.

New-Mum and Dad are hurrying across the car park to meet me.

My heart freezes. 'What? What did you say?'

'You'll wish you never came,' Sad-Ape repeats.

I don't get a chance to say more because my New-Mum takes hold of my arm and pulls me away.

'Dad says we can go out to dinner,' she tells me.

He draws alongside me and I'm somehow trapped between them as they walk me to the car. 'Chinese?' he says.

'Crispy wontons.' My New-Mum smiles.

I arch my head back and try and get a look at Sad-Ape. He stares at me with a glazed look; it might be because of the glass eye, but in every other respect he looks defeated. No Ape in any universe is ever beaten, but this one – whatever has happened to him – has died over and over until he's little more than a husk.

We approach the car and New-Mum and Dad flank either side of me. They're rabbiting on incessantly.

'How was your first day at school?' she asks.

'I had a great day at work,' he tells me.

'Did you make a friend?' New-Mum asks, gesturing back towards Sad-Ape.

'I got so wrapped up in things I don't know where the day went,' Dad laughs.

'Is that big boy nice?' New-Mum quizzes me.

'How come you were late getting out today?' Dad asks me.

'Got detention,' I mumble, pulling open the rear car door.

My dad's eyes find mine as the September evening encroaches with a chill in the air.

'Detention on your first day?'

'Was no big deal.' I climb into the back seat and shut the door before my dad can say more. But he stands there, looking at me for a long moment, weighing me up, as if he's in the middle of a puzzle or an equation he can't find the answer to.

I've got my own puzzle going on. What is it with this world? I need to talk to someone else.

Someone with brains.

As New-Mum climbs in behind the wheel and my dad slides stiffly into the passenger seat I spot the New-Moth squeezing out of the main exit. He's hunched over, ashamed of either himself or the others in detention, but he looks singularly unhappy.

Which to me is a good sign.

New-Mum shifts in her seat as she pulls the seat belt around her shoulder.

'So tell me, what did you learn today?' she asks me.

My dad is sitting still and silent directly in front of me. I can almost hear his brain ticking over. Something has got him on edge and I can't resist adding to it.

'I learned that when a noose goes round a human neck, it very often, if not always, leads to death.'

New-Mum's face loses its smile.

I can see my dad tensing.

'That's ... interesting,' New-Mum eventually says and beams at me. Nothing can wipe that incessant smile off her face.

Well, we'll see about that, I think.

I watch New-Moth trudge past our car. He doesn't know it yet, but he's about to become my saviour.

BLURRED VISION

Train brakes have a very distinct odour. It's an acrid, pungent smell that bites at your nostrils, but whatever the Ape has done he has managed to bring the train screeching and whining to a halt.

Roughly two centimetres from flattening GG.

I can't believe it. GG survived falling off the side of a speeding train. He's standing there, looking battered but unbowed. Maybe he did float and land in a lovely GG heap of powdery cotton gentleness.

'Rev?' There's hope in the Ape's voice.

'It's him. It's GG!' I scream.

It takes us ten seconds to climb out through the broken window and walk round to the front of the train.

The Ape draws alongside me and then increases his stride, hurrying to meet GG. He's more excited than I am, forgetting all about his pain-wracked shoulder. He dips a great hand into the pocket of his giant black overcoat, thoroughly dried out now, but stinking of stale river water. I know what he's searching for.

'Hey!' he bellows at GG.

I join him. 'GG!'

'Hey!' The Ape's voice rises into the night.

GG waits silently for us which seems odd, but maybe he's injured and can barely walk?

The Ape is moving more quickly now, his hand back in his pocket. I'm right behind him, slipping and stumbling on the sleepers. GG watches us approach and then produces the most flamboyant gesture that only one boy in the universe could manage. He adopts a John Travolta pose from *Saturday Night Fever*, the iconic hand in the air, while the other dangles at his side, one knee bent and pointed, ready to take to the dance floor.

'You should be dancing,' he sings. I only know the song and the pose because GG came as John Travolta to a prom night and no one knew who he was until he commandeered the DJ's microphone to explain in great detail.

I dart past the Ape and reach GG before he does.

'OhmyGodohmyGod!' I squeal and scream at the same time. I doubt I form an actual word.

'*Vroom vroom*!' GG squeals in recognition.

The Ape lumbers forward and before he knows it GG, injuries not able to slow him down, has leaped into the air and landed in the Ape's arms. Again the Ape swallows the pain from his shoulder, or maybe he just doesn't notice it, he's so overjoyed.

'Oh, my magnificent monkey!' GG throws his arms round the Ape's neck and kisses him hard on the cheek. The Ape tries to arc his square head away, but GG is all over him, dotting kisses across his cheeks and forehead. 'It's you, it's really you!'

The Ape from before detention would have hurled GG away, probably under the wheels of the train, but now he holds on tight to his friend, pretending to put up with his kisses, to suffer and endure them, when we both know he is lapping up every second of them. He awkwardly reaches into his pocket and pulls out GG's shoe.

He doesn't say anything as he brings it up to show GG. He's kept it with him all this time, through the Black Moth attack, the near drowning in the Thames, through everything, and now he can return it.

But GG hesitates, his eyes falling to the shoe.

'You shouldn't have,' he jokes.

I don't understand the hesitation until I look at his feet. At his two pristine shoes. There isn't one missing, even though the Ape and I both know that he lost one of them when he was ripped from the side of the speeding train.

'And we were getting along so well,' GG sighs.

The Ape looks confused, but I already know what's happened.

It's pretty obvious when you think about it.

Billie's back.

New-Mum and Dad are getting ready to go out to dinner. They go out to dinner every night to the best Chinese restaurant in town. Sometimes I've gone with them; sometimes I've stayed behind. But they are very keen that I join them tonight.

'Crispy wontons.' New-Mum smiles as she pins her hair into a bun that reveals more of her delicate and pretty features.

My phone rings. 'Hold that thought,' I tell New-Mum and quickly disappear into my bedroom. New-Billie has called me, just like she said she would.

'Hey,' I answer, closing the bedroom door behind me,

'Don't be long,' New-Mum calls out, rapping on my door. But I ignore her.

'Hey to you too,' New-Billie says. 'So . . .'

'Yeah,' I say.

'It's not the Ape they're angry at,' she tells me. 'It's really not.'

'What then?' I ask. Outside my door I can hear my dad

161

asking New-Mum where his best shoes are. He does this every night before leaving for a Chinese meal.

'So where have you been hiding?' New-Billie asks me.

'Hiding?'

'What I mean is, how can you have stayed indoors all day long, over and over?'

'I didn't. I only just got here. Two weeks or so ago,' I say.

Another silence develops between us as New-Billie processes the information.

'Say that again,' she asks.

'I'm not from this world. And I know how that sounds.'

She laughs, but in surprise, not with cynicism. 'You actually sound like you mean it.'

'I do,' I summon as much honesty as I can when there's another hard rap on the door from New-Mum.

'Come on, we want to get a table.'

We always get a table, the restaurant, and even more so now that the restaurant's clientele seems to shrink every time I go there. There's always one less person, or even one less family. They are about the only changes to the mind-numbing repetition.

'I'm not lying,' I whisper to New-Billie. 'I swear to you. In another world we're best friends.'

Again New-Billie falls into a long deep silence. There's another harder rap on my bedroom door.

'I've got to go, can we talk later?' I ask New-Billie.

'If you're not lying, then yeah, we really do need to talk.'

'This is the truth,' I state. 'The absolute truth.'

I hear her suck in a breath. 'I dunno where you came from, but if there's a way back then show me.'

'I was pretty much out of it when I, uh . . . arrived.'

'Convenient,' she sighs.

'Not for me.'

'Call me later. I'll be up ...' New-Billie trails off. I'm about to hang up when she speaks again. 'Rev, I'm sorry you're here, no matter if you're telling me the truth or not.'

I need to know more, but New-Mum walks into my room with a big smile. She has bright red lipstick on and her even, near-white teeth look even brighter against the scarlet hue.

'Come on, we're starving.'

I look back at my phone but New-Billie has already hung up.

'Do we have to have Chinese every night?' I ask New-Mum.

But she just smiles. I slip my phone into my pocket and think about New-Billie. I think she likes me, maybe even wants to be friends with me.

It feels like I'm starting to win.

'Rev, I'm sorry.' Other-Johnson is back in my head which means he must be close by as well.

'You blew it,' I transmit to him. *'Didn't you?'*

He takes a long moment to respond.

'I tried,' he broadcasts. *'I tried my best to look like I loved her.'*

'What's that?' The Ape has heard something. I can't make out what it is at first, but then a faint humming comes down the line I'm squatting on. It vibrates very gently through me.

'But she figured it out,' Other-Johnson tells me. *'And she's mad as hell.'*

I can just picture Billie, broken all over again. The first time she imagined a reality where she was with Johnson and I blew that out of the water for her. This time she's got Johnson for real only in reality she hasn't so I make that two heartbreaking losses in quick succession. One is bad enough, but two?

164

The hum is turning into a vibration. The Ape drops GG who lands hard on the railway line. The Ape then rises to his full height, trying to peer into the distance, but the dark of night has enveloped us. We can't see more than a few metres in front of us.

'Where is she?' I ask Other-Johnson.

'The question is: where isn't she?' he repsonds.

Billie is going to be doubly angry. Twice now she has believed that Johnson was hers, and twice it's been a lie. Yet another echo in this world, history repeating itself and events flowing in mad circles round us, happening over and over, but in ever more transmuted ways. I wonder where the first ripple started. Was it with us? Or was there an original Rev out there somewhere who broke her best friend's heart? Maybe it was a simple thing, as easy as telling her that Johnson wasn't interested in her? And now that simple thing has sparked an emotional fire across worlds, igniting flames that melt, reshape and re-form the same moment over and over again.

The line is humming on both sides of the track now. The Ape steps over to the line parallel to the one I'm perched on and bends his ear so he can listen. He then clomps back to my line and bends and listens to that. Satisfied, he arches his broad back and squeezes his shoulder blades with a crack. He loves a war, which is a good thing, considering whatever's coming down the line.

'They're coming,' he says.

'Johnson,' I transmit.

'Yeah?' he replies.

'You put the Moth's face in my head, right?'

'Clever girl.'

'Where is he?'

165

'In the shopping centre.'

He means the giant spider-shaped construction that squats over the tunnel we were just in, seven or so miles back. Back where I now think that Johnson and Non-Ape lost their war.

'The Black Moths took him there,' Other-Johnson tells me. But his voice sounds weaker than before.

'You OK?' I ask him.

'I'm amazing,' he lies. *'Rev, listen to me, if you can – then get back in the train and run.'*

'I'm done running.'

Other-Johnson takes a long moment, and I'm sure he's in pain. The whine of the railway line is steadily increasing. *'This time's it for real,'* he tells me. *'Billie is coming to finish this.'*

'What's she done to you?' I ask.

'I was the starter,' he says quietly.

My breath catches in my throat. *'What did she do?'*

'Forget me. You can't fight her, you've got to hide.'

'I'm not going to fight her. I'm going to help her. Make her remember who she used to be.'

The railway track is singing.

The Ape works his shoulder, trying to make his arm as battle ready as he can. I don't want Billie hurting him for real this time. But what if she can't help herself? What if she's been totally consumed by the pure violent essence of the doppelganger blood?

'Rev.' Just that one word seems to take so much effort. Even thinking has become a struggle for him. I don't know how close he is, but his next words provide a chilling answer. *'She's here.'*

FORTUNATE COOKIES

Our Chinese food is served by a quiet waitress who looks frail and exhausted, despite the fact that we're the only three people in the restaurant. I remember this restaurant in my world and it's always packed. It sits above a clothes shop and in the empty world I almost died of pneumonia under the light from its first-floor window.

The food is actually pretty tasty, but my mind is doing cartwheels as I try to establish what the heck is really going on in this world. My dad has barely spoken a word since we left the school, but New-Mum more than makes up for it. If anything, she is becoming increasingly happier.

'Fortune cookie!' she exclaims, picking one from the plate the silent waitress hands us after the meal. She has done this every time I've accompanied them in the two weeks that I have been in this world.

"'Today it's up to you to create the peacefulness you long for,'" New-mum reads out, then sighs. 'Isn't that lovely?' She reads the saying again to herself, her lips

moving silently as she does. 'Open yours, Rev,' she encourages.

I crack open a cookie.

'A good way to happiness is to eat more Chinese food.'

New-Mum claps and laughs. 'I like that, that's funny.'

'Comedy gold,' I mumble. I'm finding it hard to keep up the pretence that everything is fine and wonderful. My dad is struggling too; he keeps snatching glances at me, clearly wrestling with something that bothers him.

New-Mum pushes the last fortune cookie towards my dad. 'Your turn.'

Dad snaps out of his anxiety and a broad smile replaces his taciturn mope as he pushes the fortune cookie back towards her. 'You do it – you love them.'

'It's yours.' She bats it back playfully.

'I insist.' His eyes light up as he gazes at a woman he thinks he loves. But it's not real. She's just an imitation. This is not where we're from.

Dad's shaken off his earlier frown and is enjoying the silly game. So much so that I reach over and smash my fist into the fortune cookie, shattering it and bringing the playfulness to an abrupt end.

Bits of fortune cookie are stuck to the bottom of my hand and I brush them off, flicking them on to the carpet, causing the waitress to hurry over with a hand-held carpet sweeper.

'Sorry,' I mutter to her as she squats to scrape the few crumbs into the sweeper.

New-Mum and Dad look at the smashed cookie lying in the middle of the table between them. It takes a long second for them to recover their earlier joy. I snatch up the saying written in lyrical italics on a small piece of white paper.

"'You're both insane,'" I say aloud, pretending that these are the words that were written in the cookie. Which completely blows my attempt to keep a lid on things.

The short drive home is carried out in silence. New-Mum drives and for once there is no sign of her hideous, overbearing upbeatness. My forehead is pressed against the window as I stare out at a town I know so well and yet don't know at all. A few people wander the high street, but unsurprisingly everything is done in silence, they are just going through the motions. Waiting til they can get to bed and go to sleep. The buzz of life is in short supply.

By the time we are back in our cramped little flat New-Mum has a headache. Dad gets her some pills and a glass of water.

'I'm going to my room,' I tell them and slip out of the lounge before they can say a word.

Somewhere in this flat or at Dad's office is the equation that somehow has the power to transport me out of here. It's my only hope of leaving this strange version of my world and getting back to my real life. I'm not going to look for it now, I'm going to wait until the flat is empty and I can sneak back and ransack the place. Dad will be out working and New-Mum has her waitressing job so at some stage I can engineer a fake illness and get the day off school. That's the sort of plan Reva Marsalis excels at.

I slump face first on my bed.

There's a light rap on my door and my dad enters

without being asked. I can feel him standing just in from the doorway for a moment, staring at my back.

'Tell me about detention.'

'Not much to tell.'

'Didn't you like school?'

'Does anyone?'

I feel him step towards my bed after quietly pulling the door shut.

'Reva.'

'Yeah?'

'It's important you like school.'

'No one really likes school, Dad.' I call him Dad because I think he will enjoy that. It'll make him think I'm buying everything he's selling.

'But it's also important that you are happy there.'

I don't reply.

'Are you listening?' he asks.

'I'm listening.' I turn round and he is actually standing closer than I realised. He's all but looming over me.

'If you're happy there, you'll be happy here.'

'Here?' Does he mean this new world?

'At home,' he clarifies.

There's something troubling behind his eyes, a desperation he is fighting to keep to himself.

'At home,' I repeat.

He nods quietly. 'Detention would suggest you weren't happy.'

The desperation is in his voice too, and for a second I feel sorry for him.

'Happiness is the key.' He smiles, but it's not a proper smile, it's a forced grimace. 'The key to everything.'

I nod, but only for his sake. 'You should tell everyone in town that.'

He falters, screws his eyes up in thought.

'You have seen them, haven't you?' I push. 'No one's happy.'

My dad rubs his temple. 'They are what they are,' he eventually says. 'And it's not about them, this is about you. You, me and Mum.'

'Being happy,' I state.

He nods and smiles again. 'Now you're getting it.'

'Can I ask a question?' Which I've long thought was a weird thing to say. Asking a question so you can ask a question.

My dad nods.

'Where are we?'

His eyes find mine and he tries to look as honest as he can manage.

'Home.'

'But I know there are loads of homes. I've seen four of them now.'

'This is our home.' He is gentle but there's steel there too. 'This is where you and me and Mum live. Where we're happy.' He reaches down and ruffles my pink hair. 'You saved me and, because you saved me, you saved this. Us. You're my little hero, Rev.'

Delusion is a wonderful thing and for a moment I'd love to give in. It would be so easy to sink into this life and find whatever misguided happiness he thinks is here for us. But that's not the way Reva rolls. I smile because a little bit of ingratiation never hurt anyone with a plan to get out of Dodge. 'You're my hero too, Dad.'

He walks to the door and opens it. But then he stops

and turns back to me. 'The fortune cookie was right.' He beams. 'A good way to happiness is to eat more Chinese food.'

Though a much better way is to find a door out of here, *I think.*

I wait until I'm sure my 'parents' are asleep next door before calling New-Billie back. She answers on the second ring, as if she'd been on high alert waiting for my call.

'Hey,' *she says. It's about two in the morning and she sounds tired.*

'Tell me about this world.'

'You must have figured it out,' *she tells me.*

'Figure it out for me. I was never top of the class in any subject.'

'We're all dead.'

Which makes me sit up straight. 'What?'

New-Billie's bed creaks as I hear her shift positions. 'I mean, not really dead.'

'Like zombies then?'

'Zombies?' *She laughs and I hear the same laughter my Billie had.*

'It's a living death. We're dead in so many ways that isn't actually death but just feels like it.'

'I'm listening,' *I say.*

'This is it, Rev. This is all there is. Every day is the same. Every single day. But you don't wake up as if it's a new day; you wake up knowing it's going to be the same day. And nothing you can do will change it or make any real difference. We all go through the motions because the motions are all we have. Can you imagine what that feels* *like? Never going forward, no making plans, no going anywhere – ever. There's no escape from this.'*

'There's always a way,' I tell her. 'I came from somewhere else.'

'But you don't know how that happened, so it's of no practical help. And by the way you got me hugely excited for a moment.'

'Sorry.'

'Actually, I enjoyed it. Excitement is rare here.' She laughs but it's laced with despair.

'How about we meet tomorrow?' I ask her. 'I mean, later today.'

'Of course we'll meet,' she says.

'Yeah, just you and me though.'

'It'll happen.'

'I was just making sure—'

'We will meet, Rev. That will absolutely happen. And more times than you can imagine.' Her voice takes on a weird deep tone. 'But only until one of us can't take it any more. And we decide to end it.'

I think of Mr Balder and the dwindling number of Chinese restaurant guests.

Her voice fractures. 'Welcome to Suicide World.'

They're coming down the track.

Fast.

The rumble is almost upon us. The fake GG is lying on the railway line and the fall may have broken his spine.

'Might need a little handy wandy,' he breathes through his agony. But I ignore him because I doubt he even exists. Presenting a living, breathing GG to us like that was the cruellest of the cruel.

'Rev!' Other-Johnson is back in my head. *'Get back on the train!'*

'And go where exactly?'

'Home!'

I grab the Ape's arm. 'We've got to go.'

The Ape stands rock and stock-still. 'I got this.'

The lines are whining at a pitch a dog would howl at.

'We end it now,' he tells me.

And then out of the gloom they come. Lucas upon Lucas,

blurring on the spot as they walk, moonlight bouncing off their talons.

'They're not real,' I tell myself. 'Not real. Don't exist.'

The Ape watches the Lucas-blurs backing up behind each other, the ones standing on the railway lines shimmering so fast the lines are juddering.

'Make me believe they're not there.' I transmit to Other-Johnson. *'The more I buy it, the more real they become.'*

'Wait!' Other-Johnson says; it's like he's using the last of his strength just so we can have this conversation.

The Lucas-blurs are forming a circle around us, the railway lines vibrating so hard they're coming loose from their moorings.

'Rev, you should've run.' There's hopelessness in his voice.

The railway lines are practically jumping from their beds, the shale scattered between them rising into the air.

Other-Johnson climbs back into my head.

'They're not there, they're not there,' he says over and over, a hypnotist on full power. The Lucas-blurs are starting to blink out of existence. All around us they pop, leaving holes in the air.

'Where they going? We got a fight to have.' The Ape watches the Lucas-blurs disappearing and he looks faintly annoyed. 'I had that.'

'Johnson it's working!?'

'Yeah, now listen carefully—' His sentence ends abruptly mid-flow.

'Johnson?' I strain to hear him in my head. Nothing comes back. *'Johnson, you there?'* I wait, holding my breath.

The train horn hoots for no logical reason. The doors

open and shut, over and over. Hissing into the night air while the horn hoots again and the lights in the carriage flash on and off . . .

The air moves, or ripples, and suddenly Other-Johnson is flying out of the darkness straight for me. He is unconscious and he is upon me before I can react. We go rolling into a heap before slipping down the slight incline of the train embankment.

'I believe this belongs to you.' Billie emerges a few seconds after hurling Other-Johnson at me. She is calm but raging underneath and I can hear a quiver to her voice. The Ape readies himself, but this time I don't think she's going to be messing with our heads. She's got the power to eviscerate us. The only upside is that it probably won't take long. Swiftness will be her only mercy.

New-Mum and Dad had driven me to school and, just like yesterday, I'd arrived at least half an hour early. New-Mum had another present for me.

'I raided my savings account,' she told me, handing over a large leather schoolbag. Hand-stitched, real leather, and when I opened it there was a note inside:

Have a great day every day, love Mum.

The kindness in the words caught me off guard and I felt a lump form at the back of my throat. I looked up and she had tears in her eyes, despite the fact that she was smiling widely, a full toothed beam. She nodded rather than spoke, then squeezed my hand.

'Like it?' my dad asked.

'Wow,' I managed to mumble. 'Just wow.' I'd decided to play the Happy Game to string them along. But that note – it was killing me. I wasn't her daughter, but for a second I may as well have been.

'I knew you'd love it,' she said.

177

I climbed out of the car and slung the schoolbag over my shoulder; it smelled new and leathery. Just like yesterday the morning was cold, but I knew it would soon develop into a warm September day, not too hot, not too cold, just perfect. Every day here has exactly the same weather. I heard New-Mum clapping behind the steering wheel and was about to ask her why when my dad stepped out of the car and drew close to me, keeping his voice low. 'Happiness is more Chinese food,' he whispered.

Our eyes met and that pain was back behind his eyes again. Lurking deep inside him, but rising, always rising, until it was ready to pour from him. He blinked a few times, fighting back the swell of desperation.

New-Mum climbed from the car and clapped again. 'The schoolbag suits you,' she said. Then she pulled out her mobile phone and made me pose while she took as many photos as she could.

'Amazing. Gorgeous. Lovely,' she mumbled to herself, over and over, after checking every photo she'd taken of me.

A thirteen-year-old with his hands shoved deep into his pockets appeared by the car, his head bowed as he kicked lamely at a small stone. I could tell he didn't want to be here either.

'Try and stay out of detention,' Dad joked.

'We'll be waiting right here for you,' New-Mum sang and took one last photo of me with my dad while I stood, feeling the weight of the schoolbag trying to drag me down to who knew where.

The first person I wanted to find as soon as I got into school was the New-Moth. I really wanted to see New-Billie or

New-Johnson, but I also wanted to give them hope; cast-iron, concrete, all of those things, hope. And excitement. I wanted to present New-Billie with something that would light up her soul. And I had to do it quick. If she did really think of this world as some suicidal earth, then the thought of ending it all was already boring deep into her. Right now no one can help me as much as New-Moth with his big, giant space brain.

My biggest fear though is that New-Mum's simple note hit me hard emotionally. The longer I stay here, the more she'll become attached to me. I don't want to break any parent's heart and with New-Mum being so mentally fragile and delicate I know I'm going to hate myself for taking away the one thing she adores beyond anything else. But also there's a clawing belief growing inside me that I'm on my last legs. I can't keep going from world to world, I don't have the energy. So I'm going to give it one last superhuman effort and I'll create merry hell if I have to, but I need to find the New-Moth.

Miss Hardacre is behind her perspex window and isn't expecting me to yank open the door to the reception room and join her.

'What on earth?' she exclaims.

'Gimme the register.'

'Do you mind?' she says, collecting herself.

'Is that it?' I grab what I think might be a school register, archaic and handwritten. I know it's all on computer as well, but the Miss Hardacre from my world didn't like to move with the times, so hopefully it's the same here. She still insisted that the schoolteachers sign in the students before she then had children from each class deliver the morning registration forms to her.

This Miss Hardacre is no different.

She tries to drag the attendance records from me, but I turn my back on her, shielding myself as I rifle through the names of the pupils to find where New-Moth will be. The sooner I get talking to him the better. He's in a physics class right now and I'm ready to burst in there and add a little of my own chaos theory to that lesson. I swivel and shove the registration book back into Miss Hardacre's chest.

'Must be quiet without Mr Balder.' My eyes meet hers and I watch her flinch.

'Get out,' she says quietly.

'I'm going,' I tell her. But I mean I'm going for good. 'And when I do I'll leave a map.'

Miss Hardacre doesn't respond.

'You listening? I'm going to find a way out of here.'

I can see I'm not going to get much of a response so I head for the door.

'You think you're the first?' Her fractured voice stops me dead.

I turn. Miss Hardacre has found some semblance of strength as she gazes hard at me.

'You think others haven't tried to leave?' She clearly knows more than I've given her credit for. 'There is only one way out of here. And Mr Balder – he took it. So don't come here and think we have all just given up like weak, lost people. But until someone finds a way there's nothing to do but get through the days until . . .' She trails off.

The warning tone in her voice should fill me with a chill, scare me half to death, but I know she's wrong. There will be a way because, if there's one thing I've learned, there is always – always – a way. I don't look back at Miss Hardacre as I head for the physics block.

I'm not trapped here.

I can't be.

New-Moth will make sure of that.

WATERBOARDING THE TRAIN

Her long slender limbs are as unmistakable as her rage.

'Billie,' I say in a dull monotone. It's a thud of a word that slumps and dies in a heap between us. I'm up on my feet and back on the railway line, but Other-Johnson still lies unconscious at the bottom of the incline.

'You keep on doing it to me, don't you?' she says.

'Haven't you noticed that everything we do keeps repeating?' I tell her.

The Ape grips GG's pointy-tipped shoe like a dagger. He takes my arm and manoeuvres himself in front of me, protecting me from Billie.

'That's going to help,' Billie smirks.

'Make your move.' The Ape is ready for war.

'I'll cut you open for real this time, Ape.'

'I've definitely broken my back,' GG whimpers.

'Shut up.' Billie doesn't even blink as the fake GG disappears into nothingness. She's growing accustomed to her outrageous power, turning it on and off with barely a thought.

'I knew it was too good to be true,' Billie tells me. 'It

felt like Johnson, it spoke like him, obviously looked like him, but when you can make up reality then you sure as hell know what's real and what isn't.'

I step forward, drawing level with the Ape. 'Billie, I can get us all home, and then – well, then – you and me can have it out. You can do whatever you want to me, just let me get the others safe.'

'You're so heroic, Rev. So caring and wonderful,' she spits. 'It must be amazing to be as good as you are. Really, we should bow down in your saintly presence.' She scowls. 'I might actually throw up if you carry on like that.'

'What did you do to Other-Johnson?' I'm peering out from behind the Ape. Not because I'm scared, but because every time I try and step forward he sticks out his sore arm and blocks my progress.

'Stay behind me,' he warns.

Billie's smirk shines through the darkness. 'Oaf.'

'What are you going to do, Billie?' I feint one way, confuse the Ape and emerge on his other side. There's no way I want her to think I'm hiding from her. 'You really going to kill us?'

'It's on my agenda.'

'You think I'm going to let that happen?'

'I'm definitely going to vomit.' She is raging under her faux calm. I know her well enough to be able to see what she's really about.

'How though? Are you going to create a thousand Moths? A million Lucases? Only I don't believe in them. And if I don't believe then they can't touch me.'

'I don't need them,' she replies. Her smirk is captured in the glow from the train carriage. She looks like an evil pumpkin head.

'This is not you,' I tell her. 'Not the real you.'

Billie allows a talon to slip from her fingertip. She holds it up in front of her face and I can see her black eyes either side of it. They're smiling eyes. Insane eyes. I'm going to try and reach her, break down her defences and find the human hidden behind the mutation. If I can keep her talking, I can hopefully reach past her misguided carapace of violence and animosity. She's clearly in the grip of something ugly and vindictive and it's not her fault. She stares solely at me, eyes boring into my brain.

'Let's do this,' she says.

It happens somewhere between the start of a second and the end of that same second. That's how quick the Ape moves. He lurches forward and snaps Billie's taloned finger straight back towards her.

'Shut up!' he tells her.

Billie's taloned finger is driven straight back into her throat before she can register the outrageousness of the Ape's daring. He grips her hand in his huge paw and holds it in her throat until her life seeps away and she sinks to the ground, landing softly in a clump of dandelions and grass. The Ape doesn't bat an eyelid as he turns back to me.

I can barely move I'm so numb.

'You killed her.'

'I'll heal her later,' he tells me.

'No ... You ... You killed her. That's my best friend!' I shout at him. 'I was going to talk to her, reach out to her.'

'Got there first.' The Ape marches over the railway lines to collect Other-Johnson.

'Wait, I'm talking.'

Even with an aching shoulder, he drags Other-Johnson's

body back past me until he's at the train doors again. He presses the button to open them and this time, without Billie's powers to make us believe they were locked, they open easily. He hefts Other-Johnson into the carriage.

'Hey!' I yell after him, but then drop to my knees beside Billie. Her hand is still bunched against her throat, the talon driven almost clean through to the nape of her neck. Her dead eyes stare up at me.

'Billie,' I whisper. 'Billie ...' I don't know why I'm talking to her. I know she's dead.

'Don't worry ... We can make this better. Cure you. We can. We can change everything back. The other you, she'll do it, I promise you.'

'Chuck her in with the others,' the Ape calls back. 'I'll drive us home.'

The Ape punches the CLOSE button on the carriage door containing Other-Johnson, Carrie, Evil-GG and Non-Lucas then marches back to me. I know Billie may well have eviscerated me and, as ever, the Ape came to my rescue, but watching her die in front of my eyes has left a residue of hopelessness. Not just about her, but about how this world has changed so much about us in such a short amount of time. The Ape can kill without blinking and I wonder if we're actually fit to go back home. Who knows what we have all turned into?

'Tickets, please,' he says, picking Billie up by the shoulders and fireman-lifting her towards the open carriage door. He lets her slump in a heap on the floor and then bangs the CLOSE button, shutting the dead Billie inside.

'Want to ride up front?' the Ape asks me as he makes his way to the driver's cabin.

'Can you give me a minute?' I ask him wearily.

185

'For what?.'

'For whatever . . .' I tell him. 'I just need a minute.'

'Well, I really don't blame you.'

The voice emerges from the darkness. It's unmistakable. It's GG.

And he staggers weakly towards us, and at first, because of the darkness around us, I think I'm imagining things, but as he draws closer I see it's him. His right arm hangs loose, probably broken, and he drags what looks like a shattered left leg behind him. His beautiful face is cut and scratched and one of his eyes is black, blue and broken-veined. Bloodstains have dried on his clothes and he's probably closer to death than life.

But he's still GG.

'I told you I float,' he says in a whispery version of his singsong voice.

'GG?' I ask stupidly.

'I saw the lights, I heard the sounds and I came a-limping . . .' He grins, revealing a mouthful of broken, jagged teeth.

I'm so stunned to see him that again I don't have time to react as the Ape attacks him.

'What, no, wait!' I cry.

GG's eyes widen as the Ape launches himself bodily at him. The Ape thinks it's another copy and GG collapses under the weight of the Ape's massive body, landing with a shrill, agonised squeal and a crunch of already dislocated and broken bones.

'AAAAGGGHHHHHH!' he screams as the Ape grabs his throat and gets ready to land a meaty fist.

'I got him!'

186

I throw myself at the Ape's fist, lassoing both hands and arms round his thick wrist to try and stop him punching the poor defenceless GG.

'It's him, it's him!' I shout.

'It's me, it's me!' GG echoes.

'It's not, it's not!' The Ape tries to twist away from my grip and I slip and slide as his brute power overwhelms me.

The huge fist is a centimetre away from mashing GG's face when I see his shoe-less foot. 'No shoe! No shoe!' I scream.

The Ape's fist stops, almost completely blotting out GG's fine if battered aqualine features. The Ape looks back at GG's swollen and distended foot. That's missing a shoe. GG moves his head a little and his blackened bruised eye blinks a little GG stardust at the Ape.

'Kiss me, Hardy.'

GG is back.

How many times have you walked past a fire alarm and wanted to set it off? To smash the little plastic square and press the button? Well, let me tell you, it feels good. Even though I scraped my knuckles punching its little face in. But I was in that sort of mindset.

The alarm went off, screeching throughout the school, and finally – finally – there was movement. Classroom doors were flung open, teachers stood in doorways and counted the schoolkids out; some did it vocally, some did it silently but there was definitely a flurry of movement.

I waited, pressed flat up against a wall that would usually display the artistic endeavour and achievement of the art classes. But this wall was bare. No one had drawn or painted a thing, it seems. Herds of the disaffected and disillusioned shouldered past me as I tried my best to spot the New-Moth. He's not tall and as the door to the physics block opened I almost missed him carefully and quietly making his way to the playing field.

188

I moved fast, cutting through the oncoming tide, getting butted and jostled, so much so that I heard my new blazer rip and tear as it caught on the metal buckle of someone's satchel. I didn't care because I needed to get to the New-Moth while he was just a face among hundreds. It felt like I was back on the cobbled town square in the evil world. The Ape, GG and I were ambushed there and almost died for about the hundredth time until Rev Two's mum rode to our rescue. The memory still haunts me because Rev Two's mum will never know that her daughter died in vain, and all because of my dad the liar.

New-Moth is swept up in the orderly swarm and is trying to follow the physics teacher, Mrs Collins, a short woman in her thirties with a large nose, who holds her arm straight up in the air while gripping a white hanky and telling her class to follow the hanky. It looks like she's used the hanky recently and most of the class following her share a mutual grimace. I home in on New-Moth, shoving harder and faster to get to him. I don't care that I get glared at. I burrow through the swell and before he knows what's happening I've grabbed his arm and started marching him backwards.

'Hey, what are you doing?'

'Shut up!' I'm in no mood to stop and explain as I keep ramming him back through the crowd.

'Hey, wait,' he says trying to twist his arm out of my grip. But he'll never break that grip, not today.

'I need you,' I whisper at him.

'Excuse me?'

'I want you.' My eyes meet his as they widen behind his glasses.

'You-you what?'

The Moth has never really been popular with girls and I can already detect the same abject failure to attract the opposite sex in this Moth which is something that's going to work hugely in my favour.

'Come with me.' I'm still pushing him back against the tide and he's getting buffeted by everyone but he doesn't care because all he can think is that he's finally got a date with a girl.

'OK,' he whispers. 'OK.' He grins what he probably thinks is a suave and sophisticated smile, but his glasses slip down his nose and he looks toothy and myopic at the same time.

'Good. We don't have much time.' I think we've got until they read out the fabled register and tick off all our names to do this. When we don't answer, they may even think we burned to death in the non-existent fire. But who would care? These people are living their lives just waiting to die at some point. I've at least figured that much out.

The New-Moth hurries to keep up with me as we head into the physics block and slam the door behind us. I turn to start explaining everything when the Moth launches himself at me. Puckered lips first.

'I've been dreaming of something like this,' he says as he tries to plant a kiss on my big fat full lips.

'What the hell?' I duck and the Moth ends up kissing the door.

He turns, looks back at me, his brilliant space brain unable to compute. 'You said we don't have much time.'

'I didn't mean for that!' I tell him.

'No?' His brow furrows, creasing in disappointment.

190

'I get it. Yeah. I see what you're doing. Making fun of the Moth. Lonely old Moth, easy victim, easy target, yeah, thank you, you've had your laugh – goodbye.' He makes for the door, but I get back in front of him and grip both his biceps, forcing him to look at me.

'We're getting out of here,' I say through gritted teeth.

Somewhere in the main body of the school someone has found the fire alarm and switched it off and the howl dies away, leaving only silence.

'You mean school?' he asks.

'I mean this world,' I tell him.

The New-Moth laughs. Which surprises me.

'Don't laugh, I know a way.'

He shakes my hands from his biceps. 'Yeah, sure you do.'

'Listen to me, my dad is a scientist,' I tell him as earnestly as I can. 'He's got a formula.'

'Reva. It is Reva, isn't it?'

I nod.

'Well, Reva, you need to know there is no escape. D'you think people haven't tried to figure a way out?' Which are pretty much the words the school receptionist uttered. Does everyone think the same thing? I presume they must do if so many of them give up and end their lives.

The New-Moth almost looks sorry for me. There's pity in his eyes. 'This would've been so much easier if you had just wanted to kiss me.'

I'm not giving up. I can't allow the apathy and torpor to claim me. I grab him by the shoulders.

'There's a formula that my dad worked out and, if I can find it for you, then you can put it to work, rearrange the fabric of reality with it, open a portal. I know you can.' I

am not going to let this go, I refuse to. 'We'll grab whoever wants to leave and we all go, out of this hell.'

The New-Moth weighs me up.

'Meet me tonight,' he says eventually. 'You show me yours, I'll show you mine.' It's a smart joke considering, but in that quip is a sense of the absolute. This New-Moth knows something I don't.

WE ALL FALL DOWN

'I knew you'd be back for me. Knew it. No one can live without a little GG in their lives. Where's the magic in that? I touch everyone I meet. Not physically, not like that – obvs – but I do touch. I am the magic.'

GG is driving the train back in the direction of the tunnel where Johnson and Non-Ape were fighting the Black Moths. His voice is cutting in and out of the tannoy system while I stand guard over the dead Billie. I mean, she could be faking that as well. But so far she hasn't moved a muscle.

'We tried to find you,' I tell him. 'We searched but only found a shoe.'

'And what a shoe,' he declares proudly.

'We called out. I even had Other-Johnson try and find you telepathically.'

'When I floated away, I did hit my head rather hard on the side of the train. Knocked me clean into the land of slumber.'

Which could explain why Other-Johnson couldn't scan for him. Maybe his powers only work on the conscious.

'Oh, the dreams I had.' GG's trying his best, but I know he's hurting. The Ape and I could barely wedge him into the driver's seat without his broken flappy arm getting in the way. I made a makeshift sling to put his arm in, but he grew alarmed that it didn't match the colours of the rest of his frayed and filthy outfit. 'In one dream I was riding on the back of a Black Moth, inspecting my kingdom. I was waving a silk monogrammed hanky at faces crowding the streets. Trouble is I got so taken by waving the hanky, making sure I didn't miss flapping it at one single person that I ended up breaking my arm. That's how hard I was waving. But that's me all over. Lord Eager of Eagerland.'

It's good to hear his voice. But I also know that when Johnson, the Ape and I went looking for GG along the railway track we never ventured this far. We found his shoe over ten miles further back down the line. Which would suggest that GG couldn't have been unconscious. Or if he had been then he was sleepwalking along the track. I don't know how he ended up where he did – and more incredibly how he just emerged from the darkness like he did. It's too weirdly coincidental.

The Ape barges through the interconnecting doors of the train.

'Everyone's still dead.' He slumps in a seat. 'Couldn't heal any of them.'

The Ape still believes that he can perform miracles. 'Johnson is dead as well.'

But I'd already guessed that because I checked Other-Johnson's body and blood was pooling around his chest and it looked like Billie may have stuck a talon clean through his heart.

'Got to get this healing thing working.' The Ape takes a seat beside me, inadvertently crushing me up against the window. He checks his healing hand and then pokes a finger at my forehead. 'Anything?'

I can't bring myself to respond. The images of death and dead friends filling the carriage are overpowering.

He jabs his finger repeatedly at my forehead, trying to reignite his non-existent healing power.

'Anything?'

'Please stop,' I say gently, my voice barely above a whisper.

'Anything?'

'Seriously. . .' I know he thinks we're in some big video game where people die and then spring back to life – maybe he has a point – but he's not seeing the reality of it. The harsh and stark horror of bodies piling up all around us.

'Anything?'

'Ape, please.' My voice catches in the back of my throat. Death has never stopped coming for us. From the first moment that Lucas hanged himself I have had to kill. To extinguish life, alien life, doppelganger life, call it what you will, and I never quite took it in because to do so would have stopped me in my tracks. We had to keep running and fighting and there was never much time to allow that stark harshness to bed in. But seeing Billie and Other-Johnson without life – I realise it has bedded in: it's in my DNA, in all our DNAs now. I want more than ever for an end to this, to make everything right and never, ever encounter death again.

Thankfully GG's voice interrupts the Ape's assault on my head.

'How come there's another train?' He's not expecting a response. 'And where did it come from?' He adopts an eerie ghost voice. 'Answers tonight at eleven.' Then he executes a horror-movie laugh. 'If you're still alive by then.'

GG is evidently staying as far from reality as he possibly can. And who can blame him?

I watch the Ape listening to GG and see his mouth curl up at the edges. He's smiling at GG and I know he's glad that he's back. On GG's part he was only too happy to let the Ape shove his shoe back on to his foot. GG didn't say one camp word about the fashion disaster of being without a matching pair of shoes for so long. He was just too happy.

'Hello, hello, hello,' GG chirrups into the tannoy. 'The shopping centre is on your left. And thank the Lord for that because I need some serious retail therapy.'

The Ape and I glance out of the window and see the bright lights of the shopping centre radiating through the darkness. Underneath is the tunnel where a Black Moth battle may or may not still be raging, but the train switches tracks and heads towards the tiny station that is roughly two miles from where we'd ideally like to be. Which means another trek if we're going to find the Moth and hook up with Johnson and Non-Ape. But it also means we can do it stealthily, that with any luck we can get in and out without detection. The Moth won't have his wheelchair but Non-Ape, if he's still alive, can carry him.

The train slows to a stop and the station is silent and still. Shrill beeps signal that we can open the automatic doors. But as I do I see a person in the shadows, sitting on one of the blue metal mesh benches, way down at the bottom of

196

the platform. The shadows cast from the small brick railway office obscure the figure, but I've been here before and I know exactly who it is.

'Wait here,' I tell the Ape and leap off the train and walk as quickly as I can towards the figure. As I approach, he leans forward and my dad sits there, smiling, handsome, well-groomed, with shiny shoes and a dark grey pinstripe suit. It's another apparition. And another repeat of something that happened before.

'Rev,' he says quietly.

'Dad,' I breathe.

'You're meant to be in hurry,' he says with a dry smile.

'My friends need me.'

'I need you.' He leans further forward and his handsome features and soft eyes beguile. 'And you need me.'

'I'm working on it, Dad, promise you.'

'If the other Rev finds me . . .' he says.

I am anything but ready to hurry and I sit down beside him. Slump would be a better word. I want to reach out and touch him, but I'm scared that if I do he'll disappear and the illusion will crumble away. I want to be able to smell his aftershave, to 'feel' his presence, just for a second, just for old times' sake, and for the missing years when I never had this opportunity.

'Dad?' I ask.

'You really need to get moving,' he says with more urgency.

'I'm tired. I hurt all over. I don't know how long I can keep going.' It's the first time I've come close to admitting defeat. But I'm not sure I've got anything left in me.

'And you're Reva, little Rev, and it's almost over. I promise you.' My dad looks like he wants to reach out and touch me, but I know he can't. 'All you've got to do is get here,' he says, and starts to fade out.

'Dad!' I shout.

His image lingers.

'How can you do this? Talk to me like this? Contact me?'

My dad looks quietly at me, semi there, semi not there.

People in the world I know and grew up in don't possess any sort of powers or abilities. But I've got some psychic thing going on here. 'I can sense danger and I can see you even though you're not there . . . what does that mean?' I ask him, desperate for an answer.

My dad starts to fade away. 'Dad, please!'

But he's gone and all that's left is the night.

The train horn sounds twice and . . .

. . . I sit up suddenly. I'm back on the train and I must have fallen asleep, with my face crushed up against the Ape's shoulder. I have been drooling and there's a wet stain on his T-shirt.

'Sick,' the Ape says, trying to brush away the damp patch.

My dad came to me in a dream before, another repeated moment to drive me crazy. I'm beginning to get an ominous feeling that I'll never be able to break this insane cycle of recurring events.

We pull into the station, again eerily silent, but this time there is no dad sitting waiting for me. I sit upright and gather myself.

'Let's find the Moth.'

The Ape clambers from his seat and stands and stretches his battered body. He winces because his ribs ache a whole lot more than he's ever let on.

'Once more unto the breach,' GG's voice sing-songs across the tannoy.

We're going to make a fine trio. Me, exhausted, the Ape with his broken ribs, sore shoulder and GG with his arm in a horrifically mismatched sling.

But that's never stopped us before.

THE APE ON THE EDGE OF TOWN

Getting out of the flat proves easier than I thought.

'Mum, I'm not going for Chinese tonight. I'm meeting a boy.'

It's all part of my happiness plan and New-Mum is all over this, grinning and squealing and clapping.

'Someone's got a boyfriend,' she sings, pinning her hair up as Dad waltzes past, looking for his shoes.

'What's that?' he says.

'Rev's got a boyfriend.'

'I'm only meeting him.' I pretend to look bashful.

'Who is he?'

'This kid Timothy asked me out. He's sweet.'

'Sweet. Did you hear that? Aw ...' New-Mum is excited to say the least. She claps her hands again. 'You'd better have a bath first.'

My dad is less enthusiastic and I know he doesn't fully trust me.

New-Mum picks up his missing shoes. 'Got them!' she sings.

He stares at me and I can see that he's curious. 'So that happened quickly,' he says.

'All the best love stories do,' I chirp back. He can be as suspicious as he wants, all I care about is finding his formula.

New-Moth meets me at the rec, a scrap of land that is all things to all people. From a pre-schoolers' rubberised playground to dingy, graffitied public toilets for drug pushers and users. There are fields where people play sport or throw sticks for their dogs, sometimes at the same time, which causes all manner of ill feeling – and head injuries. But this rec is deserted and only two of the tall street lights that illuminate the meandering pathway are working. Under one of them stands the New-Moth. I wonder if he's planning to try and kiss me again.

'Hey there,' he says in a cool, heroic Johnson way that fails miserably. He's wearing a leather jacket that doesn't suit him and jeans that billow rather than cling. On his feet are bright white trainers and he's brushed his hair back and tried to apply hair gel to make it stick up like GG's quiff. He's also swapped his glasses for contact lenses, but sadly none of what he's done has made him any more attractive. All it really does is highlight all the faults he had in the first place.

'Hey,' I smile. I'm wearing more new clothes given to me by New-Mum. Black T-shirt, hipster jeans and a three-quarter-length black donkey jacket. I have a wardrobe packed with new stuff, it's about the only good thing in this world.

'Hey,' he repeats and I realise he's already run out of cool words. He clears his throat. 'Anyway, shall we?' He does some sort of half-bow and sweep of his arm like he's now a knight in shining armour and I step past him. 'After you, m'lady.'

I think he's trying all manner of what he thinks are cool or attractive male stereotypes in the vain hope that I will fall for one of them.

'Smoke?' He offers me a cigarette from a brand-new packet.

'I don't,' I tell him.

'Me neither,' he says and immediately tosses them into the nearest bin.

We follow the serpentine pathway through the rec until we cross a small bridge that spans the skinny, dribbling river that simpers its way through the middle of town. It's the same river that was frozen over and somehow turned out to be about three metres deep once. As we cross the bridge, the New-Moth clumsily slips his hand into mine.

'What are you doing?' I ask. 'This isn't a date.'

'Yeah ... I know that.'

'So why hold my hand?' I don't like having to keep him at bay in such a cold way, but there's too much at stake here.

'I, uh, I ... I don't know.' He lets my hand drop and I can feel him retreating into himself. 'Sorry.'

The street lamps bounce off his bulging forehead, revealed in all its glory now that he has a stiff quiff. I can smell some sort of middle-aged aftershave on him and I quickly grab his hand and together we take proud strides towards the north side of town. On the way the New-Moth describes the hideous world we are trapped in. I listen, never once interrupting because I want to hear everything. The more the New-Moth talks, the more confident he becomes.

'Every day is the same. Over and over. It's pretty much the exact same day. We don't get any older, or any cleverer or even go anywhere. There's no ambition; there's no dreaming,

there are no magical, inspired thoughts that light up anyone's face. No hope. No future. Just this. Played out again and again. You have any idea what it feels like not to move forward? It's a killer. It kills you slowly though. Some people give up, like Mr Balder, but if you do that, you're saying there is no chance at all. But the sad truth is that everyone will give in one day, because that's the only thing you have any power over. So people go through the motions until they can't take it any more.' The New-Moth hesitates and then offers a fractured grin. 'Not the best fairy tale you ever heard, is it?'

'Is it the same for everyone here?'

He nods. 'Until they check out.' He grimaces. 'One day this world will be empty.'

I tighten my grip on his hand and we keep walking in silence as we head past a row of Victorian two-up, two-downs, cramped together as if there's safety in numbers. It's only now that I can feel the fear and despair that lurk within every brick and blade of grass.

'I think my dad is a part of this,' I tell the New-Moth. 'After twelve years away, he's gone crazy. We could gather everyone and march on his flat. Force him to send us all home.'

'I did wonder where you'd come from. Everyone said that you'd just been home-schooled until now.'

'My dad probably started that rumour,' I say.

The New-Moth muses for a moment. We are now beyond the street of Victorian houses and emerge on to the main road that leads out of town. 'If your dad has a magic formula, then won't there be thousands of your dads in thousands of other worlds with the same formula?'

'I guess so,' I reply. 'I mean the empty world had a formula, and I think the doppelganger world did as well.'

'So where are they all? How come it's only one version of your dad who appears to be doing this? And why?'

I'm starting to like this Moth, despite his clumsy attempts to look cool and sexy. He speaks with a gentle wryness, but everything he says is honest and thoughtful. I doubt he ever lies which sets him on a pedestal in my view.

'We're here.' He stops suddenly.

As far as I can tell, the 'here' isn't really anywhere. We're halfway down the road and all I can see is it stretching into the darkness of the evening, being swallowed whole by the gloom. There are no street lamps to light the way.

'This is "here"?' I ask the New-Moth.

'This is here,' he echoes.

I peer into the dimness, trying to make out more of what lies beyond the town, but it's almost impossible.

'I'm not seeing anything,' I tell him.

'Nothing to see,' he replies.

I go to step forward, but the New-Moth whips out a hand and drags me back. 'Nothing is nothing, Reva.'

My shoulders tingle, but I can't see where the problem or the danger lies. Until the New-Moth points to the sky. It's littered with sparkling stars.

'See those stars?' he asks.

I nod.

'Look how it all stops.' He points to the dark maw of space way above us and I see he's right; it suddenly comes to a lurching halt. It becomes nothing.

'This is as far as we go,' he says. 'This town is all there is. No way in, no way out. It just exists.'

'So if I take a step . . . ?'

'You can't take a step into nothingness.'

204

I'm not smart enough to understand that but I'll take the New-Moth's word for it.

'It's not a world we live in, Rev, this place – it's just a town. There's nothing beyond it, otherwise don't you think we'd all be out of here?'

'How's that possible?'

'This – all of this – is all there is,' he says calmly, matter-of-factly. He has clearly grown used to the horrible truth. 'The shops, the restaurants, the lights, the electricity and the fuel and everything else we need to live reappear day after day. You'd think it'd be Nirvana, wouldn't you?'

Before I can respond, car headlights sweep round a bend in the road and highlight us in silhouette. The New-Moth isn't surprised by this.

'Like clockwork,' is all he says as the car eases to a stop about twenty metres from the nothingness. The car is small, a Fiat, and it's similar to the one the Ape broke into in the Tesco car park in the empty world about a thousand years ago. Inside I can make out a large bulk behind the wheel. It's Sad-Ape and he sits quietly revving the engine, a gentle murmur rather than the roar you'd expect. The driver's window is smashed, just like it was smashed by the Ape in the empty world, and at least that's a sign that somewhere deep inside this frightened, meek version of an Ape is a real Ape. He stares into the nothingness, but even the beams from the car's headlights end abruptly as they hit the blackness and just disappear. Straight into nothing.

'That's death,' New-Moth tells me. 'That out there, that's got to be what death is.'

The thought chills me but I'm now more interested in

205

Sad-Ape and why he's sitting in what is obviously a stolen car, quietly revving its engine.

'He does this every night,' New-Moth says.

'What's he going to do? Ram the blackness?'

'He's thinking about trying again.'

'Again?' I ask.

'Escaping. Busting through the blackness. It's how he lost his eye. He's lucky he didn't die, if you call that lucky.' The New-Moth turns his gaze to Sad-Ape as he revs the engine again. He looks like a getaway driver with nowhere to get away to. 'No one leaves, Reva. Not alive anyway. But worse, I think the blackness is getting closer. That nothing, it's creeping towards us, I've been trying to measure it and I'm pretty sure that one day it'll crawl all over this town and snuff it out.'

'Why were the others so angry at him though?'

'Because he didn't make it,' he says. 'The Ape proved that there is no way out. And that's pretty hard to take.'

I try to peer at the darkness that is really just nothing. Is New-Moth right about it eventually smothering this town? For now it's the perfect world for my dad. He can live the same happy day over and over with his beloved wife and daughter. Not that we are his real wife and daughter. But I guess after twelve years of searching, when you find a world like this, unchanging, unescapable, then I can almost understand his unmitigated joy.

Sad-Ape revs the car engine, willing himself to try and smash his way out of town. It's the first really positive sign I've seen in him. It means he's still got a residue of Ape-ness in that he, too, likes to smash things.

SHOP TIL YOU DROP

Only GG would know a short cut from the train station to the shopping centre. He can barely walk and with every step he sucks in a grimace, but he sure knows his way to a sale.

'We take this little turning, then we take another, then another, and then we should be able to smell the price tags. We're that close,' he says as we lumber through the night. The street lights cast long shadows that make the Ape especially resemble his alter ego Non-Ape. There is no longer any sound of battle coming from the tunnel. Someone has clearly won.

A huge car park weaves its way round the exterior of the forbiddingly huge shopping centre before it turns into a multi-storey. There are restaurants and a cinema at the far end of the car park, but I'm only interested in the giant doors that welcome us to the main shopping area.

'You sure the Moth's in here?' GG asks.

'Positive,' I tell him, remembering Other-Johnson's last transmission before Billie drove a talon deep into his heart. Thanks to Another-Billie's healing powers, I know he's not dead forever, but what my Billie did to him still chills me.

The Ape yanks open one of the tall doors to the shopping centre.

'Promise me one thing,' I tell GG as we edge inside. 'Don't ever leave me again.'

'Never in a month of nevers.'

As we edge into the shopping centre and pass a small wooden cabin where lottery tickets are usually sold, I can feel GG's eyes on me. I turn to him and he's just quietly staring at me.

'What?' I whisper.

'I didn't think I'd ever see you again.'

The words ripple through me like a chill. 'I thought the same,' I tell him. 'I didn't want to believe it, but it kept jumping into my head.'

GG leans forward and I can see that for once he's being serious. 'I'm glad you came looking, knew you would, but I'm glad I was right.'

In that moment I know we will always be bonded; no matter what happens, GG and I will always be there for each other.

We find the escalator that rises relentlessly and silently towards the first floor of the shopping centre.

'Be on your guard,' I whisper to GG. 'You never know.'

GG nods, but as we rise to the main floor and step off the escalator my shoulders start tingling like crazy.

The shops are identical to the ones in my home world – another carbon copy of the earth I know so well – apart from Black Moths covering every square centimetre of the shopping centre. They are inside shops – so many of them that they're crushed up against the reinforced plate-glass windows – and outside on the concourse where they fill the entire area with their unforgiving ferociousness.

As soon as they're aware of our presence, they turn as one and stare hungrily at us. The Ape has somehow found the one remaining unoccupied space and he stands, staring the Black Moths down. I expect him to utter his immortal catchphrase: 'I got this.' But for once he seems struck by the challenge ahead and he stares me straight in the eye, a flicker of concern visible.

'Lot of Moths, but not our Moth,' he tells me.

'Eeny, meeny, miny, mo . . .' GG says quietly.

The Ape swivels his great chunk of head and scans the packed concourse. 'He's not here.'

The Black Moths tense and coil as one. They bare their metal teeth. They're getting ready to attack.

'It's OK. Remember they aren't real,' I tell GG and the Ape.

'Wait, what?' GG asks.

'They don't exist. Billie imagined them into being,' I explain, one eye on the Black Moths as they stretch their powerful limbs and reveal their talons.

'I'd pretty much say they are definitely there,' GG says.

'Imagine they're not.'

'I so wish I could. They stink to high heaven.' GG screws his nose up, but he has a point, the Black Moths do emit a strong animal odour. 'Someone's getting deodorant for Christmas.'

I'm not sure why the Black Moths do exist, especially now that Billie is dead-ish.

The Ape stops to listen for a moment. Yet again his

remarkable hearing has alerted him to something. 'OK,' is all he says as he turns and heads for the down escalator.

'Ape?'

'We better go.' Yet again his impeccable hearing has picked up something no one else has.

'What is it?' GG cups his bruised and bloodied ear with his good hand. 'Can you give us a clue?'

The Ape starts down the escalator.

BOOM!

The noise is unmistakable.

It's the fist of Non-Ape sinking into the very foundations of the shopping centre.

BOOM!

GG grabs my elbow and starts herding me back down the escalator. Never mind his pain he's moving like an Olympic athlete now.

I take the metal escalator steps two at a time, not bothering to look back. I don't really care if there are Black Moths leaping and charging after me. Not one of them is going to be fast enough to catch us.

BOOM!

Shop windows shatter.

BOOM!

The entire concourse rises like a concrete and marble wave and the escalator comes loose from its mooring, swinging free and sending me, the Ape and GG flying over the rubberised edge. I crash through the wooden roof of the small hut that is usually home to the lottery-ticket seller, landing on my back amongst a thousand lottery tickets. I hear a horrible thud, like a wet slap only magnified tenfold, as GG hits the shiny floor of the entrance lobby.

And finally the Ape comes flying down on top of me, landing hard.

BOOM!

The large exit doors splinter and collapse as the entire shopping centre lists to one side. The strengthened glass roof cracks and huge chunks of broken glass start to rain down.

The Ape climbs off me and I see a massive shard of glass falling from the sky, arrowing straight for me. I roll to one side and it lands, shattering and throwing jagged splinters everywhere. I shield my head and face but the glass flies into my back and legs, jabbing and sticking into me. The Ape grabs me, forgetting his own injuries, lifting me clear off my feet as huge sheets of glass continue to rain down and then explode into a million deadly fragments that fly off at incredible speeds. Black Moths are falling from the teetering edge of the first-floor mezzanine as the centre rips apart. Those that aren't killed by the fall are battered by the rainstorm of glass and sliced to ribbons.

BOOM!

'Couldn't he have waited till we were out of here?' GG garbles as I grab him and try to hustle him out of harm's way.

The Ape snatches a side of the wooden hut and with every sinew of strength he raises it above his head.

'Get under!'

BOOM!

Glass continues to pour down and Black Moth limbs are sliced clean off as the entire structure of the building roars in futile protest. This place is coming down and there's nothing anyone can do to stop it. I drag GG under the shelter of the Ape's makeshift wooden umbrella. Glass crashes down on it, but even though his knees bow from the force the Ape bunches his muscles and stands tall again.

'Go, go, go!' I yell.

The Ape starts heading for the smashed exit. Walls are caving in upstairs on the concourse; shops are dying on their feet, collapsing like giant dominoes into one another and crushing the swarm of Black Moths. I pray that the Ape is right and that our Moth is not up there somewhere. He had a hotel fall on him before and that's surely enough for anyone.

Another chunk of glass hits the Ape's wooden shelter and drives right through it, stopping centimetres from GG's cowering body.

'I used to shop here all the time!' he shrieks. 'The bargains you could find.'

We crab our way under the Ape's protection to what's left of the exit. Glass lands and erupts close enough to send grenades of shards our way.

BOOM!

The tall exit doors no longer exist, but as we head outside I hear the shopping centre groan, a sound louder than anything I've ever heard before. It's sliding the same way we are heading. The floor is erupting around us. Black Moths try and sprint and weave round and through us, but none of them make it as ceiling and glass and wall and concrete fall in a deluge of destruction and black blood. The Ape's knees buckle again as something horribly heavy smacks on to our wooden protection, but on he ploughs, shaking the impact off. We are in a race to reach the exit before the entire shopping centre slides down on top of us.

BOOM!

I have no idea why the Non-Ape has decided to punch the shopping gallery to death. But knowing he's alive means that surely Johnson is too.

We reach the exit and the Ape shoves me outside, then drags GG with him. He casts off his wooden shield and escapes a second before the entire shopping centre comes sliding after us, like a racing horse buckling at the knees and going over on its neck.

The Ape picks GG up and throws him into a fireman's lift and keeps running. I stop to look back but all I can see is the enormous exterior starting to fall my way. I turn and run for all I'm worth.

BOOM!

The buckling shopping centre is tumbling fast towards us, throwing up dust and debris, before completely engulfing us.

DUCKING SCHOOL!!

The morning ritual went smoothly. They had their tea and toast and then drove me to school and parked illegally on the shale and tarmac so that I could get a peck on the cheek from my 'mother' and a nod from my increasingly disaffected father. I was so eager to get into school that I broke into a sprint, until I remembered that I'm meant to hate the place. I eased up and tried to walk with sloped shoulders, head bowed, until I saw New-Johnson and New-Billie kissing by the bike sheds. That made my stomach flip and it had no right to. They're not the Johnson and Billie I know but I guess there's a residue of something or other. I've become so wrapped up in my Great Escape plans that I haven't thought about where I can actually go. What if there are even worse worlds than this one? As I mulled over my plans last night, I started to convince myself that perhaps these new versions of my friends could come with me and somehow take up my lost friends' mantle. It's a pretty hideous idea, but having copies of the people I've come to love is better than not having them at all. Just about. Or I could bring these new friends home and no one would be any the wiser. Apart from the Ape's glass eye. Condemning New-Mum to a life of abject sadness will be hard to do but what choice do I really have? I truly don't belong here.

The school bell rings and I head into school with a slow troop of the listless and lost – and then make straight for the rear exit. New-Mum is working early as usual and my dad claims to go to work every day so this is my chance to get into the flat.

I duck out of school and race back to our flat in record time, sprinting until my lungs burst and my mouth tastes of iron. I find the key under one of the plant pots outside the front door and let myself in. I should have a good three or four hours before New-Mum arrives home and I waste no time striding straight into their bedroom. If there's an answer anywhere, it's going to be there. I know Dad keeps old notebooks and battered briefcases in his wardrobe, and I also know that in the evil doppelganger world my Non-Mum found the formula rolled up and stuffed into the sleeve of one of Dad's leather jackets. Why should it be any different in Suicide World?

The wardrobe is so old it still has a tiny ancient and ornate key in the lock. I swiftly turn it and the ancient oak door swings open with a dreadfully clichéd creak. On one side are New-Mum's clothes, nothing too fancy or flash, or anything that would draw too much attention, and on the other side are my dad's suits and – thank God – four leather jackets. I take the first one down and start patting the sleeves when I hear the front door to the flat open.

I almost gasp at the sound, but quickly clasp a hand over my mouth. I stand stock-still and listen to a familiar footfall.

215

It's my dad. And he's coming down the hallway. Heading straight for his bedroom. I probably have five seconds to put the jacket back, close and lock the wardrobe and find a hiding place. Yeah, like that's going to happen.

The footsteps stop outside the bedroom door. And I stop breathing. I can't possibly explain being here. There is no story or tale that I can weave other than to tell the truth and then blow any chance I have of escape. The handle of the bedroom door slowly dips and I brace myself, quickly formulating a plan to hurl the leather jacket at him, and then run for my life. I won't ever come back here I'll hide out at New-Moth's until he and I can think of another plan.

I'm ready for my dad.

I'm going to leather-jacket him and run like I'm in the Olympics. He'll never catch me.

A phone rings.

Not mine, thank God.

Dad's mobile.

He lets go of the bedroom door handle and answers.

'Hey, you.' The tone of his voice makes me think that it must be New-Mum on the other end of the line. 'Miss you too.'

The call has given me a bit of time and I turn as lightly as I can, trying to put the leather jacket back on its hanger. As I do, a rolled-up group of papers slide from it and land on the carpet.

The formula!

'By the way, did you leave the key in the door?' my dad asks New-Mum.

What sort of idiot am I? I was so eager to ransack the flat that I left my key in the front door.

But then I spot the magic, world-opening formula lying at my feet in a curled-up tube of answers.

'You still have yours?' There's a quizzical tone to his voice. 'So has someone used the one we hide under the plant pot.'

I'm ditching the leather jacket and Olympic sprint idea. I've got a better one. I gently hide the rolled-up pages of the formula under the bed and then step backwards into the wardrobe. Far better not to be found at all than have to leg it.

'Definitely?' my dad asks again. 'OK ...' He hesitates, 'There'll be some silly explanation.'

I sink into the clothes until I'm up against the back of the wardrobe. Because it's so ancient, an heirloom from way back, the wardrobe has room and depth. I'm about to draw myself into as small a size as possible when I realise I need to pull the door shut.

The creaky door.

The door that can't be left open because it'll give me away and the same door that can't be closed because that too will give me away.

'Well, there's no harm done, and no one seems to have broken in.' My dad squeezes a jolly upbeat lilt into his voice. 'It's pretty warm out there and I wanted to grab a thinner jacket.'

Why can I never catch a break?

He can't come in here and start rummaging around in the wardrobe. I mean, that's just not fair. This world is laughing its sweet socks off at me. Everything I do and everywhere I go it is crying hysterically with laughter. I can't escape through the lorry. I can't get any further than the main

217

road. I can't even hide in a sodding wardrobe! Am I meant to just give in gracefully? Is that what it's telling me?

'Yeah, I'll take the leather one,' he laughs into his phone.

What's starting to dawn is that it seems every world I end up in doesn't want me. The doppelganger world definitely wanted me dead. The empty world ... well, that had a very good go at killing me on numerous occasions. And now in this world, this world that is just a small town in Hertfordshire and nothing else, is keen to despatch me. Because what if when my dad finds me he decides I'm far too much trouble and decides to do something about it.

'I love you,' my dad says into the phone. 'We'll go for a Chinese later.' He ends the phone call and, even though I can't see it, I know the door handle to the bedroom is being pulled downwards. He's definitely coming in this time.

The bedroom door opens.

I might as well come out of hiding.

Dad's going to find me anyway.

REUNION

Rubble
Glass. Stone. Concrete
Dust billowing

I'm imagining how Carrie would describe this in one of her poems. How the onrushing mass of ex-shopping centre stopped centimetres short of engulfing us. The dust covered us, but the rock and the rubble and cement never quite reached us.

Black Moths no more
But wait . . .
What is that I spy?
Is it hope?

Oh, yes, she'd write it exactly like this. But maybe with a rhyme. Some Black Moths got away, but very few. They disappeared into the night and I really don't care where they have gone. Though we did capture one that had broken limbs and a gaping chest wound.

From the stone
Emerges the one
Who can save us.
I am delirious.

Oh, yes, that's got Carrie written all over it. The thing with a Black Moth is it's really just Moth Two from the violent world transformed into a panther. I'm hoping this one, when all is explained to it, and Another-Billie has healed its wounds, will be able to transform back into Moth Two. If not, Non-Ape can deal with it.

And wait, who is that?
A stranger?
A friend?
Is it danger?

I could fill ten of her notebooks in about half an hour. This is so easy. Once you get rhyming.

Johnson emerged from the shadows carrying our Moth. I couldn't believe my eyes. There was so much we all wanted to say but during the two mile walk back to the train station no one said a word.

The Moth smiles.
We smile at his smile.
The train waits.
None of us hesitates.

The wounded Black Moth has joined Non-Lucas, Billie, Carrie, Evil-GG and Other-Johnson's (well, Johnson's body, but Other-Johnson's mind, I suppose – it's getting harder and harder to keep up!). The train is fast becoming the Cadaver Express. Non-Ape is back with his best pal, playing snap while they sing Iron Maiden's 'Run to the Hills'. Non-Ape is the hero of the hour, but he couldn't care less, not when he can play snap instead.

My Johnson is slumped with a lazy metal smile across from me in the first-class carriage. He has traces of cuts and bruises on his superhuman skin, but nothing life-threatening.

'We were getting swamped by those gruesome Moths,' he tells me. 'No offence, Moth.'

'None taken, Johnson.' The Moth is sitting beside him.

I'll say it again and savour it. The Moth. *My* Moth.

While Non-Ape fought the Black Moths in the tunnel, Johnson snuck away to try and find the Moth.

'I just had a feeling he was OK and that he was nearby,' Johnson had told me after our reunion. It seemed strange that he could sense the Moth, but I think maybe it was a residue from Johnson being in the wrong body. A hangover from Other-Johnson's incredible mental powers that's still lurking in his DNA.

'The other versions of me took me to the shopping centre. I don't know why though.' The Moth had filled in the gaps, but then he frowned and looked even more shaken. 'I don't even like shopping.'

'I barely got the Moth out of there before Non-Ape started punching the shopping centre to death,' Johnson added.

'Did they do anything to you?' I asked the Moth.

'Just squatted there, saying nothing, doing nothing. But if

I tried to crawl they all leaped up as one, flashed their teeth, their talons.'

'What did you do then?' I asked.

'What do you think? I stopped crawling.'

I sighed quietly to myself. Ask a stupid question, Rev.

'But they didn't hurt you or try to kill you.'

'No. They wanted me off the train and as far away from the rest of you as possible. At least that's my theory.' He frowned at that, as if trying to find a coherent thought that would explain everything to his muddled mind.

Now, as we sit on the train rushing back to town, the Moth looks more troubled than ever. There's clearly a problem he's trying to get his brilliant brain around.

I show him my dad's dust-covered papers. 'Salvaged these.'

The Moth nods, but doesn't take them.

'Maybe later.' He looks tired, exhausted.

'We got Carrie,' I tell him gently.

His dull eyes brighten a little.

'You found her?'

I nod.

'Where is she?'

'In another carriage. She's going to need a bit of TLC.' Which is the queen of understatements. 'But once we get her healed—'

The Ape hears this and thrusts a meaty finger into the air. 'Healed!'

The Moth barely notices because his heart has quickened. 'She'll be OK?'

'That's the plan.' I smile through a cut and bruised jaw.

The Moth is lifted for a moment and I tap the papers that now lie on the table between us. 'We're all going home.'

Johnson meets my eyes. 'Really think that's finally going to happen?'

'Yeah. Yeah, I do,' I tell him.

He smiles again. 'Can't wait for the homecoming party.'

It's as simple an exchange as anyone can have, but somewhere in between the words, I know he's telling me when we get back we – as in me and Johnson – are finally going to be together.

The Moth falls silent and I'm not sure, but I think he's doing calculations in his head; his lips are moving as he whispers to himself.

GG's voice erupts over the tannoy. 'So where on earth am I going to go shopping now?' He laughs.

The joke brings a smile to each of our faces as the train trundles gently through the pitch-black night. The train that shouldn't exist. The Moth sits up in his seat. We'll have to find a wheelchair for him when we reach town.

'Rev?' he says.

'Yeah?'

'I can't believe it.'

'Can't believe what?' I ask.

'This . . . reunion. I don't get how it can have happened.'

'It just did,' I offer.

'We got lucky,' Johnson adds.

'SNAP!' Non-Ape roars at the table opposite ours.

'That's not a snap.' The Ape holds up two cards. 'That's a King and that's a Jack.'

Non-Ape takes a moment to study both cards. A moment

that turns into a minute until he eases back, satisfied. 'Jacks are young Kings.'

The Ape turns the cards towards him. 'Oh, yeah.'

'Obvious.'

'SNAP!'

The Apes study the cards, their great wide foreheads touching as they pore over the Jack and the King.

Non-Ape has grown small again, able to fit into the train seat with only a tiny amount of discomfort. He's used up almost all of his power smashing the shopping centre to pieces.

'So what exactly were they doing with you?' Johnson asks the Moth. 'All those ugly Moths. No offence. Again.'

'Nothing. They just stood guard. I tried talking to them but they remained in their panther-like state the whole time. Like animals.'

The very first Black Moth turned from a brainbox into a marauding animal when we first encountered him. We were on a train – we are always on trains – and he chased us down. He went from upright to all fours and morphed into a panther, sleek, black and murderous.

'Billie created them,' I tell him.

'From what?' asks Moth, looking confused.

'Thin air.'

'Impossible.'

'It's true.' Johnson backs me up.

'Billie turns your fears into reality,' I say.

'But the Black Moths were real. I felt them; you felt them. You can't make something out of nothing.' His space brain is working overtime now. 'Unless she's the most dangerous person of all time. Being able to create matter just by thinking of it.'

224

'I think they snatched you to stop you reading my dad's papers,' I tell the Moth. 'I think Billie wanted to stay here.'

'With me,' Johnson adds.

'But this world,' the Moth says. 'This world is empty. It likes being empty. And Billie is changing it, populating it. Just like we did when we were transported here.' The Moth focuses on me again. 'It wasn't luck that there was a second train, or that we're going home.'

I glance at Johnson who looks as confused as I do.

'Why was there a train at the station when there weren't any others anywhere to be seen? Until now,' the Moth asks without wanting an answer. 'It appeared when we needed it the most.'

'Maybe the thing to do is not question it,' Johnson suggests.

'You're right. We shouldn't question it. I don't think this world wants anything but for us to leave,' the Moth says.

My shoulders ripple. A hint of fear slips through me.

I wait for more.

'It's not meant for anyone,' he continues. 'This world is about order, not chaos. It even parks the cars nicely. Nothing is out of place. Not until we turned up, that is.' The Moth takes a breath. 'And now it's going to spit us out.'

'I'm all for being spat anywhere but here,' Johnson offers.

'But I'm worried it thinks we're taking too long to leave. So if we don't escape very – and I mean very – soon then it will step up its efforts.' The Moth's words are haunting. 'Can't you feel how restless it is? It's like a dog whining at a door, getting more and more agitated. It's like a dog with fleas.'

'And we're the fleas?' I ask, even though I know we are,

225

but I'm feeling a panic rising and talking seems to keep it at bay.

The Moth nods. 'We've contaminated it, and Billie's weird power to create has infested the world. She's made everything a hundred times worse. It's not happy with us. It's giving us everything we need to leave, so I say we get out of here as quickly as we can.'

'You really think that this world has that sort of power? You can't know for sure, Moth,' Johnson argues.

The Moth is convinced. 'We all found each other again, Johnson, even after everything that's happened. It's too much coincidence to be luck.'

'Well, that leaves one question then,' Johnson says.

But I beat him to it. 'Just how much time do we have—'

'—before this world ups its game and wipes us out.' Johnson finishes my sentence.

The words linger.

The Moth stares out of the window again and spots our hometown rising up in the distance.

'I guess we're about to find out,' he says.

Bang on cue GG sounds the train horn.

'Honey, we're *almost* home!' he booms over the tannoy. 'Please remember to grab all personal belongings, and if you see any suspicious packages or dead people, please report it to the proper authority.'

My dad folds his clamshell phone closed with a plastic snap and is about to spot the open wardrobe door when there's a sudden hammering on the front door.

'Rev!' The voice is unmistakable. So is the hammering on the door.

It's the Ape.

Sad-Ape.

And, just like every good Ape should do, he steps in to save me when everything seems lost.

I hear my dad turn and head out of the bedroom. I've got seconds to extricate myself, grab the formula and sneak out of the bedroom while Sad-Ape keeps my dad occupied. Easy.

I slip out of the wardrobe. But snag my hair on a sparkling diamanté brooch thing that New-Mum has pinned to a dress and it yanks my head and neck back. I twist and turn, groping blindly behind my head for the brooch. But I'm making it worse and resort to wrenching clumps of trapped hair out of my head.

My dad has left the bedroom door ajar and I can see down the hallway to the front door where Dad is now facing the giant boy that is Sad-Ape.

'Rev?' Sad-Ape asks.

'What do you want?' Dad asks.

I yank a fistful of pink hair from the brooch and finally get free. Sad-Ape can't see my past my dad. And thank goodness he can't because he'd just point my way and say – Her, I want her. *He may have hammered on the door, but he's already retreating into his shell.*

'Uh – I just said. Rev,' Sad-Ape tells my dad.

I get down on my hands and knees and start searching for the rolled-up formula. But in my panic I've kicked it too far and I can't reach it. I get up and tiptoe as quickly as I can to the far side of the bed, my New-Mum's side judging from the day and night creams sitting on her cheap bedside table. Creams that didn't erase the wrinkles that have dug trenches in her face.

'She's at school,' I hear my dad respond.

Which I seriously wish he hadn't.

'No,' the nervy Sad-Ape replies. 'That's why I'm here.'

I duck down again and flail about for the formula, grabbing it on the third attempt because every time I touch it, it seems to want to roll out of reach.

'She's not at school?' My dad's voice reveals an edge of steel.

'Saw her leave.' Sad-Ape is killing me with every word he utters.

I grab the rolled-up formula and realise I've forgotten to shut the wardrobe door. I contemplate leaving it open, but even if I do the first thing my dad will do is reach for his thin leather jacket. The leather jacket that contained the rolled-up formula. I need to put it back before he realises what I've been up to.

'You saw my daughter leave school?'

'Yeah.'

'And you think she came home?'

'Yeah.'

My only saving grace is Sad-Ape's slow-moving brain. Having a conversation that would normally last seconds can drag into hours with an Ape.

I grab the sleeve of the leather jacket and try to wedge the formula into it.

But the sleeve's too tight. It can't be this jacket.

C'mon, c'mon, gimme a break.

'Why do you think she's here?' *my dad asks.*

I try again.

'I followed her here.'

And my life ends in that moment. Death and non-existence curl around the edges of Sad-Ape's words and then strangle them with the constrictive power of a giant python.

The formula slides inside the sleeve and I breathe a silent sigh until I spot a clump of electric-pink hair held fast by a glittering diamanté brooch. Even if the open wardrobe door isn't questioned, I can't possibly explain the hair so I grab the brooch and tear it from New-Mum's dress.

'You saw her come into the flat?' *my dad asks quietly. Too quietly. He's speaking in whispered tones because he must know I'm in the flat, listening.*

I drop down and crawl under the bed, brooch and hank of pink hair clasped in my hand. My heart is going faster than a Lucas-blur.

229

'She found the key,' Sad-Ape tells my dad.

'Under the plant pot?'

I'm imagining Sad-Ape nod his great head.

They fall silent.

'She in?' Sad-Ape asks.

'No,' my dad replies.

And then I hear the door close and the turn of the lock.

Which is the worst sound I've heard in a long while. Until I hear footsteps making a measured pace towards my bedroom door. He knocks on it lightly.

'Rev?' I hear him ask. 'You in there?'

I'm not certain but I'm pretty sure this is a game he's playing. He knows full well I can hear him and he knows there's no way for me to escape. We're six floors up so I can hardly jump out of a window.

I hear my bedroom door open and then: 'No. Not there.'

It's like a game of hide-and-seek now. But without the laughs and thrills.

He knocks on the bathroom door. 'Reva?' Again I hear the door open and close. Then the sound of footsteps heading towards the small lounge. 'Sweetheart, you home?' His voice echoes through the silent flat.

I press down as flat as I can, breathing in carpet dust.

'Nope, not in here either.' If this was a real search my dad wouldn't bother talking.

His commentary is purely for my benefit and he's dragging it out, building as much threat as he can. There are just two rooms left for him to check. The kitchen and the bedroom I'm currently hiding in.

I need a weapon and when the brooch in my hand suddenly sparkles I realise that I'm holding one. It's about seven centimetres long which means the pin that fastens it is probably just short of that length. I turn the brooch round and raise my head to get as good a look at it as I can. I immediately stab the back of my head on the twisted metal knots of the framework that holds the mattress in place. I have to swallow a pained yelp.

'You making brunch?' my dad calls out. He's enjoying dragging this out. 'Mmmm. Smells good.'

What a joker.

The pin on the brooch is solid metal, not flimsy; it will make a great weapon. He won't see it coming. This is between me and him and I've got the edge. I'm a fighter now, ironically because of him. Because of what he put me and my friends through. He doesn't know that and that's going to be his biggest mistake. There's a new plan and it's simple. Keep my dad at arm's length, grab the formula, find the Moth, go home.

Great. After twelve years of his not being there I now have to threaten him if he comes anywhere near me.

And if he does then I'll have to act. I'll have to stop him anyway I can. But can I really leave him lying in the bedroom with his throat cut open for New-Mum to find?

Jesus.

Can I do that to her? Can I do it to myself? What the hell have I turned into? As I hear the bedroom door open I let the brooch drop from my hand.

I can't hurt my dad. No matter what he's done.

He walks in and shuts the bedroom door gently behind him.

The train pulls into darkness.

GG stops it with a gentle shunt and three toots of the horn. The beeps that signal the opening of the doors pierce the night and I stand up and look into the pre-dawn maw and realise that almost all of the lights in the town have gone out. Dawn is maybe half an hour away, but to all intents and purposes we're looking at a blackout.

Then Johnson is at my side, staring at the tiny station and the road that will take us into the heart of town. 'Run the plan by me again,' he whispers.

'Phase One: find Another-Billie. She heals everyone we've brought back with us. Phase Two: Other-Johnson swaps people back into their rightful bodies.'

'Phase Three?'

'My dad sends us all home.'

'Where's Another-Billie?' Johnson asks.

'You know the private hospital? In the posh part of town?'

'Up the posh hill?' Johnson asks.

'Up the posh hill.' I nod. The same one Other-Johnson roared up on his gleaming, powerful motorbike. The thought gives me a quiet tingle.

I step on to the platform and see GG limping towards us. How he's still standing I have no idea, but I've already put him to the top of Another-Billie's list of patients.

'Tickets, please,' he jokes through his relentless pain.

'You'll have to fine us,' I smile back, playing along.

'That's *fine* with me.' He cackles. 'Do you see what I did there?'

Johnson jumps down from the train and lands with alien grace. He turns and holds out his hand for me to take. I reach for it, but he grabs me instead and sweeps me into his arms. I shriek and then laugh as he cradles me for a moment.

'Gotcha,' he says quietly.

'But who's got you?' I tease.

I stare into the black pools of his eyes and wonder if this is the moment that he finally kisses me. He's in Other-Johnson's body and surely some of his swagger is going to rub off on him. Other-Johnson didn't hesitate when his moment came. He kissed me like there was nothing in the world that was going to prise us apart. So c'mon, Johnson, I'm waiting. I'm ready.

He sets me down gently. Without a kiss. So I decide to hell with it and go to kiss *him* when the Ape yells—

'My turn!' He leaps out of the train in a vain attempt to be caught and swept up in Johnson's arms. But Johnson is taken off guard and he falls down under the Ape's bulk.

'Dazza!' Johnson lets out a muffled yell.

'My turn!' Non-Ape leaps out of the train and lands even more heavily on the Ape and Johnson combined.

GG looks at the sprawling mess on the platform.

'I love those guys,' he grins.

Even with his super-sinewy strength, Johnson can barely dislodge the combined meat and flab of the Apes, who are laughing hysterically. Non-Ape gets to his feet first.

'My turn!' In less than a second he leaps back on to the train and then dives off it again. Crashing back on to the Ape and Johnson.

'For God's sake!' I snap and start dragging at Non-Ape. 'None of this is appropriate behaviour.' I sound like a teacher, but I am so tired, so sore all over, and all I want is to go home. 'Get off him!'

Non-Ape climbs to his feet again, sheepish, head bowed. 'Just cos you want to be on him,' he mumbles.

'What? What did you say?'

'Nothing,' he mutters, chin still bowed towards his chest.

The Ape joins his comrade. He's less cowed by my outburst. 'You used to be fun.'

Johnson lies groaning on the platform. 'Good job we're heading for a hospital.'

I reach down and help heft him to his feet. He cracks his rubbery-skinned neck and cricks his spine into place. 'Let's go find Another-Billie. No way we can drag all the bodies to her. She needs to come to us.'

'Let's not forget Lucas,' GG tells us.

He's talking about our Lucas who hanged himself the first night we were sent to the empty world. GG beams through the dark. 'Look at little GG, the walking, talking school register.'

'Rev Two is out there,' I warn them. 'Don't forget what she can do.'

Rev Two has a hand that turns blue and steals life, sucking it out of you until you're just a grey husk. She did it to Other-Johnson by accident and she sees us, our kind, as her mortal enemies. The only reason she hasn't done the same thing to my dad is because Another-Billie promised not to tell her that he was human. But, as my dad said when he contacted me in the Ferrari's wing mirror, Rev Two now knows that he's not her dad.

I turn to Non-Ape. 'You need to stay here with the train. Keep guard.'

Non-Ape nods. 'There's going to be trouble?'

'Maybe. Probably.'

'Good.' A grin ripples along his wide mouth.

'How come I can't keep guard?' the Ape asks.

'Because we might have trouble in town, so you have to come with us.'

'Good. I like trouble.' A grin ripples along his wide mouth.

'How come I can't help with trouble in town?' Non-Ape looks put out.

'Because you're guarding against trouble here. Remember?'

'Good.' Another grin ripples along his wide mouth.

'How come he gets all the fun?' the Ape asks.

Please, shoot me now, I think.

'Look, we don't even know if there will be trouble—'

'—Gotcha!' The Ape laughs right into my face. 'Every time!'

I look at his laughing face and then lean forward and press my head into one of his huge shoulders. I let it rest there until I can gather what's left of my brain. Johnson pats me on the back.

235

'We need to get moving,' he says.

GG tightens his sling round his broken arm. 'Got to get me some healing.'

We set off into the night. The Ape, GG, Johnson and me. Leaving Non-Ape on high alert, watching over the bodies of our friends and doppelgangers. Until we hear a loud rapping on one of the windows of the first-class carriage. It's the Moth.

'Hey! Why do you always forget me?'

We all look suitably apologetic, but turn and head for the electronic gates that lead out of the station.

'Relax, my little amigo, we'll be back to forget you later!' GG calls to the Moth.

As we walk away, I try and stay alert for any type of contact from my dad. Whether it comes in person or in a dream or a mirage in a mirror: I'm desperate to hear from him. To talk to him. To be able to finally be with him.

Twelve empty years are about to end.

My dad sits down on the edge of the bed and his weight squashes me even further into the dusty carpet. He knows exactly where I am and I probably can't roll away even if I wanted to. I'm trapped by his weight. This is the same man I never thought I'd ever see again. A man I helped bring back to life and who, when I saw him lying in that private hospital bed, made me want to cry. I nearly died several times over and every single near-death was worth it because I knew I'd be seeing him again. I'd be waving goodbye to twelve empty years; to starting again with him and my mum, picking our lives up and piecing them back together. Not so long ago he was going to be my saviour, and here he is the complete opposite. There's a lesson there. You don't always get what you think you deserve.

He takes a long moment before eventually speaking.

'I wanted to be a hero.' He speaks quietly. 'Her hero. Your mum's.'

This isn't quite the anger I was expecting.

'I lost you.' Here it comes, I think. The liar is about to

237

tell the truth. 'A silly, stupid accident. You walked into the road . . . I'd left the door open. You were always brave and adventurous. Until night-time. Then you got scared. But the flat door was open. And you, little sweet four-year-old you, toddled out of it. Passed all those other flats, and of course no one saw you. Not a single person stopped you going down the flights of steps.'

He stops, giving himself a moment as the memory eats into him. 'I was wrapped up in my discovery. An amazing discovery. It's all numbers, you know. The only true universal language – and I miraculously wrote them down in the right way. Or the wrong way. Still don't know which one it is. But I performed an experiment and created a key, a molecular key from an equation, and opened a door. In my lab late at night I made the biggest discovery in history.'

He stops again and then his next words sound like they're trying to climb out over a small boulder in his throat. 'I was so thrilled. I raced home, woke Mum up, tried to explain and then thought no, no, I can't tell her, I can't tell anyone. Not until I know the rules. Because there's always rules. If you break open the fabric of everything you know, there's going to be a price to pay. Unless you take it one step at a time. And then there was you. I was so amazed by my discovery I forgot about you. I forgot to go into your room like I did every morning and wake you up. So brave, adventurous little Reva gets up by herself and heads outside. Goes down the steps, probably singing or playing a game in her head, going on a great adventure. It probably takes a lot of effort to keep climbing down those steps. But you don't fall or tumble. And I wish you had, because what's a few bruises compared to what actually happened?'

He's silent once more as the sharp, twisted knots of metal from the bed frame continue to dig deeply into the back of my head.

'While I'm making history, dreaming about publishing the papers, about winning awards, being famous and all the things that seem meaningless now, you walked out into the road. Our precious Reva.' He swallows and I think, from the jerky movement transmitted through the bed he wipes his eyes. 'The van driver didn't even know he'd hit you.' Silence. 'I'm ecstatic, running round the flat with joy, until I see the open door. I looked for you in the flat, then ran out, nearly breaking my neck as I leaped down those steps, yelling your name. I saw your hand first. Your tiny, unmoving hand sticking out from under the van.'

It hits me like a ton of bricks. I'm not me. I'm not who he said I was and I'm not who I thought I was.

'I got you out from under the van, ran back to the flat to call for an ambulance. But you weren't breathing; you were just lying in my arms and I knew I'd already lost you. My little Reva.'

I start crying for the little me. And for everything that's built up over the last weeks. It all comes flooding out in a silent stream of tears.

'I held you and thought that if I'm feeling like this, like I want to die, then what will it do to your mum?' He sniffs. 'That's when my eyes settled on the papers. My amazing discovery that had made me so happy ... I almost tore them up, so angry that I'd lost you because of a few numbers. And then I realised: I could use those numbers to find another you. To enter another world and take another Reva for us. You've got to understand I was desperate, broken. So

I did what I insanely thought was the right thing to do. I left as quickly as I could with you in my arms. I thought I'd get back easily as soon as I swapped you. No one would know. Another version of me would find a Reva by the wheels of a van. It's wrong, it's hideous, but I did it nevertheless.'

I am so squished I can barely move my hand to wipe the flood of tears from my eyes.

'But there are so many variables. Worlds where you didn't exist, where I didn't exist. Where you're not something that is as human as we are, or maybe you're older or younger because time isn't straight-forward. I carried you across worlds and couldn't find the right you to make the switch. But I did eventually find a place. A lovely place. It was empty. Totally empty and totally beautiful. So I left you in that heaven. You know the place; you've been there.'

The empty world.

He buried me there.

Is that why the empty world never wanted me? It already had a Reva Marsalis. It despised chaos, and what's more chaotic than too many versions of one person?

'I took you to the church in the centre of town. I cried for weeks there. But I had to carry on, had to find you. Had to make everything right again.'

My dad has tampered with the laws of the multiverse in an unimaginable way. He's probably changed the fabric of a thousand realities. Leaving only one truth: his Reva died and he should have tried to accept that.

'I opened door after door to so many worlds. Once I had the key, it was so simple. I created new matter with my formula. There's a finite amount of molecules in any world and if you add to them then you need to make room

240

for the new ones. They elbow their way into existence and squeeze the old familiar molecules right up against the edge of reality. So much so that something's got to give. And a door opens. Over and over and over I did that. Until I realised I was lost. I didn't know how to get back to my own world.'

He rises from the bed and I listen as he closes the creaky wardrobe door. Then there's the sound of the lock turning. I can see his polished shoes level with my eyeline.

'I almost gave up. Resigned myself to never finding a replacement, never going home again. Then I got caught in a dying, burning world so I opened one last door to escape and finally there you were. Older, but I knew it was you. I panicked, the flames were coming for me, so I used the key and tried to reach you. But this time something went wrong. I don't know how it happened – maybe it was because I'd given up; maybe it was because I was so panicked about dying in the flames – but rather than me moving to another world I pulled us both back to that empty world. A place I'd have time and space to talk to you and finally take you home. I didn't expect two versions of you to emerge. I was burning to death, I was desperate, and somehow made a mistake. But that won't happen again, I swear on my life to you. We don't need to go anywhere any more.'

Something lands beside my dad's shoes. It's a set of rolled-up papers. And they're on fire. His impossible formula.

As soon as I see them, I start to scramble out from under the bed but my dad presses down hard on it, trapping me there.

'Reva, listen to me.'

I kick and fight and pull and push, but he pushes as hard as he can down on the heavy old bed.

'This is us now.'

'This isn't even the world you came from!' I scream at him. The formula is igniting; the flames are burning brighter.

'This is us now, Reva! I'm done searching. I'll never find my real world again.'

'That's not your wife.'

'But she is in so many ways.'

'She's stuck in a repeating day, so what does twelve years really matter to her? Why does she keep celebrating something that hasn't happened? I didn't die; you didn't leave. Not in this world. It only exists in this one day. She can't have memories, can she?'

My dad takes a long time to respond. 'All that matters is we're here now,' he says as gently as he can muster. 'Maybe what happened to my Rev transcends the worlds, echoing its tragedy over and over. Reaching out to all of the versions of your mum in some way. Hurting them, debilitating them. But I beat that tragedy, I got past the heartbreak. I made us whole again.'

'But what about all the other Reva dads?' I am so panicked I'm now looking again for the brooch I dropped. If I can find it, I can scrabble out from under this bed and force him to write another formula. Surely, after twelve years, he must know it off by heart. 'All of them must have done what you did and discovered this stupid formula. Just like my dad did. He disappeared, just like you did.'

'Reva, there are no other versions of me who discovered

242

the formula. I'd have met them. If your dad left, it was because he chose to, not because he found the formula.'

'No . . .' I cry.

'He walked out on you. It's that simple.'

'Never, no, that's a lie. That's what you do, you lie and you lie.'

'Believe me, I haven't met a single me crossing worlds; no one else got it right. Others may have tried, but no one succeeded. And no other version of your dad would love you as much as I do.'

'No!' I wail.

'Your real dad is probably living in another town somewhere, maybe even with a new wife and family.'

'Stop.' I continue to wail at him. 'No, no, no!'

'I'm the dad you always wanted. Because I'm the only one who wanted you. We're together again and that's all that matters. Me, you and Mum.'

'She's not my mum, you're not my dad! You can do stupid things like appear in a mirage or a mirror.' The words are pouring from me. 'You have . . . gifts. Powers. You . . . You have . . .'

It dawns so late it should be called dusk.

'How could I have believed that you were my dad? How could I have done that? All this time you were doing weird things and I was never less than convinced you were you.'

'You wanted to believe. And that's half the battle,' he tells me quietly.

When you want something so badly and for so long, then it's almost forgivable. But my blindness to an obvious fact got all of my friends killed and there's no forgiveness in that.

'But look at us, these past few weeks we do belong to each other, in a way. Look at how happy we are. I'm making up for what I did all those years ago, paying it all back.'

The formula is ash now. Just like little four-year-old Reva, it is gone forever.

'I'm not your Reva. And my real mum is out there, waiting for me. You need to get me back. If not for me, then for her. Don't let her lose me too.'

'This is us,' he repeats. 'This is how we were always meant to be. I righted a wrong. I made everything better.'

'This world isn't going to last. You've seen the darkness coming, you must have.'

'And if and when it comes we'll be together.'

His polished shoe kicks away the ash.

'This is us, Rev.' And his tears hit his shoes.

The hill is steeper than I recall. Thanks to his injuries, GG is in a shopping trolley and the Ape is pushing him. The Ape certainly loves a shopping trolley.

'Look at me, I'm flying!' GG squeals and the Ape charges up the hill with him.

I'm still looking for Rev Two and any sign of my dad. If I haven't heard from him, does that mean she's already caught up with him? We've got my dad's papers as a backup so maybe for the first time since the white light yanked us out of detention we've got all the angles and bases covered. Johnson can sense my optimism.

'When we get back, we're going for a ride.'

'Yeah?' I say.

'Out of town. Not London either. Somewhere with an open road and nothing but us.'

'I'll let you know if I'm available,' I tease.

His eyes meet mine. 'You will be.'

Despite only having the low glow of the few street lamps that still work to guide us, we eventually locate the hospital where I left my dad. The last time I was here Non-Ape hurled a car door through a ward window, and then I tried to run for my life before he caught up with me. My leg stings from the sudden reminder of the jagged nail that tore its way up my thigh. I look at the cars parked outside the entrance and remember Moth's comment about how this orderly world decided to neatly park all the cars and buses. I wonder how much time we have left before it decides it's finally had enough of us.

The automatic door to the hospital opens silently as I try to remember what floor Another-Billie had been treating my dad on.

'Stinks in here.' The Ape sniffs. 'Someone die?'

The Ape's right. The hospital reeks, and not in a good way. Johnson lets his steel talons slide out of his fingertips. 'Smells like death,' he whispers.

I know that smell. It's another echo. It's the smell of burning flesh.

The Ape's sense for danger and impending combat sends him rushing towards what looks like a supply room. It's locked, but that doesn't stop him eyeing the forbidding DO NOT ENTER sign plastered on the door and then booting the lock as hard as he can.

'What on earth are you doing?' GG asks.

The Ape kicks and kicks and the door starts to splinter and give.

'Darren, dear heart,' GG tries again.

The door buckles as the Ape kicks it off its hinges and marches into the DO NOT ENTER room. We hear him throwing things around and then after several minutes he reappears. There are five of the sharpest and shiniest scalpels you've ever seen taped hard to his knuckles. Two on one hand, three on the other. He's tried to make his own version of Johnson's talons.

'Five-pointer!' The Ape boasts.

GG stares at the monstrous pseudo-claws. 'I've got to get me a pair of those. They're all the rage.'

The Ape swishes his hand cutting the air back and forth and adding a swishing sound for good effect. He's gone from Healer to Killer in under three minutes.

'Teeny-weeny word of warning.' GG reaches out and gingerly lays a hand on the Ape's arm. 'If you need to pick your nose, give me a call first.'

The Ape stops, thinks and then, even though I know he's secretly come to love that GG is so kind and caring towards him, he scowls. 'My nose, my pick.'

Johnson touches my elbow. 'Let's go find the other Billie.'

He steps forward, ready to lead the way, but the Ape stops him. 'Me first,' he says. 'There's a stink up there. Could be trouble.' He motions for us to get behind him and none of us argue.

The stairwell is dark and cold. Dawn is approaching, but not quickly enough to warm the hospital. That will be Non-Ape's fault for creating a huge hole in its side. Would Another-Billie really have stayed in this freezing building? What if I've made a terrible mistake bringing us back here? My dad's well enough to run and escape from Rev Two but did Another-Billie go with him? As we make our way up the stairs, the Ape swishing hard at every shadow with his scalpel fists, I think about telling the others about my

247

second thoughts. *Hey, guys, guess what? I didn't stop to think.* Again.

The smell is starting to overpower and GG already has his good hand covering his mouth and nose. 'I think they left someone on the operating table.' His voice echoes like he's speaking into a shell.

Johnson hoicks up the bottom of his T-shirt and presses it against his nose, revealing his lithe stomach, no six-pack, just slim and taut. He catches me staring, but says nothing. He knows he doesn't need to.

The smell is now a putrid stench as the Ape breathes a huge lungful of it in and then points to a door in the stairwell landing. 'That way.' It seems that not only is his hearing a thing of wonder, but his sense of smell is also as keen as a dog's. He pushes through the door that leads to the second floor. The corridor lights flicker, because obviously they would have to as it all adds to the growing sense of foreboding. The last smell that was this bad was—

'This is like Tesco's.' The Ape finishes my thought before I can. Which is a first. 'When your dead dad stunk the place out,' he adds looking at me.

The Ape's right; it is the same smell. Johnson coils, almost imperceptibly, but he tenses as we head along the flickering hallway, our footsteps somehow falling softer without us even knowing. We're all on high alert: being in this world for over a week has clearly honed us into smart-thinking survivalists.

The Ape slows at the first open door and peers round it to take a look inside, and we hear him take a huge gasp of breath. But as we ready ourselves for whatever's in there he steps back out again. 'Not in here.' He takes another deep

248

breath and sniffs his way towards the stench, homing in on it, passing doors, looking in, then moving on. Finally we reach the last room in the corridor. The door is closed and the Ape presses his nose up against it and sniffs deeply.

'In here,' he whispers.

'OK,' I whisper in return and GG and Johnson gather round. 'How shall we play this?'

'Come on then, stink butt!' The Ape kicks the door open with all the might of a bucking bronco and charges into the room.

'That works for me,' Johnson quips and quickly follows the Ape. GG looks at me and even in his beaten, bashed and bruised state, he limps in as best he can. 'All for one.'

I'm last in and as soon as I'm through the door I really wish I'd stayed outside. Lying in a hospital bed is a burned and seared person. It's not as bad as before in Tesco; the flesh is badly charred all over and all of the clothes have been burned off, but that only makes it a little easier to recognise my dad.

Burned to a crisp.

We are not going home any time soon.

I think the top of my head is bleeding from where the metal twists of the mattress holder dug into me. My distraught dad eventually left the bedroom, freeing me. I don't care where he went because, as I slide out from under the bed, I roll in the ash of the burned formula. It sticks to my blazer and smudges my crisp white school shirt as I charge from the flat, tears streaming down my face. My dad's story, his abject tale of misery, has cut into me all over. There was a little Reva in another world and he failed to save her. A little kid run over by a reversing van. Something so stupid and inane and ridiculous and avoidable, but yet it happened. In the blink of an eye. It happens every day I'd imagine, senseless tragedy, but it doesn't make it any easier to understand. I'm not crying for me, I'm crying for her. But she is me . . . was me. And then she wasn't anyone.

Sad-Ape is waiting for me at the bottom of the stone steps that lead to the street our block of flats looms over. He revealed a spark by following me home, but that's gone now. The hint that he's like the other Apes out there has shrunk and shrivelled away, as he stares at me half in hope and half in fear.

'You were home,' he says quietly. 'I was right.'

I wipe my snotty nose and salty eyes with the sleeve of my new blazer. 'What did you want?' I cough, half choking on the despair caught in the back of my throat. 'I mean, do you know what just happened because you told him I was home? Do you?' I want to beat at him, bunch my fists and pummel him. I know it's not really his fault, but I can't contain the hurt or the rage that surges through every vein in my body. 'What did you want anyway?' I scream into his face.

'I was worried,' he mumbles into his chest, lowering his face so he doesn't have to meet my gaze.

'What?'

'Worried,' he mumbles again. 'About you.'

I stare at him and it takes everything I've got not to erupt into a heap of spontaneous lava I'm so filled with burning anger.

'You were worried about me?' I ask, incredulous.

'Saw you sneak out of school.' He still can't look at me and I'm having trouble hearing what he's saying.

'So?' I ask him.

'So I followed you.'

'Why would you do that?'

Sad-Ape takes an eternity to respond and he shuffles on the spot before speaking. 'You're the only friend I've got.' And he lifts his great chunk of head, his one good eye meeting my stare. 'We're pals,' he says quietly.

If eyes are the windows to the soul then his single eye is a view on to Sad-Ape's torment. I'm his only friend?

251

'Pals hang with pals,' he says, standing stock still while he waits for me to give the green light to our blossoming friendship. I look down at my blazer and to the grey smear from the ash that clings to the material.

'There's no way out,' I tell him.

'No?' he asks, even though he has no idea what I'm talking about.

'We're stuck here.'

'Then it's good we're pals.'

The Ape is my destiny. It's not Johnson, the boy I can't stop thinking about; it's not even my best friend Billie; it's the Ape. We're always going to be drawn to each other.

Sad-Ape continues to wait and seems incapable of making a move without me telling him to.

'Yeah,' I tell him. 'It's good that we're best pals.'

His glass eye catches a rare moment of sunlight and gleams brighter. He smiles, beaming broadly, and nods eagerly. 'I'm hungry,' he tells me.

'Greggs?' I ask him.

His smile widens.

As we walk into town, moving through the silent, lost people who are as trapped as I am I try to explain to Sad-Ape what I believe this world to be.

'It's just another weird copy,' I tell him.

'Of what?'

'Every other world that's out there.' I tell him.

'A copy?'

'Yes,' I nod.

'Thought I recognised it,' he says, scanning the streets and buildings.

252

We take the steps that lead from the carpark to the pathway that cuts across the tiny skinny river that runs through town. To get to Greggs we take a short cut through the church grounds that dominate the centre of town. This church is still standing, unlike the one Non-Ape levelled in the empty world, and I wonder for a moment if the flock here has tripled in size as the trapped pray for all their worth for salvation.

Then, as we pass the ancient gravestones, my eyes threaten to explode with tears again. I stop suddenly and bend over as if I've been punched in the gut. This is the exact same place where I'm buried, I think. Little Reva Marsalis is in the empty world in this very spot. All alone. No flowers, no gravestone, no memory or celebration of her life.

Sad-Ape shuffles beside me, not knowing what to do or say. The pain travels through me, shaking even more tears from my eyes. That version of me is in that empty world by herself all because her dad couldn't face what had happened. But, if I've learned anything from what I've been through, it's that we belong where we belong. Taking little Reva from one world to another destroyed the order of how things should be. He broke science.

A thick heavy hand tries to delicately pat my back. 'People are looking,' Sad-Ape tells me.

But I don't care. Why didn't little Reva's dad just live with what had happened? It was an accident, no more than that. But he just couldn't cope. And I wonder if I hate him or pity him.

'Rev,' Sad-Ape is now rubbing my back in a circular motion. 'I'm hungry.'

It hits me then that my real dad left. Disappeared. Just like Rev Two's dad probably did . . . I slowly straighten and again wipe my eyes on my sleeve. Did all of the Rev dads in every universe walk out on their wife and daughter? Did they die, go missing, find new love, start new families? Did one dad's disappearance in one world cause the disappearance to reflect and ripple throughout all of the other worlds? They may not have found keys to different kingdoms, but they definitely left a mother and daughter to fend for themselves. Which helps explain the bond I had with Rev Two's mum. I'll probably have that bond with every Rev mum, and I know New-Mum is weird and unsettles me, but given time would I revert to type and grow close to her?

'Greggs,' Sad-Ape tells me in case I've forgotten.

I manage to nod and we set off through the churchyard again.

'Got any money?' He asks.

'Uh . . . no,' I answer. 'You?'

'No.'

But we head to Greggs all the same.

KILL, KILL, KILL

Smoky tendrils rise from my dad's charred body. The walls of the room have scorch marks and most of the monitoring equipment lies on its side, broken or damaged in some way. There was a fight here and it's a fight my dad lost. The Ape prods the body with one of his taped-on scalpels. It squelches. The smell stings our eyes and Johnson looks my way, worried that I'm crying.

'Rev?'

'He said he was hiding,' I tell Johnson. 'But she found him.'

GG stares at the burned body. 'Your doppelganger?' he asks.

'I think so.' I nod.

'Why burn him?' GG asks. 'Why not just ... kill him?' He saw her take Other-Johnson's life with one touch of her hand; he knows what she's capable of.

The Ape prods my dad again. Again he squelches.

'Maybe show a little respect,' Johnson admonishes.

'It's a funny noise,' the Ape says.

We hear footsteps in the Hall and instinctively we are on high alert within a millisecond. The door bursts open and Another-Billie charges in.

255

'Thank God!' she says, exhausted and drained looking. 'I thought you were never coming back. I tried to reach Johnson telepathically, but—'

The Ape immediately goes for her. His fists are curled and his attached five-pointer drives straight towards Another-Billie. She is stunned, but can move faster than the Ape with her super-limbs. And evades his lunging swipe.

'She's back again!' the Ape yells.

'That isn't Billie!' I scream.

'Get behind me,' he says, advancing on her again.

'It's the other one.' Johnson grabs the Ape's arm, feet skidding on the tiled hospital floor as he tries to drag the Ape away from Another-Billie who has her talons out ready to defend herself.

'It's all right,' GG tells the Ape, sounding anything other than that. 'It's fine. Trust us.'

GG reaches for Another-Billie. 'Please excuse the beast. In fact excuse us all because we've been through dark days.' He looks lost and desperate as he takes her hand in his. 'And we're all just a little twitchy,' he mutters.

Before our very eyes GG starts to heal. His broken arm fuses with a grim crack and his fractured bones knit in seconds. His scars heal and broken teeth grow back to replace the ones he lost. Even his quiff returns. That's how powerful Another-Billie's touch is.

'OMG,' he whispers gripping Another-Billie's hand. 'I'm having a makeover.'

'What happened to my dad?' Who burned him?' I ask Another-Billie.

'I got him out of here, and we headed into town,' Another-Billie explains. Her eyes find Johnson and it's pretty clear she's never, ever going to be over him. She keeps snatching glances at him the whole time. 'We hid in the snooker hall.'

'We hid there too,' GG tells her. 'Isn't it a great den?'

Another-Billie regards GG for a moment and I know she's comparing him to Evil-GG, the worst of the worst when it comes to our doppelgangers. Then she collects herself. 'I didn't like sneaking away from Rev, but I couldn't trust her not to do something to your dad. It was OK for a while; he was contacting you, I dunno how, but he said you were coming back. So we waited, eating crisps and drinking coffee.'

'What did you think of him?' I ask. I can't help myself.

'He's all right,' she says. 'He's smart, nice. I like him. He couldn't stop talking about you.'

I blush at this for some reason.

'He said he'd been searching for years. He never gave up either. Not once did he think he wouldn't find you.'

I nod and feel a lump forming in my throat. 'That's what dads do I guess . . .'

Johnson slips a comforting arm round my waist and Another-Billie tenses before trying to pretend she isn't bothered and smiles through her metal teeth.

'You're lucky,' she says and I think she's talking about my dad, but she could also be talking about Johnson. 'So we were hiding and then . . . Then it got weird. This empty world is not empty.'

GG's eyes widen at this. He's been enjoying his newly healed body, checking himself in the small mirror screwed to the wall above the sink in the corner of the room. But his reflected eyes find mine. 'When you say not empty . . .' he says.

'There's something out there,' Another-Billie tells us. 'In town. So we came back to the hospital. I thought maybe Rev would still be here and, if she forgave us, she could also try and help keep us safe. She's who you need when you know there's trouble coming.'

'What was out there?' Johnson asks the zillion-dollar question.

The Ape sits up straighter at this, instincts for the fight and the kill switching to high alert.

'I dunno, but it got your dad, Rev. It ... burned him,' she answers. 'I was fast and I got him back here. But things feel different. The air, the molecules, I'm not sure what exactly but this world has changed. I'm convinced of it.'

Her words linger for a long heavy moment as I think back to what the Moth said. What if the world has finally had enough of us? But worse, has it tried to destroy my dad, our best means of escaping?

'Rev,' Johnson touches my arm. As he does, I see the Ape touch Another-Billie and start to heal as fast as GG did.

'Yowza!'

I look at Johnson and he is as fearful as I've ever seen him. 'Your dad was our ticket out of here.'

I nod.

'What if the Moth was right and this world is angry at us for being here and it's given up waiting for us to find our own way home? What if it attacked your dad because ...'

'...that's the best way to keep us here,' I finish his thought for him. 'It doesn't want us to just leave any more, it wants to destroy us. It's making sure we never come back here.'

Our eyes meet as the same thought strikes us. 'The Moth!' we say in unison. 'It'll go for the Moth next.'

BUS STOP

A few days have passed since my dad – I call him that because I don't have another name for him, it's all too confusing – burned his formula. I don't know if his was the only formula that worked, or if he's lying about all the other Reva dads running out on their families. Right now it doesn't rank very highly alongside my other more pressing needs. I went to check to see how far the darkness had encroached, but it's not really visible to the naked eye. We could have months left, we could have years. If ever there was a perfect description for the word futile, then this is it.

I always imagined that if you knew the world was coming to an end you'd go crazy, fly to Las Vegas, swim with dolphins and maybe try and steal a space rocket. But the reality is that you have to eat and drink. You have to live, despite the fact that you know you'll be dying soon. That lounging around on your sofa, or going out looting, actually doesn't mean a thing or make it any more palatable. Instead you just do what you always do, and secretly hope that the promised doom won't happen. I expected Armageddon to consist of major chaos, round-the-clock screaming and buildings in flames, but the reality is much more mundane. Which makes it doubly ominous somehow. You can't put up a fight when you don't have anything to fight. So you go about your life instead and eke out your days. Until it all becomes too much.

The New-Moth and I have become best buddies already. I know he thinks there's no escape from this world, but I have convinced him that not only was there a portal in the school classroom, but that there was one in the cabin of the lorry. We both went there during a lunch break, but again it refused to give away its secrets. I told New-Moth about the bus parked halfway up a hill which was another possibility for escape. New-Mum and my dad think I'm dating New-Moth and because Sad-Ape knocks on my door at all hours, they also think I've made a friend. They seem happy enough, but dad still has to bite down that horrible inner despair that he's experiencing. I watch him when he's on his own and I wonder how long he can endure New-Mum's madness. She seems to have grown happier with each new repeated dawn.

My dad hasn't spoken to me since that moment in the bedroom. Not properly anyway. I find him staring quietly at me sometimes, but usually he sits and talks about the simple things in life, like tea and toast and should we go out for a Chinese meal. He's trying his level best to make this work. In a hundred years' time I might have grown to accept it but I'm not like him. I can't and won't settle for this.

The New-Moth and I are on our way to find the bus. He calls me Rev now instead of Reva, as he grows more and more comfortable around me. The quiff has gone and he *is wearing his glasses again. Today we've slipped out of school during lunch. I had to make sure Sad-Ape didn't spot me because he lumbers everywhere I go. New-Moth and I start up the steep hill towards the bus. I can see it as we draw closer; it's abandoned and silent, just like the one in the empty world.*

'I heard voices,' I tell the New-Moth. 'I definitely heard voices calling to me when I was last here.'

'What did they say?' he asks me.

'I couldn't make it out.'

The New-Moth nods again and purses his lips in thought. 'I suppose it doesn't really matter. The important thing is there might be another world we could reach.'

I like that the New-Moth is with me. He's the only one I trust right now. Sad-Ape is totally trustworthy, but just doesn't understand what's going on. I've seen New-Johnson on a couple of occasions, once when he was driving on his motor bike with New-Billie clinging to his back, and once in school when he came straight up to me and didn't apologise for dragging me from the truck's cabin.

'I saved you,' was all he said. But there was something in the way he sought me out that made me think he'd been waiting for the right moment to tell me that again. He was gone before I could react, snake-hipping out of the school. I know it's pretty much the same day happening over and over, but it must've been the equivalent of three days before New-Johnson made his move. I hadn't seen him at school in all that time so part of me wonders if he made a special appearance just to tell me that. Which gives me a quiet thrill.

New-Billie and I talk all the time on the phone, usually

late at night. I'm dying to tell her about my continued battle against the apathy that is crawling all over my skin. I want her to know I haven't given up on the thought of escaping. I know I definitely can't mention my dad or his burned formula as much as I want to, but the conversations we have keep us both going. I stay as optimistic as I can, trying to imbue her with hope. Sometimes it doesn't always work.

'I'm not sure I can take it, Rev,' she said two nights ago.

'Hey, c'mon,' I said, hearing her voice crack. 'There's always tomorrow.'

She took a moment and I imagined her wiping tears from her eyes. 'Nice joke.'

'I try.'

'But some days – boy – some days you just think maybe a few more seconds of this is all I can take.'

'Yeah, but . . .' I trailed off.

'But what?'

'You've got the magnificent Johnson.' The words were harder to say that I thought they would be. Johnson is Johnson whichever world you're in. 'You've got him and his motorbike.'

'I guess. But some days we just stare at each other because we have literally run out of things to say.'

'Talking's overrated,' I joked again.

I heard her laugh quietly. Then she changed the subject. 'What's your other world like?'

I almost asked which one she was talking about, but so far I've kept the thought of a multiverse from her. I'm still not sure I can quite believe it and I lived through them. 'It's pretty much like this, but we have pasts and we have futures.'

'So what was your future?' she asked and I swear I could sense her eyes lighting up at the thought of a future.

'Well. I had plans. I was going to move to London, get a job, party a little, meet someone, have kids I guess.'

She let out a low whistle. 'Wow.'

'My mum . . .' The thought of my real mum still stopped my heart. 'I'd make her come with me. I'd have a house big enough for her as well as my little family.'

'Keep talking,' New-Billie urged me. 'Keep telling me about what and who you're going to be.'

And I did. I told her about a life I imagined. The life little four-year-old Reva might have had.

The bus is indeed empty and the door is locked. I peer in the windows while the New-Moth searches for the lever that can open the door in an emergency. 'All buses have them,' he tells me.

I have to get on to my tiptoes to see if there's anyone hiding inside – or, more to the point, lying in wait. I'm too used to danger coming for me.

The bus doors hiss open.

The New-Moth stands back as our eyes meet. He's nervous but not afraid. I join him at the open doors and take a moment. There are no voices. Just like there was no heat in the cabin of the lorry.

'I'd better go first,' the New-Moth volunteers.

'You want to?' I admire his bravery.

'Not really,' he grins. 'But I'm a gentleman.'

The New-Moth places his foot on the first step into the bus.

He waits.

There are still no voices.

He reaches for the interior railing and hoists himself into the bus.

I strain to listen for voices, but apart from the roar of a motorbike in the distance the world is silent. No voices. No nothing.

The New-Moth turns back to me. 'Stay there.'

'No way. I'm coming on board.' I reach for the railing.

'I can do this.' He holds up a hand, indicating that I should stay back. 'Doesn't need two of us.'

He has a point.

But there are still no voices and the bus is probably as useless as the lorry was. The New-Moth steps further into the bus.

The motorbike engine I heard a moment ago gets louder and I realise it's heading our way.

The New-Moth stops to listen, searching for something, anything that will reveal a portal or a white light. He moves deeper into the bus.

'Anything?' I ask, even though I know he'd tell me if there was.

'Not yet.'

The motorbike roars past the bus and carries on towards the centre of town. It's New-Johnson. He didn't spot us, but at least he's riding alone and New-Billie is nowhere to be seen. She's probably enduring a mindless lunch at a mindless table in the mindless school canteen.

The New-Moth stops suddenly. 'Rev?'

I peer into the bus. 'What?'

The New-Moth looks worried.

'What is it?' I ask him.

264

'I think . . .'

'Yeah?' I ask.

'I think I can feel something.'

I climb on board the bus. As I do, I notice in my peripheral vision that New-Johnson has done a one hundred and eighty turn and is now heading back our way. Did he spot me in his wing mirror?

'Stay back!' the New-Moth tells me.

'What have you found?'

'It's not an actual thing, it's a presence, a feeling.'

'I'll help you.'

'Rev, please, let me make sure it's safe first. It might be nothing; it might just be my nerves, or my imagination. But then again . . .' He turns slowly, trying to zero in on whatever it is that he thinks he's sensed. 'Then again . . .'

New-Johnson's motorbike pulls up outside the bus. He kicks the stand down and slides easily off the bike.

'School's out?' he asks as I step off the bus.

'Yeah,' I tell him and block his view of the doorway. Whatever the New-Moth has found is our little secret.

New-Johnson takes me in and his gaze electrifies me. This Johnson is pitched somewhere between the original Johnson and Other-Johnson. He's got the darkness of Other-Johnson, but I'm also convinced he's got the real Johnson's hesitance.

'That bus won't take you anywhere,' he tells me.

'I know.'

'Sure about that?'

'I said I know which would indicate that I'm totally sure.' I have to focus on escaping this town and don't need any more complications so I'm trying to avoid thinking about *how quickly he makes my heart beat. I also don't think I've got room in my heart for a third Johnson, so, as much as I might need his help at some point, I don't want any more than that from him.*

'You always this rude?' he asks, slipping a cigarette between his lips.

'Copying you.'

'What are you doing, Reva?' The voice is my dad's. I spin round expecting to see him standing right behind me, and he is – in a way. He shimmers like a projection, and it's the same as when I first saw him at the train station. I thought it was a dream then, but now I know this dad can do these things. 'Why aren't you at school?'

'MOTH!' I yell. 'Get out of there!'

'What's wrong?' New-Johnson asks. No one can see my dad when he does this, apart from me, and my strange outburst has knocked even New-Johnson's cool attitude off kilter.

'Reva, don't!' My dad's hovering image looks extremely worried. 'You've got to trust me; you can't leave. I burned the formula to save you!'

'Moth! Run!' I scream.

Even before I turn, the warning bleeps that signal the bus doors are closing start. The New-Moth is charging back down the bus's aisle and I reach for the doors and try and stop them closing.

'What's happening?' he shouts.

'We've got to get him out of there!' I shout at New-Johnson and he grabs the edge of a door with me as we fight with all of our might to keep it from slamming shut. But the door mechanism is too powerful and even our combined

strength is barely stopping it from closing. The New-Moth's hands join ours, but the door is dragging all of us with it. New-Johnson's boots scrape on the tarmac and the New-Moth is slipping and skidding on the shiny bus floor.

'What's with this door?' New-Johnson asks.

'Rev!' the New-Moth yells again, a different look in his eye now. He sticks his head through the gap that's left and his eyes meet mine, desperate but determined. 'Rev? Don't look! Please – don't look! This is not the way out. Turn away—'

The door slams shut.

And I don't think I can or want to describe the result.

But it does make me think back to a different time and place where another Moth got run over by a train.

I reel backwards, my heart drowning in despair and bewilderment. New-Johnson isn't faring much better as he staggers away, grabbing me by the waist.

'Don't look, don't look,' he repeats over and over. 'Don't look, Rev.'

I can't breathe, I can't feel, I can't do anything as New-Johnson draws me to him, cradling me, pulling my head into his shoulder.

'Jesus,' he says. 'Jesus.'

The horrible thing about a hill is that, if there's nothing to stop an object's progress, it can roll all the way down, picking up momentum until it reaches the bottom, in this case to career across a carpark before tumbling down stone steps that lead to a meek little river. I don't know how I can even hear the resultant splash from so far away but I do. And New-Johnson hears it too. I look up and his bright blue eyes have turned a dull grey, the life drained from them.

The horror of what just happened may mean that they never regain their colour again.

'Rev,' he says quietly, holding me tight.

I try and look for my dad's apparition, but it's gone and instead I look back at New-Johnson. 'Get me out of here!'

I'm on the back of New-Johnson's motorbike. He leans into a corner and I lean with him the way Other-Johnson taught me. I have my arms wrapped round this Johnson's waist and I can feel his taut stomach through his jacket and T-shirt; it's like a washboard and I hang on to him as tight as I can. Shortly after the New-Moth perished, New-Johnson dragged me kicking and screaming away from the bus and hoisted me on to his motorbike. He was pale and his eyes were still grey but at least he was moving and thinking and trying his best for me. He didn't breathe a word as he climbed on to the motorbike, kicked the stand up and fired up the engine.

He swept down the main high street of the town and accelerated through every red light. Taking bends at great speed, we've raced on towards the edge of town. I know that's where he's heading and I know he's going to drive straight into the nothing. The shock of what happened to New-Moth has triggered all kinds of distress and despair in him.

The motorbike is screaming towards the void. And I'm starting to think that it will be a welcome relief. Seeing New-Moth die like that has broken my resolve. Can I really keep going? Fighting. Running. Killing. I'm so tired of it all. Worn out and worn down. All of my friends are dead. I'm not going to see my real mum ever again because even if I escape from here I have no way of knowing how many worlds are out there. So why not leave the multiverse to get along without me? That's what it wanted all along, right?

The nothing is upon us and I'm going to let this Johnson drive me into its oblivion. I know the liar was trying his level best, but he went about it in completely the wrong way.

'Do it!' I yell to New-Johnson.

'You sure?' he yells back.

'You have to,' I tell him, gripping him tighter. His hand rests on mine as he steers the bike towards the nothing. But even as I say it I feel the motorbike start to slow, the speed bleeding away.

'Johnson?'

New-Johnson is braking.

'No, don't stop!' I yell. 'Please. I've had enough. I'm done, I'm through.'

But the bike keeps slowing. The nothing is looming up in front of us. He applies the brakes and we roll to within a centimetre of it and the bike falls to the right until New-Johnson kicks his leg out and stabilises us.

'You can't stop,' I almost cry.

New-Johnson turns and looks back at me, his eyes level with mine. The blaze of blue is creeping back into them.

'Can't do it, Rev,' he tells me.

'Then get off the bike and I'll do it myself,' I tell him.

'What happened on that bus?' he asks.

It's a simple question, but I'm blank so New-Johnson tries again.

'Rev, do you know what was going on with that door?'

'I thought it was an escape route,' I mumble.

'A what?'

269

'I came from somewhere else, I don't quite know how, but if I got here then I thought that maybe there's a reverse trip.'

I slide off the back seat and approach the nothing. It's just that. A dark nothing. I stare at it for at least a minute before New-Johnson speaks again.

'When you say somewhere else,' he probes.

'I was in a detention on another world.'

'Another world? Yeah, right.'

'I don't care if you believe me. That actually doesn't matter to me. Not right this minute anyway.' I wipe tears from my eyes. 'I was in a detention; a version of you and the others were there as well. A white light came and – after a journey I can barely comprehend – I ended up here.'

I stare at this version of Johnson, his blue eyes laced with disbelief. But I can tell that he wants me to give him something that he can hang on to. The shock of what happened to New-Moth has left him rudderless.

'Tell me more,' he says.

'All my friends died.' My voice is barely a whisper.

'But you didn't.'

'I'm the last survivor.' I offer him an empty smile.

New-Johnson may believe me, he may not. 'Have you told anyone else?'

'Billie.'

He raises an eyebrow at this. 'She kept that quiet,' he murmurs.

'With good reason. It sounds ridiculous,' I tell him.

'A day that repeats forever runs a close second,' he responds.

'I was hoping to surprise her,' I add. 'To show her a better exit than the one she has planned.'

270

He muses on this for a moment. 'Yeah, I can feel she's giving up.' He stares into me again. 'So the Moth believed you?'

I nod.

New-Johnson turns and looks at the darkness. 'Is it me or is that edging closer?' He squints into the void. 'Or is that wishful thinking?'

I reach out and place a hand on his shoulder. I feel him immediately relax a little. 'That's not how a Johnson thinks.'

He reaches up and lays his hand on mine. He doesn't pat or squeeze it, he just rests his hand on mine. It's enough.

'I want out of here,' he says as if daring the darkness to hear him.

THE GATHERING

Lucas is still in a daze.

Yes.

I did say Lucas.

The same Lucas from my world who hanged himself because he couldn't face the empty world.

His house was on the way back to the station so we ducked in and grabbed his body. We found him exactly where we left him and put him into the shopping trolley so that Another-Billie could climb in with him and start to weave her magical healing powers to raise him from the dead. It took a lot out of her and she has a migraine as a result. Right now she is the most important person in this world. She's under armed guard: Johnson with his talons and the Ape with his five-pointer knuckles. GG is bringing up the rear.

'I don't know what it was,' Another-Billie tells us. 'I mean, I do. It was a bolt of lightning. But the sky was clear – there was no thunder, there was just this lightning bolt . . . But it was so quick I can't honestly be sure.'

The more she talks, the more we quicken our pace.

'Like from God?' Johnson asks wryly.

'Or Thor,' GG adds excitedly. 'Go on. Please let it be Thor. Let it be a big muscly man with a big meaty hammer.'

As ever, GG is joking, lightening the gloom as best he can. But he can't lift it like he used to.

'But it didn't hit you?' I ask Another-Billie.

She shakes her head. 'Just your dad.'

I check the sky and there's no storm coming. No sign of meteorological doom heading our way.

'Let's get the others and go.' Johnson speaks up.

Another-Billie snatches a secret glance at Johnson and withers a little. 'It's definitely changed; the world's shifted, I can sense it.' She glances all around her. 'I should have fixed your dad again and then gone straight to the school.'

'You've got me.' The Ape swishes the air with his five-pointer. His way of telling her he'll protect her.

Another-Billie isn't convinced. 'We're all going to burn,' she says quietly.

When Lucas came back from the dead and saw GG, the Ape, Johnson, Another-Billie and me, he looked completely stunned. He couldn't get a grip on any of it. At first he thought his attempt to hang himself had failed and that we'd just turned up and shoved him into a shopping trolley for some reason.

'I was going to kill myself.'

'You did,' GG told him.

'Can't believe I was going to do that.'

'You did do it,' Johnson added.

'I thought I was a whole lot braver than that.'

'You're not.' GG reached out and patted him on the head. 'But hey, we all get a little scared now and then.'

'I thought everyone had gone. Disappeared.' Lucas is open-eyed and slack-jawed.

'We have,' Johnson tells him.

'Funny guy Johnson,' Lucas replies.

'We have gone, my handsome friend,' GG backs Johnson up. 'We've fluttered away to another world.'

'Where's the Moth?' Lucas asks, knowing that his best friend will be able to explain everything to him. I'm all for hurrying that reunion along.

'You might get a tiny little surprise when we reach the train station,' GG tells him. 'In fact you may actually wet yourself. But we'll understand.'

I look at Johnson who is scanning the surrounding area as the sun rises higher, illuminating us, wondering when the attack will come. We decided that my dad, not as badly burned as the first time, could wait to be healed. Our logic is that if he's already dead no one is going to attack him again. You don't kill people twice. Though recent events might argue against that. The unseen enemy that Another-Billie is convinced is out there could well be training their evil intent on us.

'See anything?' I ask Johnson.

'Zip,' he says.

'Feel anything?' I ask.

His eyes find mine and he can't hide a smile. 'That's a leading question.'

The Ape has been quiet the whole way. Every now and then he lurches forward and swishes the air in front of him. Practising his lunges. Lucas can't figure out what the Ape

274

could possibly need such a vicious weapon for, but I guess, at least for now, ignorance is bliss.

'What sort of a surprise?' Lucas asks.

'A good one,' GG tells him. 'And a bad one. And maybe an inbetweenie one.'

Another-Billie is extremely anxious. I can feel the fear emanating from her. 'This is so the worst idea ever. Being out here, exposed like this,' she mumbles. 'The worst.'

'Are you sure you didn't see anyone else out here?' I ask.

'I told you I didn't.'

'So how do you know it wasn't Rev who threw a lightning bolt – assuming it was that?' Johnson asks her.

'Because she can't do stuff like that.'

Which leaves only one obvious question.

'So who can?' I ask.

'Thor can,' GG quips.

The Ape swishes the air, rehearsing his attacks, and, as I watch him, I get the sense that he knows something is coming. He's too quiet, too focused. He's a fighter and he knows when things are about to turn bad.

THE PLAN TO END ALL PLANS

New-Billie is uneasy. She doesn't like missing lessons and she doesn't like the thought of getting detention even though she gets it every day of her life. In this world anyway. We're in the girls' toilets, hiding during lessons. New-Johnson is smoking and looks a little anxious as he sucks deep on his cigarette and then blows smoke to the tiled ceiling. He is sitting in one of the cubicles, toilet lid down, legs stretched out in front of him. His black boots leave scuff marks on the polished floor. Sad-Ape stands by the door, guarding against entry. He may be mentally fragile and missing an eye, but he's still powerful and I've told him that he can't let anyone in. If he does, it's a friendship-breaker (not really, but I need him at his all-conquering best).

'Oh my God,' New-Billie says, dry-mouthed from shock. 'Poor, poor Moth.'

'Still can't take it in.' New-Johnson's tone is still easy and almost lazy, but his brain has been rewired by what happened to New-Moth. It has jolted him into more of the Johnson I know. Correction. Knew.

276

'And Rev,' New-Billie points at me, 'still thinks she can get us out of here?'

'She came here somehow,' New-Johnson tells her, cementing the idea that I haven't been lying to her.

New-Billie casts her eyes over Sad-Ape. 'How come he's involved?'

I step forward, giving Sad-Ape a reassuring look, pushing myself off the sink I've been leaning back on. 'You'll be glad he is. Trust me.' I'm convinced Sad-Ape will come good. It's like I said. Destiny means we're meant to be in this together and somehow it's in his DNA to come to our rescue.

'Rev thinks we should round up the others.'

New-Billie doesn't like that New-Johnson and I have been talking. But she lets it go because what good will falling out over a boy do for either of us? 'The others?' she asks quietly. The death of the Moth has really scrambled her brain.

'GG, Lucas, Carrie and . . .' I was about to add the Moth to the list but that's not going to work. 'Those three,' I correct. 'Those three and us four.'

'Because that's how the universe decrees it?' New-Billie asks.

'And thus it is written in the stars,' I reply, hoping to break through her shock at what happened to New-Moth.

'I don't want to stay here any more,' New-Johnson says to her. 'Do you?'

'But say we do get out, where do we go?' she asks.

Someone pushes at the toilet door, but Sad-Ape shoves it closed. 'Get lost,' he tells them.

There's a pause outside the door and whoever is outside

is clearly thinking, Why is there a boy in the girls' toilets? *They try the door again.*

Sad-Ape places his two meaty palms on the door and, using his mighty man-arms he keeps the door from opening. As he does, I am transported back to the school in the empty world, to my Ape and how he charged into his last battle. I shake myself from the memory, I can't get tearful now. I need to hold it together.

'I'm pooping!' Sad-Ape tells the person outside the door. They groan and retreat. Sad-Ape looks pleased. Mission accomplished. 'I'm not really pooping,' he tells everyone.

New-Billie looks back at me. 'Why us though? Why not just go on your own?'

'I owe it to you all.'

'You don't even know us.'

'I sort of do,' I tell her. 'And I want to try and make up for something that happened. Something I'm not ready to explain yet because I'll never get the words out.'

My guilt is driving this and I never realised that before. The guilt that I abandoned my friends. I didn't plan to, but the result was the same. I left them all behind to perish.

'I want to make amends,' I tell them all.

New-Billie looks at New-Johnson and she knows he's sold on the idea of escape. He would be. He's the type who walks against every tide.

'I've got my dad here,' New Billie tells us. 'Am I meant to just disappear and never see him again?'

I was waiting for this. This world is killing us all slowly, but the others will likely have people here that they don't want to leave behind.

'If we find another world, then we can come back here for

278

anyone and everyone.' I don't actually know if that will be possible, but I try to look convincing.

She turns to New-Johnson. He doesn't try and influence her answer in any way, he just waits, his blue eyes unblinking.

'That makes sense to me; if we could do that, then yeah, I'd love to leave,' she says.

'Good, because I want to go as soon as I can,' I tell her. I can't afford to lose momentum.

'You've got a plan then?' she asks.

Sad-Ape looks over and stands just a little taller than he usually does. 'You'd better leave. I do need a poop now.'

Which is the best sign yet that the real Ape is emerging.

I look at New-Billie. 'The last thing I remember before I came here was fighting my way to the classroom where we have detention. I think – I can't be sure – but the answer could be there.'

'It hasn't been so far and we end up there every day.'

I'm not sure how to respond to this obvious flaw in my plan, but luckily I'm saved by a loud knock on the door. It's the music teacher – Mrs Crow.

'I've been told there's a boy in here and I can smell cigarette smoke. Whoever you are,' she calls from outside, 'you're all getting detention.'

Yeah.

We all kind of knew that by now.

Another-Billie is exhausted. She has given her all and reanimated everyone who needed reanimating. She sits slumped and dizzy in a first-class train seat while GG tends to her, brushing her hair from her eyes and telling her how amazing she is.

'Seriously,' he tells her, 'from a chipped nail to a body with ghastly holes in it, you can fix everything. Though maybe I could have a squarer jaw. Do you do plastic surgery as well?'

Another-Billie is too weak to respond. Other-Johnson and Johnson have swapped back into their rightful bodies and can't help but pick on each other.

'Where's my hat?' Other-Johnson asks.

'What hat?'

'The hat I was wearing.'

'You weren't wearing one.'

'I always wear a hat,' Other-Johnson says.

'Then you know what you can do,' Johnson tells him.

'What's that?'

'Go back to London and find it.' I can tell from the dry lilt to his voice that Johnson is being ironic. 'We'll wait for you.'

Lucas's face is a mixture of bewilderment and downright open-mouthed shock. The Moth is trying to explain everything to him, but Lucas just stands with his eyes wide open and his chin all but touching the floor of the carriage. He keeps glancing back and forth from Moth to Moth Two who is now sitting across the aisle. Lucas can't take in what he's seeing.

Another-Billie healed the Black Moth we rescued from the collapsing shopping centre. It was in the animal panther form until she and Other-Johnson managed to coax the real Moth Two out of the monster and transformed him back to normal. Well, as normal as the dopplegangers get anyway. It means we now have a backup to our escape plans. Two super-science Moth brains are better than one. Though I still can't figure out why Moth Two exists if he was merely a figment of Billie's imagination.

'As long as we believe in him,' the Moth stated, 'then I'm pretty sure he'll exist. Assuming what you told me about Billie's power holds up.'

'I think I should have hanged myself properly,' Lucas mumbles.

'You did,' GG tells him for what feels like the hundredth time.

'Can we start again?' Lucas asks, completely bewildered.

'There's no time,' both the Moths tell him in perfect unison. 'And, if we escape, then you won't need to worry about anything. Everything'll go back to normal.' The Moths are talking with the same voice and the exact same words at the exact same time which is pretty freaky, to be honest.

Lucas's eyes land on the Apes. 'He punched a hotel to the ground?'

'And a Shopping Centre,' the Moth adds. Lucas slumps down and puts his head in his hands. Non-Lucas watches him and then smiles. 'I knew I was hot, but this is smoking hot,' he tells himself, revelling in his reflected perfection.

Carrie's body was the hardest to heal and we thought she was beyond help, but Another-Billie wrung almost every last drop from her healing power and brought my ex-arch-enemy back. Other-Johnson then swiftly swapped Evil-GG back into his own body and we watched Carrie take a deep breath and sit up. She took a while to work out where she was, but when she saw the Moth she got to her feet, ignored the rest of us and staggered to his side and kissed him. But she actually kissed Moth Two and when she felt his metal teeth on her tongue she recoiled and slapped him.

'How dare you?' she yelled at him, even though he'd done very little.

'I'm over here,' the Moth told her, yet again overlooked. Carrie took a moment, weighed the Moths up and then slid with barely any embarrassment towards the Moth.

'You'd better have real teeth,' she warned him.

The Moth almost fell out of his seat, but Carrie kissed him for at least half a minute before she broke away.

'I have no idea why I just did that,' she said to him.

'No need to question it,' the Moth smiled hopefully and then Carrie turned her pointy features my way.

'Remind me. Do I hate you or did we make up? I can't remember.'

Evil-GG came back from the dead and sprang to his feet behind me, unsheathing his talons, ready to take on anyone. 'Okey-doke, now who wants a little taste of GG steel—'

Before he could finish Non-Ape backhanded Evil-GG

through one of the train windows. He flew out on to the track and landed hard on the steel tracks opposite.

'Ow!' Evil-GG groaned. 'Ow, ow, ow! You wretched oaf!'

There's still no sign of Rev Two but my biggest worry is Billie. The last to be resuscitated. Her eyes have returned to normal, from black to blue, and there's no sign of her talons either. The moment she woke up I went straight to her.

'Billie.'

'Rev?' Billie looked unsteady and dazed.

'How you feeling?'

'Uh. Odd.' Then she dredged up a smile. 'But you look terrible.'

I still haven't been 'touched' by Another-Billie and have scars and cuts and bruises all over.

'Thanks, mate,' I told her.

Billie stared at me as her memories flew around inside her head.

'You remember anything?' I asked her tentatively.

'Sadly,' she said.

'I know it wasn't really you,' I told her.

'I was so angry with you,' she whispered. 'Raging.'

'I do that to people,' I joked.

'But I wanted to kill you, Rev.' Billie seemed to shrink back into herself and pulled her arms around her with a shiver. 'Can we go back to being what we were?'

I reached for her as she unfolded her graceful arms and reached for me. We met in the middle and clung to each other as hard as we could.

'I'm already there,' I whispered to her and then held her even tighter as she began to cry.

Evil-GG climbs back in through the broken window, ready to attack. 'Who wants to taste the talon?!' he yelled before Non-Ape backhands him straight out of the window again.

'That is so not funny!' Evil-GG cried.

'It's peace and love, dude. Get used to it,' Other-Johnson called to him through the shattered window.

'Can you find your Rev?' I transmit to Other-Johnson.

'Already have,' he sends back.

'And?'

'It's going to take a bit of explaining,' he sends.

'But is she OK?'

'Yeah.'

'And is there anyone else out there?'

Other-Johnson took a long moment to scan the airwaves. *'Nada,'* he says eventually. *'Least no one I can pick up.'*

I study the Ape, so silent and so ready, on the highest alert. *'There is.'* I assure Other-Johnson. *'Or there will be. We'd better get Non-Ape fed.'*

I want him as huge as he can grow. The bigger he gets, the stronger he gets.

'Anyone want Chinese?' I ask the carriage.

Everyone seems agreeable to that apart from the Moth who sits with Lucas and Carrie. Despite her kiss and despite seeing his best friend again, he can't shake the dread that's enveloped him since we found him at the Shopping Centre. His eyes find each of us in turn and he nods.

'We need to leave,' he says.

'Right now,' echoes Moth Two.

UNFORTUNATE COOKIES TAKE TWO

My dad can't use chopsticks. He keeps trying to, but every time he raises a sweet 'n' sour prawn to his lips it falls back into its china bowl. My mum, who isn't my mum, laughs every time he does it.

Every.

Single.

Time.

We're back in the Chinese restaurant that looks out over the high street. The same waitress quietly serves us and I'm doing my best to force the food down my gullet. My dad hasn't brought up the New-Moth's murder – which is what it is, there's no other word for it – but then again he hasn't had the chance. New-Mum and he met me from school after detention as usual, and we went straight to the Chinese restaurant.

They're used to me being late because of the detention, but what they don't know is that I dragged it out as long as I could. Me, New-Johnson and New-Billie explained to New-GG, New-Carrie and New-Lucas what we

285

were planning to do. They took some convincing but New-Johnson is proving to be very charismatic and determined. New-Carrie was her usual poisonous self, but New-GG was excited by the thought of it. He seemed to be concerned that he'd never find any new fashions if he couldn't escape this town. He was joking of course. I think anyway. New-Lucas was gutted that New-Moth was dead and it motivated him to make a slightly trite speech about not going gently into the good night. We then spent the whole of detention trying to find a portal. But when you don't know what you're looking for it's actually impossible to find.

Everyone lost heart quite quickly, but New-Johnson and I kept everyone afloat – just – with the thought that there is a door somewhere. And, let's face it, we have many many recurring days to finally find it.

Sad-Ape, steadily climbing towards the bullish man-boy glory of a real Ape, was all for going to my dad and hitting him until he told us where the portal was. But I'm scared stiff that the minute my dad (or Non-Dad) gets wind of another attempt at an escape he'll send me away to another world, then go looking again for a replacement.

'Make any new friends?' New-Mum asks as she picks up the fallen prawn in her chopsticks and feeds it to my dad.

'Yes,' I smile. 'Yes, I've got at least six. There were seven . . .' I look directly at my dad. 'But he went away,' I say. 'No idea where.'

My dad drops another prawn and when New-Mum giggles I momentarily wonder if I'll ever again see my real mum laugh again. Once I sneak out tonight and meet the others, I guess I'll find out.

'Six friends is just as good as seven,' my dad tells me.

'Not when you know there should definitely be one more,' I say, not meeting his eye.

The tension between us would be evident to a blind person, but New-Mum is completely oblivious and claps when the waitress arrives to take our dirty plates and leaves fortune cookies for us. She has only had to serve us tonight. There are no other diners in the restaurant.

'I love fortune cookies!' New-Mum says, rather predictably. 'Open yours first, Rev.'

I look at the cookie she offers me and eventually take it from her. She looks on, eager, anticipating the message. I break open the fortune cookie and remove the piece of paper. I quickly clear my throat.

'This is a good one,' I tell them. 'This is almost perfect.'

My dad's eyes meet mine. He's trying to warn me not to make trouble or cause a fuss. He doesn't want New-Mum getting upset.

'Goodbye,' I read.

New-Mum falters. 'That's not a saying.' She frowns.

'Goodbye,' I repeat.

'Are you sure it says that?'

My dad's jaw tightens and I know he's becoming emotional. 'Rev, please,' he whispers.

'Read it,' New-Mum says to Dad. 'She's teasing us.'

I offer the motto to Dad, but as he reaches for it I let it drop to the carpet. Even before he can bend to retrieve it the waitress is there, falling to her knees to find the motto for him. She hands the piece of paper to my dad who nods his thanks. He clears his throat just like I did; it seems we share some habits.

'"Today it's up to you to find the peacefulness you long for,"' he reads.

'Just what I said,' I say to them. 'Goodbye. It's the same thing.'

New-Mum claps and then pushes another fortune cookie towards my dad. 'Your turn.'

Just like he will do for the rest of eternity, or until the darkness blots the last of this world out, Dad weakly pushes the fortune cookie back towards her. 'You do it, you love them.'

'It's yours.' She bats it back playfully.

'I insist.' His eyes light up as he gazes at her. A version of a woman he tore the order of the universe apart to keep happy.

'I insist,' she tells him, giggling now.

'No, I do.' Back the fortune cookie goes.

'Uh-uh, I said it first.'

I think about smashing the fortune cookie with my fist again. But instead this time I let it play out to see what happens.

'You do it,' he tells her. More forcefully this time.

'Oh, if you insist.' She smiles and cracks open the cookie. '"Your smile is a passport into the hearts of others."' The words seem to take her by surprise and she looks like she might cry. 'Isn't that beautiful?' She takes my hand in her right hand and Dad's in her left and we form half a seance as she grips our fingers tightly 'This is beautiful. This is all I ever wanted. It was horrendous without you both. Horrible. It was all the nasty words you can think of. But here we are. Back together. How it should be.'

She continues to grip my hand with a strength that defies

her slim build. My shoulders start to tingle again. 'It's just so beautiful and even the fortune cookie agrees.' She laughs. But tears roll slowly down her cheeks. Tears of happiness? My hand is starting to go numb she's gripping so hard. 'No more nasty thoughts haunting my days, no more wondering, no more loneliness. This is how things should have been all along.' She smiles then lets our hands go.

I shake my hand under the table while my shoulders scream at me. New-Mum pushes the last fortune cookie towards Dad and a flicker of something crosses his face. It looks like fear.

'Read it,' New-Mum tells him. And, despite her smile and his need to be in love with her, he knows he is doomed. This is his lot for as long as he can stand it. Living in a carbon-copy world with a carbon-copy family. I fight the urge to feel pity for him. What he did to my friends in the empty world was wrong on every level.

I can't get the taste of chicken chow mein out of my mouth. I shovelled an entire plateful down my throat because it meant I could avoid talking to them at dinner, but now it's like it's still lurking, hovering above my stomach and filling the back of my throat.

I glance at my bedside clock. Nearly midnight. New-Mum and Dad both went to bed about an hour ago. I don't know if he hoovered up the ash from the burned formula, but somewhere within the body of our ancient vacuum cleaner lies the greatest discovery humankind ever made. In flaky black slivers of ash that crumble the moment you touch them. Trying to open it and tip the contents out on to a piece of newspaper in complete silence is both painstaking and nerve-jangling. I've developed this theory about the ash; if I spread it, as if it was a cremated body, then perhaps some of its latent spirit will somehow have survived. Ridiculous, I know, but that's where I am.

I'm dressed in jeans, a T-shirt and the thickest pullover I own, hand-knitted by New-Mum, and far too long but perfect for the cold night that awaits me. My phone pings with a text. Damn it! I forgot to turn the phone to vibrate. I wait, wondering if the loud echoing ping has woken New-Mum or Dad. There is no movement in their bedroom next door so I switch the phone to silent and read the text. It's from Sad-Ape.

yowza

The word nearly knocks me off the edge of my bed. The Ape's favourite word ever, used on countless occasions. Some things never change.

Yowza, *I type back. And wait.*

u ready? *he sends back.*

:) *I head for the bedroom door.*

same, *he responds.*

I gently open the door and peer out into the darkness of the empty hall. It's such a small flat it'll take me about a millisecond to reach the front door. The chain is on and when they see it hanging loose tomorrow morning they'll immediately know I've run away, even before they check my room. It's a deliberate echo on my part because my dad will have to relive everything he felt when he first discovered his little Reva wasn't in her bedroom. This might sound cruel but that one's for New-Moth.

The plan is for everyone to meet in the school classroom and not leave until we unearth the portal. Spreading the ash of the formula in some ridiculous ritual is the best idea I've come up with so far to try and spring the portal to life.

i said me too! *Sad-Ape seems to want a response.*

The light from his text illuminates the hallway making it easier for me to manoeuvre down it without crashing into something or tripping over. I pop the edge of the phone in my mouth, gripping it between my teeth, and using both hands I very gingerly slide the chain from its latch.

My phone vibrates with another impatient message from Sad-Ape. It rattles against my pearly whites and makes a louder noise than it should.

I hear a cough.

I fall silent, not moving a muscle, not daring to breathe.

Another impatient message rattles against my teeth, and my mouth must be acting like a speaker for it because to me the rattle is louder than a heavy-metal band. I spit the phone into my cupped hand and ease it into my back pocket.

I hear whispers.

They're both awake.

The snib is still down and, just like in my real flat,it sticks because it's such an old lock. I'd forgotten that sometimes you have to shove your weight against the door to release it, not easily done quietly. My phone vibrates twice more in quick succession. Sad-Ape has no patience whatsoever and I'm surprised he isn't banging on the door and ringing the bell.

I can't make out what Dad and New-Mum are saying but a bedside lamp is turned on. I can see the flood of yellow light squeezing between the gap between the floor and the door.

Do I run?

Or do I pretend I was just going to the loo? But why would I have got dressed to do that?

'It's nothing.' Dad's voice is still a whisper, but louder now, as if for emphasis.

'You sure?'

'Go back to sleep.'

'My head still hurts,' New-Mum moans lightly.

'Hang on, I'll get you some more pills.' I hear their bed creak as he climbs from it.

That's it.

Game over.

My phone vibrates over and over and I realise Sad-Ape is now phoning me. Even after I clearly explained in great detail that he should never do that because silence and subterfuge were of the highest importance.

'Hey,' New-Mum's whisper stops my dad.

I press quietly, but with as much force as I can on the door and get ready to push the snib down.

'Yeah?' My dad stops.

I have to time this right. I have to push the door at the exact moment there's some noise to cover it. Conversation might well do it, if only they'd talk a little louder.

My phone has thankfully gone to answerphone, ending Sad-Ape's incessant calling.

'I could live these days forever,' she tells him.

They've given up whispering.

'We will,' my dad promises.

'Over and over,' she replies.

My phone starts vibrating because the answerphone is now telling me I have a message. Sad-Ape has left a message?

'Over and over,' he repeats and I go for it, ramming the snib down and even though it clicks, I'm pretty sure Dad's voice has drowned it out.

'She's not how I thought she'd be,' New-Mum adds. And I can't help it, I'm intrigued now. 'The other one was a lot more loving.'

'It's the same person.'

'I know that,' she says. 'And eventually she'll be like my little Reva.' There's some serious and confusing insanity going on here and I pull the front door open as quietly as I can. 'A mother's instinct is a strange thing. I can't have her disappearing again. It'd kill me.'

'That won't happen. I promise,' he tells her. 'She's staying right here. There's no chance she could disappear, ... I made sure of it.'

I remember the ash on my school blazer. The formula that is no more.

'Promise me?' New-Mum has a true pain trapped in her voice.

'It's all as it should be now. Nothing can change that; there are no doors she can walk through, no trains or buses that she can take. All roads only lead to home. To here.'

And weirdly I hope he's right. That all roads, or even just one, will lead me to my home. My real home.

Tonight's desperate mission has to work. I ease out of the door and close it very gently behind me, praying that when my dad eventually does go and fetch some headache pills he doesn't see that the chain is off the latch.

The shadows are darker than ever, but I've become used to the concrete steps and glide serenely towards them. Until a

293

huge figure lumbers out of the darkness and grabs me. It's all I can do not to scream the neighbourhood down.

'Why you not texting?' Sad-Ape asks. He's out of breath because he has hurried here. He's sweating even in the cold and he smells strongly of BO. I ease from his bear-like arms. He was worried about me and I like that he charged up to see what was happening. He's turning more and more into a real Ape.

'Was trying to sneak out,' I whisper.

'Why not tell me that?' he asks.

'Because I was trying to sneak out silently.'

'But I didn't know that.'

'You did – I told you earlier!'

'No need to shout. You're meant to be doing this quietly,' he says. 'Stupid.'

'I'm not the stupid one,' I whisper to him.

'Ha – gotcha!' he whispers back as we hit the street that will eventually lead us to the others.

He's already driving me mad.

'So gotcha.' He snorts.

We pass under the light from one of the street lamps and for a very brief second I can see the Ape again. My Ape. And because of that I can forgive him anything.

Rice.

Mounds of it.

Heaps upon heaps of it.

Filling plate after plate and spilling over the edges on to the carpet.

It's all anyone knows how to cook. Rice. And some soy sauce if you want to add a little flavour. GG has been arguing with Evil-GG over who is the best chef and their argument can still be heard from the kitchen of the Chinese restaurant.

'I can do a million things with rice,' one of them says.

'I can do a million and one,' the other GG says, and no one can tell which is which without seeing them.

'Name them.'

'Name them?'

'Name the million and one things you can do with rice.'

'Have you got a spare lifetime?'

'I have got that, yes, indeed I have, right here in my pocket.'

'OK. Here's the first name of a rice recipe. You ready?'

'I'm almost wetting myself in excitement.'

'Thought you were just standing funny.'

'The recipe.' One of them snaps his fingers impatiently. 'What's it called?'

'George.'

'George?'

'Your face. So perfect and yet so frowny.'

'Then let me step aside and allow the master chef take over with his million and one recipes for a rice based dining experience.'

The last time they met, Evil-GG left GG tied up in a kitchen, while vowing to come back and gut him after he'd killed the rest of us. So this conversation is actually a big improvement.

The Apes know how to use chopsticks which amazes me because I can never get the hang of them. Non-Ape is on his nineteenth plate of rice and has grown huge again.

'Feed me,' he keeps repeating. Even though he's feeding himself, shovelling a trillion grains of soft white cereal grain into the dark maw of his huge mouth.

The Ape is also shovelling down as much as he can manage, but there is nothing as magnificent as Non-Ape's way with food. He lifts a plate and tips the rice into his mouth, half of it spilling down his cheeks and neck. He's also trying to speak at the same time which means thousands of rice grains zing across the restaurant, showering us with increasing force the bigger he grows.

'Feed me!' He laughs, then coughs and chokes and splutters, sending even more rice flying towards us.

'Ape!' Carrie feels the side of her stung face as tiny rice bullets strike her.

296

The Ape starts laughing and then Non-Ape joins him and even more rice starts to rain down.

'Uh, guys . . .' The Moth is sitting with Carrie and they've been holding hands under the table. I know this because I dropped my fork and when I retrieved it I witnessed Carrie take the Moth's hand in hers. 'You're spitting rice in our rice,' the Moth tells them.

'Rice in rice!' The Ape finds this hysterical for some reason.

Non-Ape laughs loudly as he tips another plate into his mouth, half of which turns into a saliva/rice blizzard.

Johnson pushes his plate away from him. 'I'm not so hungry any more.'

Other-Johnson is standing with Another-Billie at one of the leaded windows that look directly out on to the main high street of the empty town. He's been talking to Rev Two telepathically but so far she has refused to join us. He hasn't explained why. Another-Billie is more focused on whatever pyromania-dealing death is lurking outside and keeps her eyes peeled the whole time.

Moth Two stands in the doorway, impatient to get moving. 'We should just run for it,' he says and then turns to look at the paralysed version of himself. 'Or just get moving,' he corrects. 'In your own time of course.'

No one is going anywhere without Non-Ape at full power. If this world is coming for us then it's going to have to go through the boy-monster first.

'I didn't cause a tidal wave,' Billie tells me.

'You probably forgot.'

Billie and I have been talking non-stop since she returned to normal.

'A tidal wave? Seriously? I left with Johnson – or who I thought was Johnson – and that was that,' she says, basically confirming everything the Moth has been fretting about. Could this world have created the wave to kill us? 'I mean, why would I do that?' Billie asks. Which is a reasonable enough question. 'If I had Johnson, then I had whatever–' she looks at Johnson '–I foolishly thought I wanted. I didn't want to kill anyone after that.' She then gets hit by a smattering of rice bullets. 'Well. Maybe some people,' she says aiming a scathing look at the laughing Apes. But at least this time I know that she's being ironic.

'You did sort of kill the other Johnson,' I remind her.

'Well, apart from him, but I was so far gone by then. And that was a good while after your tidal wave.'

Johnson leans forward and keeps his voice low and gentle. 'No one did get hurt. Not even the Big Ape. Not ultimately.'

I watch the Moth and Carrie for a moment as he picks rice from her hair. It seems incredible that she was sent straight into my arms during the tidal wave. The chances of that were beyond astronomical. So what if Moth's right, that we've been rounded up? Like lambs to the slaughter?

The Lucases are seated together in a far corner of the restaurant. They're not necessarily ignoring us, but our Lucas is still having a deeply disturbing time trying to comprehend everything. He has taken sanctuary in his doppelganger, primarily because his best friend the Moth is otherwise occupied, but also because Non-Lucas has gravitated towards him. They're both boys-who-would-be-prefects. Perfect prefects in fact. They exist in the rarefied air of being physically and mentally wonderful. When Non-Lucas shows Lucas his talons and then makes his loam skin ripple into a form of armour, Lucas claps quietly.

'Man, that's something,' he says.

I study the doppelgangers in the room, then hear Evil-GG bickering with GG in the kitchen.

'You're not adding that to rice,' one of them scolds the other. 'I really thought you, of all people, would have had the best most exquisite taste in the universe.'

Now we're all together like this it's actually going to be strange to split everyone up. Although I know that Johnson is relieved that Other-Johnson is about to be a footnote in a very weird personal history.

And then my heart leaps into my mouth.

They can't possibly go back. That murderous town made it clear that they were all hated.

I glance again at the Moth. There was something he said once. It's scratching at the back of my mind. Something about them pouring through to this world; that once they worked out my dad's papers, his formula, the doppelgangers from the violent world of talons and superpowers will come here. He was convinced of it. And, if Billie didn't cause the tidal wave, are some of them here already?

More booming laughter brings another hailstorm of rice. The Lucases are glad they're safe in their corner but Carrie is directly in the firing line. 'So not funny!' she barks at them. Which makes them laugh even harder.

I get up and go to the window. Other-Johnson has probably been reading my mind, invading my thoughts without my knowing. He knows it's getting close to the moment of truth and that this time he'll definitely never see me again.

'I'm glad we're leaving,' he lies telepathically. *'You've been nothing but trouble.'*

I smile to myself.

'Billie,' I turn to Another-Billie. 'I know it's pitch-black and you're scared to go outside but I think we need to get my dad healed. As quickly as possible.'

'We might be too late,' Other-Johnson transmits and I glance over to see a worried look on his face just as my shoulders erupt in the most violent tingling sensation ever, so much that I shudder hugely.

The Apes stop eating and turn to the window. Instincts cutting in quicker than thought.

Other-Johnson's talons slide out. All at once.

The door crashes open and Rev Two stands there, my carbon copy, eyes wild with alarm, her hand the colour of ocean blue and throbbing, pumping in time with her racing heartbeat.

'I don't care whose dad it is,' she pants. 'I want out of here.'

Other-Johnson transmits the images to all of us at the same time. Images I will never forget in the rather short lifetime that I have left. The world has turned dark and the small tiny river I almost froze to death in is starting to bubble and rise and flood. Snow begins to fall, turning into a blizzard in seconds. Lightning bolts crash from the skies and set cars and trees and buildings on fire. But, when one huge and errant lightning hits the school bus parked on the side of the hill the doors are torn off. The electricity snakes throughout the bus, lighting it up inside, turning it as white as the white light that transported us here in the first place. So bright it blinds.

The Chinese restaurant shudders and tables lift and slide as the earth underneath swells like a wave and ripples along the floor, tearing the restaurant's foundations apart. The ceiling cracks and splinters; the window shatters into a million pieces.

'I told you there wasn't time to eat,' the Moths say in unison.

It's no longer safe inside, but it's even more hazardous outside.

Rev Two is thrown face to face with me by the earth tremor and her blue hand misses brushing my skin by less than a centimetre. For a moment we are trapped in time, staring at each other.

'We've got unfinished business,' she tells me.

'You want to do this now? Really?' I ask as the ceiling gives way above us.

She lunges for me, but with her non-blue hand, and drags me out of harm's way with her super-speed and strength.

'Tell me one thing,' she demands as the others take cover wherever they can find it. 'Did he kiss you?' She means Other-Johnson.

'No,' I lie.

'I knew it.' She can spot my lie easily. She is me, after all.

More ceiling collapses around us and the super-powered versions of ourselves are doing everything they can to protect us. It surprises me that they do, even if we have become 'friends', but there's little time to question why.

'I could let you die here,' Rev Two tells me.

'If we don't stop bickering, we'll both die.' I meet her

301

deadly look. 'You and Other-Johnson can work it out for yourselves when you get back.'

Rev Two continues to waver between sapping the life from me and doing her level best to see sense. 'This really isn't the time or place,' I tell her, hoping she'll settle for common sense. But then again I did kiss the boy she loves and maybe for her that takes precedence over a potential apocalypse.

'Guys!' Other-Johnson is back in our heads, filling them with images, showing us that this stupid empty earth has opened up the portal in the bus on the hill. So it turns out that it either takes a brilliant formula or just several strikes of megawatt lightning to tear holes between worlds. There was already a fragility to the walls of reality in that bus, so perhaps it's a weak spot between worlds.

People from the violent world start to stream through, led by Del, a boy with a glowing burning head. A teacher follows him. Mrs Crow – the mild-mannered music teacher – and she points to a tree and it erupts into flames, keen to do battle with the freezing cold elements. I'm as stunned as everyone else as Other-Johnson relays image after image to us.

Lightning strikes rain down, scorching the deepening snow as the winds begin to pick up all around the town.

The Moths, sheltering with Carrie, look at one another as more and more doppelgangers career from the bus and try to find shelter immediately. 'Oh, no,' they say in stereo. 'That's not good.'

The restaurant lurches to one side as another earth ripple tries to force us out into the open.

Both Moths hesitate and then the same thought strikes them. 'This is one careless world,' they say over the roar of snow and storm and lightning crashing in through the broken windows. 'It needs to think about what it's doing.'

More people from the doppelganger world alight from the bus. Teachers, teenagers, business people in suits, shopkeepers, scruffy students stagger and stumble out as they try to adjust to the maelstrom of elements swirling around them. Talons immediately come out, powers are turned up to eleven, as they try and take in what is happening them to them.

The Moth looks to Moth Two. 'More people—'

'—which is definitely what this world doesn't want—'

'—mean it's going to have to up its game.'

'Oops!' Moth Two is stricken by the horrifying thought. The world tried to use lethal weather to finally rid itself of us and somehow managed to tear a huge hole between worlds and drag even more people in. The precise thing it doesn't want.

GG and Evil-GG emerge through the wrecked kitchen door. 'Rice is off,' GG says.

I turn quickly to Non-Ape. 'You've got to get to the bus,' I tell him. 'And then you have to do what you love doing the most.'

'Smash it!' He grins.

'Yeah. Smash it so hard that no one else can get through.' There are already over fifty of them gathering and there's no sign of them stopping. 'Can you do that for us?' I ask him, knowing that he might not be able to withstand their combined might. They are not happy to be here and the second they think it has something to do with us is the moment they cut loose. They have the shortest fuses I have ever met; quick to anger and even quicker to attack. But we need the onrush of displaced doppelgangers stopped. The Moths are right; the more people making chaos then the more violent this world will become and there goes all hope of escape.

'Easy.' He picks a single grain of rice from my hair and swallows it.

'Let's go,' the Ape says, joining him.

'No, Dazza,' I tell him. 'There's too many, they're too powerful, you won't survive.'

'I beat them before,' he tells me, forgetting that Rev Two's mum sort of beat them for us.

'No, please listen to me.' I can feel my heart lurching in my chest, somersaulting until I want to throw up. 'You need to be here with me. So say goodbye to Non-Ape, wish him well, but you can't go with him.'

The Ape reaches out to me, puts a warm hand on my shoulder, careful that two of his five-pointer scalpels don't take my eye out. His eyes meet mine and, for the first time in his life, I think he's going to say something gentle and profound, but I really hope he doesn't because I'm going to dissolve into tears when he does.

'Yowza.'

And with that he disappears with Non-Ape, charging out of the broken restaurant, down the carpeted stairs and out into possibly the last September day they'll ever know. Him and his best buddy. Off to war. To crush the bus and save the day.

Johnson knows what this means to me as I watch from one of the smashed windows as one giant Ape and one smaller one thunder down the high street, yelling something about buses, crashing through the snow and lightning. Non-Ape

304

strides through the growing winds as if they didn't exist and the Ape is tucked in right behind him. 'Rev, we've got to go,' he says quietly.

'I know,' I respond equally quietly. I can barely talk as my heart thumps at my ribs. What if this is it? What if I never see the Ape again?

I turn to the others and summon as much courage as I can. They all look back, expecting some rallying cry, or maybe a speech. 'We need to get Another-Billie back to my dad. Soon as he's healed we'll meet at the school. That same old detention room. But for the last time.'

'We're splitting up?' GG asks and turns to Evil-GG. 'We were getting along so famously.'

'What's the plan?' Non-Lucas asks while Lucas hangs back. He just isn't equipped for this; he hasn't been in the battles we have.

'You've got speed, you can get your Billie to the hospital in seconds.'

'Sure.' His skin forms its armour again, rippling up and down his hands and arms and all across his face and neck. He glances back at Lucas. 'We'll be waiting in the classroom. Make sure you get there.' They do some sort of ghetto handshake and before we can react Non-Lucas has taken Another-Billie and disappeared into the violent weather outside.

Rev Two steps forward. 'Johnson and I will catch up with them, make sure they get your dad to the school after he's been healed,' she tells me, meaning Other-Johnson.

'We need one of you to carry the Moth,' I tell her.

She looks at Other-Johnson and then at me. 'If you think you're going with her think again.'

Other-Johnson transmits a brief thought to me. *'Can't wait to get back home. She is going to kill me,'* he jokes, but it catches in the back of his throat. For a moment I think he's going to transmit another farewell message, but I guess we've already said our goodbyes enough times now.

'Moth,' he says to Moth Two, 'we're up.'

Moth Two looks at the Moth and bumps his fist with his carbon copy. 'The odds of success are astronomical,' they tell each other in unison, then grin. Moth Two turns back into the panther creature and gets ready to run to the hospital.

Moth Two leaves with Other-Johnson and I can't help but sneak a look at Other-Johnson before he disappears into the snowstorm. That boy nearly stole my heart forever. And again I wonder if this is the last of us now. The last of all of us.

'See you in the classroom,' I call too late, they're gone at speed and I don't know if he heard me.

Rev Two squares up to me. 'I'd love to hear every single thing that went on between you two. But I guess that's not going to happen. When this is done, you're going your way and I'm going mine.'

'Deal,' I nod and only remember just in time not to shake her proffered glowing blue hand.

Other-Johnson continues to transmit images from the bus to us. He is seeing it all though the eyes of various doppelgangers whose minds he invades.

I watch as the Apes arrive at the bus.

The swelling numbers of bewildered doppelgangers can barely make out Ape in the raging snowstorm. The winds are ripping the autumn leaves from the trees and making visibility even more difficult as they blow and swirl and circle in the frozen air. But Non-Ape, at the size he currently is after eating so much rice, is hard to miss. As soon as they see him coming with the Ape drawing alongside him, they react just like I thought they would.

They turn instantly aggressive, talons emerging, powers switching on.

But there's hope in the slash of fear that slices through the ever-increasing crowd of violent doppelgangers. They're petrified of Non-Ape, and I think to myself, just wait until you see what *my* Ape can do.

HOPELESS IN HARDACRE

We're gathered in the classroom and it's two a.m. in the morning. It's freezing in the room and New-GG seems to hate the cold as much my GG did.

'I hate any type of non-warmth,' he whines even though he is wearing his faux-fur-lined WAR(M) jacket. 'And the dark,' he adds. 'The dark and the cold are not my idea of a good time. Or the wet.'

'We're not here for a good time,' New-Johnson replies.

'Now you tell me,' New-GG says with a layer of cynicism in case we miss his joke. 'I wouldn't have responded to the invite if I'd known that.'

Which was a text from New-Billie to the others, telling them where and when to meet.

Sad-Ape sticks close to me, so close I can smell his body odour creeping up my nostrils. New-Carrie is with New-Lucas and both are a little on the quiet side. They're talking about New-Moth.

'I was growing to like him,' she says. 'Well, as much as I like anyone.'

I've spread the ash and dust from the vacuum cleaner, but so far nothing incredible has happened. No flash of white light, no key, no portal.

New-GG cups his hands and blows into them. 'I'm not even sure why I want to escape,' he suddenly announces.

'Because from this point on everything becomes inevitable,' New-Lucas tells him. 'We are facing the end of days.'

'Very dramatic,' New-GG whistles.

'You know it better than anyone,' New-Carrie tells him. 'You're the one who picks on the Ape the most. After he proved there was no way out of town.'

New-GG falls silent. A miracle in itself.

But the dust and ash remain just that. Nothing magical happens even though we wait until it's nearly four in the morning, once again combing every square centimetre of the classroom and coming up with nothing.

I want to scream. The desperate plan has failed desperately.

'So what now?' New-Carrie asks.

'I guess we live the day all over again,' New-Billie declares and I watch another piece of her die, a light switching off behind her eyes. She squeezes my arm. 'Nice try though,' she tells me.

'Let's tear the floorboards up,' I suggest. 'Peel the plaster from the walls. There's got to be a way out.' My voice is turning high-pitched in desperation.

But one by one the light diminishes in all of them.

'I'm going home,' New-GG yawns. 'That's enough non-excitement for one night.'

New-Lucas watches him leave and then New-Carrie

heads past him towards the door. 'See you back here after school no doubt,' she says to no one in particular. Resignation in her normally shrill voice.

'Guys ...' New-Lucas calls after them. But they don't return.

New-Johnson lights a cigarette and blows a stream of smoke towards the ceiling.

'They're bad for you,' I say half-heartedly. I have nothing but trivial thoughts left in my head. The disappointment has crushed me.

'They can't be,' he replies. 'I wake up with fresh lungs every day.'

New-Billie takes his hand and he lets her have a puff on his cigarette. 'We all do.'

Which is when the light-bulb moment hits like a heavyweight's right hook.

Oh.

My.

God.

And suddenly everything looks bright again.

IN THE TIME OF WAR

Other-Johnson, even while he's racing with Moth Two to the hospital, is jumping from one violent world interloper's mind to the next. He's doing this because Non-Ape is attacking them one by one. My Ape is there by his side, in the middle of the battle, cutting and slicing his way to the bus. Over a hundred doppelgangers have emerged through the portal now. Non-Ape has only one thing on his mind; to reach the bus, to crush the bus. They use their powers and their talons on him, but on he roars, fuelled by the bucketloads of boiled rice he's just eaten. Invincible, unbeatable, absolutely and utterly invulnerable to anything they throw at him. He can't stop them all and some evade both him and the Ape and fly, run, jump, even blink from one spot to another, swarming their way across town. The bus spews out evil doppelganger after evil doppelganger but on the Apes fight.

The world gets angrier and more belligerent as the river floods and the snow fills every pocket of air. It knows it has made a huge mistake by accidentally opening the portal and is getting ready to put a stop to it.

We're taking a less combative route to the school, using the empty alleyways and sneaky shortcuts that proliferate throughout the freezing town. Rev Two is strong enough to piggyback the Moth with ease and he hangs tightly on to her. Evil-GG could also probably carry him, but he claimed he had a ricked back and a broken fingernail from being thrown out of the train window – twice. My GG, Carrie and Billie are barely breathing in case a doppelganger hears them. Lucas is still trapped in his world of wonder and disbelief. He staggers through the hurricane winds as best he can.

'We'll freeze to death out here,' he whispers as we edge into the churchyard, where the levelled church is barely more than ancient, hallowed rubble thanks to Non-Ape. But it provides cover from the elements as we lie low for a few moments, studying the steepest of the steep hills that leads back to the school. A hill that is blanketed by snow and battered by winds that carry lightning bolts. The swollen river has already submerged the wide expanse of empty car park and shows no signs of receding. It won't be too long before the town starts to drown. But luckily we are going uphill, a very steep hill at that.

'If we divert to the south there's a twisty overgrown pathway that leads through a clumps of houses,' Rev Two says, taking command of the group, possibly like I did without ever realising it.

'Near that big cemetery?' I ask through chattering lips.

She nods. 'We can take that path and head down another alley way before emerging above the school. Sound like a plan?'

'My ears are so cold I can't hear,' GG says.

'What?' Evil-GG immediately jokes back.

Rev Two's route is a good one, but at some point we will have to reveal ourselves and navigate at least fifty metres of open road before taking the corner that will lead us to the school parking area. We'll be lucky if we do it without being seen. The doppelgangers that got past the Apes will be lapping up the fact that there really is another world for them to try and exploit. They don't realise it doesn't want them either.

'We'll freeze before we get there,' Lucas warns, his voice immediately whipped away in the violent winds.

'Don't worry, you'll probably die before you freeze,' Evil-GG tells him. 'Those people from our town, they are not fans of ours. Especially not if they blame us for this. Which they will do because really they are awful people.'

'They're worse than awful,' GG confirms. Like me, he's seen them up close and personal. 'No offence,' he quickly adds in the direction of Rev Two.

Carrie eyes the car park and is the first to see movement. 'Get down,' she whispers.

We duck as five boys from the violent world, led by burning-headed Not-Del emerge from a hole in the fabric of reality and start splashing through the empty car park. One of them must be a teleporter. They are bewildered as they scan the town. 'What the hell? I mean – seriously – what the hell is happening to our town?' Not-Del asks, clearly not grasping that they have been shunted here.

'D'you know all of them?' I ask Rev Two. She nods. 'What can they do?' I ask.

'Power-wise?' she says and thinks for a moment. 'Some can't do anything.'

'But they've got talons,' the Moth reminds her.

'We've all got talons.' To prove her point she shows us one of hers. A gleaming steel death-dealer. 'Some of those boys can do stuff, like the tall one can spit acid.'

'Gross,' GG groans. Then thinks for a moment. 'Unless of course you can't find your nail-varnish remover.'

'The short one with the dark hair, he can spin.'

'Spinning doesn't sound that scary,' Carrie whispers, teeth chattering from the insane cold. 'Maybe we can cut through them, because we really need to move before we turn into statues.' She shivers and wraps her skinny, pointy arms around herself.

'He turns like a hurricane, a vortex. He can suck you in and shred you,' Evil-GG tells us.

'Makes you giddy just thinking about it,' GG quips half-heartedly, like the rest of us he is freezing to death. We have to go. As in right now.

'We're at the hospital.' Other-Johnson enters my head again. *'Billie's healing your dad as fast as she can. She doesn't know how long it'll take but he's already looking better.'*

'Can you take them?' I ask Rev Two.

Rev Two's full chest swells a little further. 'I can take them,' she purrs.

Johnson joins us, watches as one of Not-Del's mates is suddenly burned to a crisp by a bolt of lightning, leaving Not-Del stunned, quite literally, as the electricity from the bolt travels through the water they are trudging in. All of the boys are blown off their feet. This world has obviously had enough of playing nicely.

'Looks like we caught a break,' Johnson whispers and leads the charge for the alley that'll take us up the hill. 'C'mon! Move it!'

As we run, the white sky erupts over where the bus is and we watch plasma beams arc through the air as the Apes continue fighting their way to the bus.

'Jesus,' Rev Two whispers. It's my whisper, my voice.

The night crackles and fizzes as the battle rages. But there's a new group of violent doppelgangers surging into the car park now, at least twenty of them, angry and bewildered in equal measure. They're not quite sure why they're here, but their awe is taking a battering as the empty earth rains everything bar a plague of frogs down.

'They've seen us!' yells Billie.

'I've got this,' Rev Two steals the greatest line ever spoken, but I'm not going to split hairs as she shoves the Moth into Evil-GG's arms. 'Get to the school.'

Rev Two's hand erupts into a luminescent blue, brighter than ever, as she goes to meet the gang of murderous doppelgangers. The lightning and snow don't faze or slow her.

'She's buying us time,' Johnson tells us, but we are all aware of that and her probable sacrifice bites deeper than the icy winds.

'She's magnificent.' The Moth speaks for all of us, as Rev Two seems to glide on top of the rising flood, graceful as graceful gets as she meets the gang of doppelgangers head on. The rest of us head for the dark, overgrown alleyway as fast as we can.

When I glance back, practically all I can make out in the blur of snow is a slashing blue blur. But then Rev Two's entire body glows blue as she momentarily looks in my direction. I don't know if she can see me or not, but she raises her arm in the air, in complete defiance. She's raising it my way, her blue hand dazzling and crackling like never before. She makes a fist and I raise my hand and make the same fist in recognition of her gesture. And then the doppelgangers surge towards her.

Please beat them, I think to myself, *beat them all, Rev.*

We probably have about five minutes before we die of exposure – that's if we don't get ambushed first – so we charge up the snowy sludge of the alleyway as fast as we can, slipping and sliding, scrabbling for purchase only to slip back again.

Evil-GG reaches the top of the alleyway before the rest of us are halfway up it. He takes a moment to set the Moth down, making sure he's as shielded from the elements as much as possible before heading back down the steep alley and collecting GG.

'Shouldn't it be ladies first?' GG squeaks as he's swept up into Evil-GG's sinewy arms.

'It is, babe,' Evil-GG smirks as he darts back up the alley again.

Johnson sees me slip and grabs my hand, pulling me to him. 'I'm quitting school,' he tells me as he pants hard, breathing in great gulps of snow-filled oxygen.

'You and me both,' I cough as we hold on tight and fight our way to the top of the alley.

Billie catches my other hand. 'I'm signing on the minute we get back.'

Evil-GG comes back for Carrie and is ready to return for Billie when a new group of doppelgangers appear at the top of the alleyway. There must be a dozen of them. One of them is a toothy, rotund woman, and her carbon copy from my world works in Specsavers.

316

Evil-GG spots them first. 'Time to let the beast out,' he yells over the raging, roiling elements. Back in his world, Evil-GG is feared by one and all. He is the worst of the worst according to Other-Johnson, and he unsheathes his talons and starts firing them back up the alleyway as he charges towards the doppelgangers, a violent, merciless whirl of spite.

'You think so?' A deep baritone voice booms down through the snowstorm, and it comes from an exact copy of our red-faced town crier who marches up and down the high street on a Saturday, ringing a bell and bellowing loudly. 'YOU REALLY THINK SO?!' he yells and his voice rumbles with such force that it comes rocketing down the alleyway and catches Evil-GG, hitting him like a concrete wall and smashing him backwards. The voice continues to pick up momentum and force as it sends Evil-GG slipping and sliding and tumbling back towards me, Billie, Johnson and Lucas. He clatters into us and we are thrown backwards in an avalanche of limbs until we reach the bottom of the alleyway, landing in the freezing waters of the ever rising river.

Evil-GG springs to his feet, shakes himself then yanks me and Johnson to our feet before pulling a cowering, shivering Lucas to his feet.

'I hate this, I hate this,' Lucas says over and over.

'You OK?' Evil-GG asks me and Johnson.

All we manage between is a nod.

Billie gathers herself. 'Can't you shut that guy up?' she asks Evil-GG.

'The safe word for today is *schtum*,' grins Evil-GG and is about to take the attack back to the doppelgangers.

'They've got the others!' Lucas points through the storm and we can clearly see GG making Carrie get behind him as he tries to protect her and the Moth from the doppelgangers who have now turned in their direction. There is no way we can reach them on time.

'Save them!' I scream at Evil-GG, as if he can magically get there in time. And bless him for trying, he starts back up the steep alleyway as fast as he can.

'Hey, big mouth!' he yells, but his voice is nothing compared to the town crier's.

Johnson takes my hand and we start climbing up the alleyway again. Now is not the time to give in. Even Lucas follows, his mind genuinely scrambled but still able to recognise that the Moth is in danger. Billie brings up the rear.

'Rev,' she pants.

'Yeah?'

'Get Evil-GG to cut me.'

'What?'

'If he cuts me, I can turn back to . . . whatever I was. You need that version of me.'

If ever I wished that she was still infected and able to create reality, then this is the exact time.

'No. No way,' I pant. 'I couldn't let you go through that again.'

Up ahead the doppelgangers are gathering in front of GG who is clearly saying something to them. Maybe he's pretending to be Evil-GG again, but whatever second he buys before the doppelgangers descend on him is a godsend. From nowhere the bus comes spinning out of the sky and lands directly on the doppelgangers. All of them. Non-Ape has reached it, smashed it and then thrown it away. The bus squishes the crowd instantly. It's doubtful he was aiming for them, there's no way he could see them from where he is, but we needed luck and it came our way, so I'm not going to complain.

'You know how you can miss the bus and you get really angry,' Evil-GG babbles as he helps drag us uphill. 'Well, look what happens when it doesn't miss you.'

A mighty roar booms into the sky and it starts raining broken alien bodies as Non-Ape hurls doppelgangers this way and that. They hurtle down, plummeting and landing hard all around us, some are still alive but after impact they probably wish they weren't.

'We're going to be all right!' Billie says, reaching the top of the alley. 'We can do this.'

The Apes have stopped the invasion. They've closed the portal down.

Billie's right. For once we are winning. We've got a chance now.

As long as this earth doesn't swallow us up.

REPEAT AFTER ME...

So the answer is staring me in the face. It is so obvious I feel like I'm the most stupid person who ever lived.

I snuck back home just before five in the morning, didn't sleep a wink and then pretended to be up early, making tea and toast for my two favourite parents. My Non-Dad seemed pleased when he saw a plate of toast and a mug of tea waiting for him on the kitchen table. I could tell he felt we were making headway and it lifted his spirits no end.

As usual, they drive me to school early; as usual, I do something wrong; and, as usual, I'm told to go to detention, which suits me just fine. But also as usual, the dark nothing that threatens to engulf the town has grown closer. It's the only thing that seems to break the rules of repetition. I can see for myself that it has blacked out the dwindling edge of town. Time is most definitely running out.

I'm soon on my way back home during the lunch break. I'm walking quickly and New-Billie, even with her ultra-long legs, is having trouble keeping up. I've been waiting

320

to make this journey all day and nothing's going to slow me down now.

'What if you're wrong?' New-Billie asks.

'I'm not.'

'You keep building my hopes up.'

'Trust me, Billie,' I urge.

'I don't know if I can take another disappointment.'

'You won't have to,' I assure her,

New-Billie and I slip into the flat and I can barely breathe as I march down the short hallway and straight into Non-Dad and New-Mum's bedroom. I yank open the wardrobe and drag a leather jacket out.

New-Billie watches in silence, not daring to speak in case she curses the moment.

I grip the leather jacket, stopping to take in the odour of old leather and Non-Dad's aftershave. I know what he has done has been done from the depths of heartache and love. That he isn't a vicious man, just a very sad and desperate one. But when New-Moth died it changed everything and I feel no remorse for Non-Dad's pain. He made a terrible mistake but too many have paid for it.

I slide my hand up the inside of the jacket's sleeve.

New-Billie's eyes meet mine. She is holding her breath.

I slide my hand further up . . .

And there it is.

The formula.

We're on repeat. Every day contains the same things: food, cars, petrol, heat and light. It can all get used up, eaten, digested, whatever – but then it all comes back again, ready to nourish and enrich. This version of my town is stuck in its own version of a black hole so it can't replenish

321

from the outside; instead it just recreates what it needs everyday anew. People may die and never return, but that doesn't stop the day returning with all it has to offer.

Including the formula.

I pull it out, unroll and flatten it, then show New-Billie who can barely believe her eyes.

'OMG.' She breathes. 'OhmyGod, ohmyGod, ohmyGod.'

My hand is trembling as I hold the formula and she reaches out and places her hand on mine. But both hands are shaking.

'Rev,' she whispers, unable to find her true voice.

'I know,' I nod. 'I know.'

'Don't we need someone to understand what to do?' she says quietly.

'The Moth was our best bet,' I tell her. 'But my dad also said something – I mean my Non-Dad, the man who brought me here. He said something I think we can use.'

We share a hopeful smile as the light behind New-Billie's eyes returns.

BATTLE ROYALE WITH CHEESE

We meet Other-Johnson, Another-Billie, Non-Lucas and my limping, barely-conscious dad at the school gates at the top of the hill.

'Dad!' I run to him and slip a shoulder under his arm. He looks weak, but he nods and mumbles to me. 'The classroom, get me to the classroom.'

The Apes are coming our way, thundering through the raging elements. The Ape's five-pointer drips with black blood and he looks like he's in pain. Non-Ape has grown smaller and his leathery skin is repairing itself again after he has taken all manner of hits from the doppelgangers. I'm sure he's dragging his left leg a little. They keep coming though because Apes always, always keep coming.

'Go!' Non-Ape bellows.

The Ape waves his arms. 'Run!'

Other-Johnson's breath catches in his throat. 'Where's my Rev?' he gasps. 'I can't scan for her.'

I open my mind to him, show him the flashing blur of her blue hand as she went to buy us time, the bravest of the brave.

Other-Johnson's thoughts fall deathly silent in my head. The snow thickens, the river rises, the wind howls and the lightning gathers but he doesn't notice any of it as he instantly regrets all of the mistakes he ever made.

'She loved you,' I whisper pathetically. I don't know what else to say.

Other-Johnson is crushed. '*Get out of here,*' he yells into my brain.

'She did,' I repeat, 'she really did—'

'*Go!*' he screams through his heartache.

Then I see them. Coming up the hill behind the Apes. A swarm of doppelgangers. Which means more than we ever realised got through. The world shudders and cracks underneath us and a tremor hits so hard it tears a chasm under the deepening snow. Half of the furious, bewildered doppelgangers fall into the chasm as it spreads towards us. We move as fast as we can through the storm, but already some of the fallen doppelgangers are using their powers to fly or levitate out of the widening fissure.

A fissure that is snaking its way to the school. If it swallows that then it's game over. My dad is convinced we need to be in the classroom.

Non-Lucas unsheathes his talons and goes into a blur but the split second before he does he glances my way. I know he doesn't expect to survive.

'Make it to the classroom,' he tells me.

'You can't fight them all.'

'We were born this way.' He then turns into a stationary blur, moving faster than ever, maybe as fast as he possibly can.

Other-Johnson enters my head. '*This is the last goodbye.*'

'We'll wait for you, all of you,' I tell him.

'If we buy you this chance, then take it.'

'Wait—'

'Go, Rev. Go home.'

And with that he turns to face the swarm coming up the hill.

Non-Ape braces himself, cricks his great neck and punches his fist over and over into his great meaty palm. He's watching them approach. He has no doubt he will beat them. Crush them. Grind them to a pulp.

I however have no doubt that he will fail. There's just too many. But more than that you can't fight a world that doesn't want you. Already the river is rising, climbing the hill that leads to the school. Taking the thick snow and turning it into a dreadful river of sludge.

Evil-GG brushes past me. 'Excuse me please.' He joins Non-Ape and Non-Lucas. 'You and me, big boy, was written in the stars.'

'Homo,' Non-Ape grumbles. A lightning bolt strikes him hard and . . . has no effect whatsoever.

'You light up my world!' Evil-GG cackles.

The snarling panther version of Moth Two has lost all sense of its brilliant-minded humanity, but it doesn't stop the Moth stroking his back in silence.

Non-Ape gives the Ape a gentle tap on his arm. 'Save Boob Girl.'

The Ape is ready to stand and fight. 'You save Boob Girl.'

'I said it first.'

'I said it second.'

'I said it third.'

Collectively our doppelgangers are gathering as one, ready

to fight to the death, and I wonder if Other-Johnson is putting the thought into their heads. He must be. He's at the edge of despair having lost Rev Two. So he's going to make sure the same doesn't happen to me by using all the resources he can. Maybe he's been doing that since we got into town?

Non-Ape won't budge on this. 'You gotta save Boob Girl.'

The Ape visibly stiffens at this. He must sense that it is the end of their perfect friendship. Non-Ape's big giant cow eyes can't hide his sadness though.

'No one fights like you,' he tells the Ape.

'Yowza,' the Ape responds. They bump fists for the last time and I know for certain that Other-Johnson has used his mental powers to split them up. He could barely find a thought in their heads before so he's operating on full wattage.

The Ape turns away from his best ever friend and swings the Moth on to his back.

Evil-GG glances at the onrushing crowd as they pick their way past the widening fissure. 'That's it, come to the GG.'

Carrie's hand lands on my wrist. 'Rev, sometimes you've got to run. Don't let what they're doing go to waste.' Carrie knows me better than I realised. I want to stay and fight beside them.

Another-Billie gives Other-Johnson a quiet glance as she prepares for the mass attack. 'Rev?' she asks him and he solemnly shakes his head.

Another-Billie barely holds her grief inside.

Non-Lucas lets out a howl before speeding towards the advancing doppelgangers. He moves so fast I doubt one single snowflake lands on him

Johnson joins us as we move as quickly as we can to the

school, racing through the thick snow, trying to get there before the crack in the earth opens its jaws and swallows everything. I keep glancing back as Non-Lucas tears through the doppelgangers so fast that all I know of this is the falling bodies, standing one second, cut down the next. But there are still so many of them.

Non-Ape bellows. Evil-GG cackles and the living blur that is Non-Lucas rejoins them, shimmering so fast that he is igniting dust particles in the air. They spark and glow and burst into small flames all around him. Other-Johnson and Moth Two protect Another-Billie and I can only guess that they expect her to heal them if they fall. It's vital the swarm of doppelgangers doesn't reach her.

Non-Ape takes one last look my way.

'Yowza!' he shouts to me, his voice rising above the hurricane and cracks of lightning.

One word.

But one of the best words ever.

'Yowza!' I respond, but I doubt he can hear me because the swarm arrives and tries to overrun them.

I run as fast as I can, pushing my dad along with me. He's getting better all the time but he's still some way from his best. Carrie's spindly legs sprint alongside mine as we move as quickly as we can to the school. But it's so cold and we're soaked through and weighed down by sodden clothes. Up ahead the chasm grows like a hungry mouth as it ripples towards the school.

But on we plough because this is our last best chance and we all know it. The Ape grips on to the Moth, cradling him like a baby as his mighty strides outpace the fissure. The wind batters at him, the snow tries to bury him under giant flakes and the sky fires electricity at him, but nothing, not in this life or the next, is going to stop that boy. His mountainous determination fires my veins and I redouble my efforts. Carrie and Johnson are similarly inspired and we crash onwards, led by the invincible Ape.

Billie is right beside me and she can only marvel at the Ape.

'I get it now,' she pants. 'I finally get why you like him so much.'

The Ape is the first to reach the school door and he yanks it open. We've got four flights of stairs to navigate. The windows of the stairwell look out on to the hill and as we reach the first landing I see – or imagine that I see – the Lucas-blur speeding through the rampaging doppelgangers. He cuts them down before they even know he's there. Non-Ape rips bodies apart as they try to swarm him. They have powers, they can jump and fly and grow tall and strong but Non-Ape has a mountain range's worth of power and he repels them all, punching and crushing and ripping them to pieces. Evil-GG lets every shred of his inner bitch out and turns into a remorseless killer, never once stopping to think or show pity. He shoots talon after talon like a machine gun from his fingers, while spinning and twisting through the masses. Moth Two is fast and vicious and with Other-Johnson at his side, he is spectacular, never letting anyone within a hair of Another-Billie.

But, by the time we reach the second floor landing Evil-GG is dead. I see him go down as a lightning bolt strikes him and, while he's stunned, a gang of doppelgangers overpower him. Another-Billie can't reach him to heal him, despite Other-Johnson and Moth Two trying to cut a path towards him. The Lucas-blur and Non-Ape are holding their own and for a fleeting moment I think that together they can still win.

The third floor looms and a body flies through the reinforced window. It's a doppelganger without a head. Carrie shrieks. Echo after echo after echo is following us to the bitter end.

'For the love of God!' Billie yells as she cowers from the shattering glass. I drag my dad onwards; there is no time to stop. The Ape is panting hard and only now do I see that he is cut badly, bleeding real blood from the first encounter with the doppelgangers. But on he ploughs, carrying the Moth, who desperately clings to his neck. Lucas is an emotional mess, crying the whole time. I don't blame him.

The fissure, the widening chasm is at the school door and the empty world is reaching round it. Ready to embrace and then crush it.

'It's all right, tears are good, tears are healthy. It's just water. Salty. Like the sea,' GG says, trying to spur the nerve-shattered Lucas onwards.

Through the next window I see the Lucas-blur come to a bone-crunching stop. Something has grabbed him, something invisible or maybe it's a telekinetic thing, but the minute he stops blurring is the moment the doppelgangers strike. They descend on him with talons gleaming. Black blood fountains like a geyser and I look away. But the doppelgangers are thinning as the empty world assassinates half as many as Non-Ape does. The river is almost at the top of the hill but again this IQ-challenged world reveals it's less than clever master plan because the rivers of sludge start to pour straight down into the open chasm it has created.

Up we go. One more flight of stairs. One more desperate race for the classroom. My dad had better be ready to do his thing.

The fourth-floor landing welcomes us and as Carrie charges for the classroom I dare to stop and stare out of the window. Non-Ape refuses to buckle even against the worst odds he's ever faced. He fights on, a snow-covered mountain of a boy, struck over and over by lightning and hurricane winds, and as I watch him I see my own Ape reflected in him. It's not difficult, they're the same person, but it's the first time I've not been able to distinguish between them. And then I realise that Non-Ape's grown a lot smaller. Can you *grow* smaller? Does that make actual sense? Whatever, it's terrifying, because it means he's running out of power.

'Rev!' Carrie is screaming at me, having only just realised I'm not running alongside her. I look back along the hallway and she's standing at the open door to the classroom.

Billie helps the labouring Ape alongside her. 'Come on, hero!' she urges him.

I try to wrench myself away from the window when I see movement out of the corner of my eye. Other-Johnson goes down. My heart snaps and I cry out. Johnson has seen it as well and it makes him jolt. He staggers for a moment, looks gutted.

'Rev!' he calls.

'I know, I know,' I say, fighting back tears.

Next to where Other-Johnson stood, Moth Two is now surrounded. Another-Billie is nowhere to be seen; have the mob got to her already? Moth Two stands back to back with Non-Ape who has climbed to his feet again. They know they are there for each other and even from here I can see that they like that they are. Back to back they're ready for what's left of the swarm. Not nearly so many now. But the world is going crazy outside; it really isn't enjoying having guests.

'Rev! Come on, we're going home,' Billie says.

But I can't take my eyes off the last battle.

'Rev,' Johnson urges and drags me away.

I shove my weakened dad into the classroom. 'Do it!' I yell at him.

But already I can hear footsteps careering up the stairwell corridor. Some doppelgangers are in the school and they're coming for us, fast. The Ape looks my way and raises his five-pointer. 'Be right back.'

'No!' I scream. But he disappears before I can say another word. 'You're still carrying the Moth!' I yell. How could he possibly have forgotten that the Moth was clinging on to him?

'I need time,' my dad breathes to the others. 'Just another minute! Keep me safe. I can fix this. I can fix it all!'

The school cracks. That's the only way I can describe it. The school is encircled as the chasm reaches all the way round it like a giant claw – and then squeezes.

GG doesn't hesitate, picks up the nearest chair for a weapon and charges into the corridor. Lucas watches and when he sees Carrie step up and grab a big thick heavy book he goes out after her. Billie looks at me.

'You've got exactly a minute,' she says.

'We've got so much longer,' I tell her. 'When we get back we'll have all the time in the world.'

'Let's do something nice tomorrow.' She manages a smile. 'Something that doesn't get us into detention.'

331

Johnson strikes a match and lights a cigarette. He slips a hand into one of his tight jeans pockets. 'You know ...' he starts. But then stops and instead tosses his cigarette away and crosses the few metres towards me. He takes me in his arms and kisses me. It's a kiss that steals my soul and I kiss back with all I've got. *I love you*, I think to myself, *I love you and I love you on top of that*. The kiss has to end, but a billion years have passed and they've been the best years of my life. Other-Johnson came close, but after this kiss I know why I was always holding back from him. The real thing, *the very real thing*, is the only thing.

'Don't leave town without me.' And then he's gone to help the Ape and the others keep the doppelgangers at bay.

I glance up and my dad is writing a formula on the whiteboard. A whiteboard that slips and falls from the wall as the school experiences a terrifying shudder. The hurricane winds blow the windows to smithereens.

'Molecules!' my dad yells across the flying debris. 'You add molecules to one world then they have to push other molecules out of that world. That's the key to all of it.'

A blizzard crashes into the classroom.

My dad finishes the last digit on the large formula.

'It's time, Rev.'

My eyes widen in horror. 'Wait, what about the others—'

The white light claims me before I can move. Half of my thoughts are still in the empty world and half have come with me. I know I will never feel complete again.

There's always an Ape staring at someone.

There's always a detention.

And there's always a way out.

New-GG is performing his best John Travolta impression. Over and over. Sticking a leg and arm out. Over and over. He's that excited.

'White light, where are you?' he sings.

New-Johnson is buzzing more than at any time I have seen any version of a Johnson buzz. He has lost his cool – almost – and is on his sixth straight cigarette.

New-Billie is sharing puffs of his cigarettes and coughing every time she inhales too deeply.

New-Carrie in a quiet fug of anticipation. She has thought to bring a suitcase with her, packed and straining with clothes, make-up and every slim volume of poetry she has ever committed to the page. New-Lucas has polished his shoes and they shine under the classroom lights. He's writing my Non-Dad's formula on to the large whiteboard at the front of the classroom, one number at a time.

I am watching each digit as it appears, checking it against the formula, making sure it's completely correct, right down to the smallest squiggle.

'So what happens when I finish writing?' New-Lucas asks.

'I have no idea,' I tell him.

'That's positive,' he responds.

'What if we blow up?' New-GG stops posing like Travolta.

'I guess we blow up,' New-Johnson replies, then turns to me, puts a finger to his temple and gives me a casual salute. It's only a small thing, but it brings everything galloping back to me. The real Johnson executed the exact same salute and I suddenly lose all feeling in my legs and crash to the floor.

'Rev?' New-Billie is with me in seconds, slender arm wrapping round my waist as she bends level with me. 'What is it?'

'Nothing,' I bite back my tears as I crawl like a crab to the nearest school desk and take a seat. 'Just went a bit dizzy.'

'Hey,' New-Johnson is with me now, squatting till his face is level with mine. New-Lucas has stopped writing. New-GG and New-Carrie have fallen silent.

I wipe my eyes, suck in a few deep breaths. 'It's OK,' I tell them. 'It's OK. Keep writing.'

Non-Lucas looks reluctant to do so as if the formula might turn out to be a prescription for food poisoning.

'Please,' I tell him. 'Finish the formula.'

New-Billie makes slow circles on my lower back with her hand, soothing me. 'It's all right,' she says over and over. 'It's all right.'

I nod, suck in more air and straighten. My eyes find New-Johnson's. For a moment something crosses between us, a sliver of something deeper, but New-Ape looms up behind him and pulls New-Johnson out of the way.

'That's my friend,' he tells New-Johnson. 'Get your own.'

New-Ape squats level with my eye line, his one good eye finding mine. 'You going to spew?'

I shake my head. 'I'm good,' I say.

I straighten then get to my feet in time to hear New-Lucas declare, 'Finished.'

We all turn as one as New-Lucas steps back from the whiteboard and there is it is. The equation. The formula. Written large in front of us.

We wait a moment.

Then another.

And another.

'Nothing's happening,' New-GG speaks first.

I'm waiting, hoping the molecules will start shoving and pushing until they force more molecules to open a door into another world. 'Come on,' I mutter under my breath. 'Come on.'

'Rev?' Already New-Billie is anticipating another crushing disappointment.

I cross to the whiteboard. 'COME ON!' I yell at the formula.

'What did your dad do? Exactly and precisely,' New-Carrie asks.

I try to think back to when I was trapped under the bed.

'He said he built a key, created new matter. Matter that doesn't belong so it forces a hole; it pushes the boundaries of reality and cracks it open from the pressure.'

'But is it the right formula?' New-Lucas asks. 'Is this the actual one? Only on the way here you said it comes from this world. Which means it isn't the one that brought you here.'

My stomach lurches, climbing all the way to the back of my throat before thudding back down again.

'But he burned it,' I say weakly. 'Why burn it in front of me if it wasn't the right formula?' I'm scrambling for clarity as I grab the formula from New-Lucas and make sure he has written it out properly, checking every number twice over.

'I think we were drawn to this world for a reason,' I tell them, trying to keep my voice from cracking with hopelessness. 'Me and my Non-Dad came here because it's a moment in time. It's twenty-four hours and nothing more.'

'So?' New-Billie asks as her spirits sink right in front of me.

'So . . .' I'm talking just for the sake of it, as my eyes flick back and forth between small formula and giant formula. 'So maybe it captured a moment from Non-Dad's old life. Who knows how the multiverse works.' I'm saying anything that comes into my head because I'm scared that if I stop talking I will run out of all hope.

New-Ape stands beside me, his good eye flicking from the formula to the whiteboard until a big stubby finger lands on a single digit. 'You wrote a two, not a three.'

The hairs on my neck rise as I check New-Ape's spot-the difference brilliance.

'I've got great eyes,' he tells me.

'Make that one great eye,' New-GG calls out.

'Why does it have to be written out?' New-GG asks. 'You've already got it in your hand?'

Rather than answer I reach up and erase the number two digit. I take the black Sharpie that New-Lucas was using and, after a moment I write the numeral three in its place.

'Rev?' New-Billie asks. 'Does it have to be written out?'

'Molecules,' I tell New-Billie. 'It's the last thing I remember from the empty world.'

Then I glance at New-Johnson. 'You ready for an adventure? Like nothing you've ever known or felt before?'

New-Johnson strikes a match and lets it burn before flicking it away.

New-Ape places a big meaty paw on my shoulder and it's the best feeling in the world. An Ape taking care of you.

'We got this,' he grins.

The white light appears before I can say another word.

HOME IS INDEED SWEET

Sometimes you get a lucky break. Sometimes you open a portal to another world and it leads straight back to where it all started.

Detention.

I can hear a fire alarm, I can hear people raising their voices and before I know it Mr Allwell strides back into the classroom.

'It's nothing,' he tells me.

Correction. Tells *us*.

To help make his point, the fire alarm rings off, leaving only a tinny echo in my ears. The excitable voices outside die away just as quickly.

Allwell takes a seat and barely glances our way.

New-Ape kangaroos his desk and chair towards me. 'Did it work? Did it?'

New-Lucas and New-Billie let a small laugh escape from their lips. It's the laugh of the astonished, the barely able to comprehend.

New-GG squeals in delight, which makes Allwell look his way. 'Yes?' Allwell asks New-GG.

New-GG waggles his fingers at Allwell. 'Just so glad you're back,' he jokes.

Allwell doesn't engage with New-GG and instead goes back to marking some papers. New-Carrie is staring all around the classroom, taking it in, until I watch her subconsciously pinch the skin on her bony wrist.

I hear New-Johnson let out a slow sigh. 'I thought you said this was going to be the adventure of a lifetime.'

I have to turn in my seat so that I can face him as he lounges at the back of the class.

'Patience is a virtue,' I tell him. 'Not . . .' I grin at him.

Allwell clears his teacherly throat. 'Is there someone missing?'

We turn as one to face him.

The Moth.

His absence kills all sense of wonder, relief and excitement dead.

I have to remind myself not to act as though I haven't seen my mum in what must be weeks. That I expected to die – many times over – before that could happen.

But I have raced home and my lungs are aching, along with all the cuts and bruises I'm not going to be able to explain to her.

The others were less keen to split up. They felt safer in each other's company, but I told them no one will ever know the difference, that their family, friends and relatives will accept who they are.

It's so far from ideal that I think one of them will crack.

339

We're going to discuss saving their original families when the dust settles. It'll involve asking for help and revealing to the world that there are other worlds. I know the Moth would warn against it. He'd tell me in no uncertain terms that that would spell disaster, that humankind would inevitably become greedy or envious about what another world has, and, before you know it, there'd be interdimensional warfare. No one likes a change, he'd tell me. It never goes well. We have agreed to stay silent on New-Moth's absence for now. But when the time comes our story will have to be told.

I'm waiting in the flat when Mum walks in from her waitressing shift in the restaurant. All decorum flies out of the window as I literally hurl myself at her and throw my arms around her in a hug an Ape would be proud of. I crush her half to death as I cry and wail and slobber all over her. Mum is instantly worried because she's a worrier on a professional level, and she keeps asking me what's wrong. I mumble and blub that nothing is wrong, that everything is just peachy. Then she starts crying because I'm crying and we slide to the floor in a truly daft heap of tears and hugs. But when we look at each other and realise what we're doing we start laughing.

I love the sound of her laugh.

The next day I don't get detention. Other people do, and I hope that none of their dads or mums happen to have opened doors into other worlds. That they haven't died in those worlds, that their parents were watchful.

It's only when I leave school amongst the throng of a

hundred other schoolkids that I realise what needs to be done.

It's New-Johnson who takes my arm, coming up from behind me and leading me to one side. 'Rev,' he tells me. Then points. 'Look.'

The Moth's parents are at the school with a female plain-clothes detective and two uniformed police officers. Some teachers and the head of school are in grave talks with them.

But it's the Moth's parents I focus on. They have that pale, lost look of yearning and pain and fear that is near unbearable to witness.

'What are we going to do about that?' New-Billie joins us from the throng.

'What can we do?' I mutter, but to myself.

'We can't just take another Moth and bring him back here.' New-Carrie has also found us by now. 'We'd only hurt that Moth's family.'

'We can't be that selfish.' New-Lucas has silently emerged behind us.

'We're going to need a bigger formula.' New-GG skips and glides through the schoolchildren before stopping beside us.

'It's a shame we can't pluck one out of thin air,' New-Billie says.

Which is when I look at her and think back to my own Billie and the things she could do. The thought of Billie doubles the pain I feel for Moth's parents. Loss is a dreadful thing, but, as I have learned from a version of my dad, it also fuels us. It impels us to do what we hope is the best thing even if it turns out to be the worst.

I set myself and find clarity in everything that has happened to me. I get what it is about me now: I really don't know how to give up.

'Whatever we do, it'll only take a second,' I tell them. 'Time is one weird, screwed-up dimension.'

'A second?' New-Johnson asks.

'That'll feel like a lifetime,' I tell him.

New-Ape barges through the crowd, a boy turned proper Ape now, and looms over us. He's eating a Greggs' steak bake, shovelling it down his throat. 'I thought you said you were somewhere else. This is the same place.'

'So let's go somewhere else,' I say.

The formula is at home in my bedroom, hidden at the bottom of a creaky old drawer. I have only just got back and, as much as I yearn to be here with my mum again, I know that we're not complete without a Moth.

CODA

The brute laid waste to them with all the fury that comes from a broken heart. He stood at the gates of certain death and held firm, no matter that the black-panther boy fell beside him, no matter how many of his own kind came at him and no matter how many tried to defeat him. He broke them all. He beat every single one of them until all that was left was a man-boy with a loud bellow.

The rotten weather, the floods, the blizzard and the giant holes in the ground didn't faze him because he knew there was nothing in any world that was stronger than him.

He waded through everything, kicking a path between the broken and the dead. As usual, he had only one thing in mind and nothing would sway him from that single thought. He stomped into the school, his left leg dragging badly, but he didn't care as he leaped over the widening hole that cradled the school. By now the weather was dying away; the silent earth had done whatever it could. The big boy was just too strong and it gave up and accepted defeat. *Hey, you can't win them all*, it silently

343

thought to itself and the winds died down like a giant defeated sigh.

The big boy then found the smaller version of himself, his best friend, his kindred spirit, his brother of the soul, and picked him up from where he'd fallen. He arched his great neck and looked to the ceiling and tried not to cry. For a moment he wanted to bellow again but didn't. He couldn't find his voice. He passed the other friends he'd made. The one who couldn't walk, then the skinny one, the homo and the cool guy. All dead, but they had clearly died gloriously in battle because doppelgangers with busted and bloodied throats were strewn all around them.

He felt pride swell in his great chest; he hadn't known them very well before, but he could now see they were definitely worth being friends with. GG was brave and refused to give up. The Moth was clever and even with useless legs he kept on going. Lucas was a scared mouse, but it didn't stop him from trying his best not to be. Carrie seemed too skinny to do anything worthwhile, but she proved everyone wrong. Johnson, whom he should still hate, turned out to be a decent fighter. The man-boy then saw the tall, mixed-race Indian-Irish girl lying at the top of the stairs and he'd always had a soft spot for his version of her. He stopped to reach for her hand and his bad leg seemed to feel better already. He wasn't blessed with the most intuitive or imaginative of minds. Thoughts came and went like strangers in a park, never connecting, never meeting, but this one time it felt good to hold her hand. In truth he still dragged his bad leg, but he was convinced it definitely felt better now that he'd touched her. That's probably why he liked her the most: she made him feel good.

344

The exit door to the school was kicked off its hinges as the man-boy limped back into the night. He found the other supermodel, her twin, and while the very last drops of her life ebbed away he took her broken, twisted arm in his meaty paw and placed her wickedly bent hand against her heart. He knew what he wanted from her and he had no doubt that he would get his wish.

The moment her eyes had opened and she had managed to sit up he told her to go to work, to do what she was born to do. She started by laying her hand on the smaller of the man-boys.

Until he woke up. And belched.

After several hours the boy who couldn't walk was grinning and crying at the same time. His athletic friend, the Perfect One, still looked apprehensive. Unsure. The skinny, pointy girl clapped and twirled on the spot which made the boy with now good legs cry and laugh some more. The smoking boys watched her the whole time, even though both seemed irretrievably lost and weren't really looking at anything.

'Where's Boob Girl?' The Ape asked.

'She's gone.' Carrie stopped twirling.

'Gone where?' the Ape asked.

'Just gone,' Billie said sadly.

The Ape breathed out slowly. 'She isn't gone,' he said with complete assurance. 'I'll find her.'

Somehow they knew he would. Because when an Ape first stares at you it means he has locked on to you. Forever.

But what you also have to understand is that you lock on to an Ape in return; it's a fundamental part of the silent bargain they strike with you. Whether you like it or not, it goes both ways.

Which is when the air started to burn around them and the Ape purred as his true best friend emerged. Her pink hair was unmistakable.

She saw him and immediately ran to him, not believing that he could possibly still be alive.

'Ape!' she cried. 'Ape, Ape, Ape!'

As more people appeared behind her, more copies, even one of himself with a funny eye, the Ape looked at Rev and gave her a gentle reminder.

Some people never learn, he thought.

'It's Dazza.'